GRABMORE

By Glenn Miller

Martin Sisters Publishing

Published by
Martin Sisters Publishing Company, Inc.
www. martinsisterspublishing. com
Copyright © 2016 Glenn Miller
ISBN: 978-1-62553-096-7
Mystery
Cover design by Wendy Bublaugh
Printed in the United States of America
Martin Sisters Publishing Company, Inc.

DEDICATION

To my parents, John and Charlotte Miller, who instilled a love of reading in me long ago. And to Kathy Grey for her love and support and early reading of the manuscript.

DISCLAIMER

Any resemblance to persons living, dead, undead or merely unwell is purely intentional, er, I mean coincidental.

CHAPTER ONE

We all remember the day, that Monday when Chesterfield E. O'Riley IV, our CEO, the man we called "O'Really?" - vanished.

It was a cool January day in Florida, one of those rare winter afternoons when a robust cold front had chased humidity south to Cuba. The sun was a friend instead of something to hide from on such days.

It was a grand day for a killing or kidnapping, a grand day, indeed.

O'Riley sailed into town for his annual inspection tour/bacchanal on his 99-foot yacht, Never Enough.

His boat and all-female crew were objects of much mirth and even more anger in the company, Grabmore Publications, the country's largest newspaper empire. The crew's women ranged in age from eighteen all the way to nineteen. They hailed from Lapland, Iceland and Ireland.

Maybe one or several of them conspired in his disappearance or dismemberment. Nobody knows, well, almost nobody. Maybe he was alive and carousing somewhere in Dublin or north of the Arctic Circle.

Maybe one of his vixens hijacked O'Riley to a dungeon somewhere.

Maybe.

Maybe they were driven to it by the bizarre uniforms or lack of uniforms he allegedly coerced them into wearing.

Maybe I'm responsible. I'm a sports writer for one of Grabmore's papers, The Fort Myers Tropical-Times. My name is F. Scott Bond. No jokes, please, about either James Bond or The Great Gatsby.

I have motives: no pay raises and unpaid furlough weeks. Then there's Furlough, the rat in the newsroom that scurries under and between desks. When I say rat I mean that as in a small four-legged critter and not a human being.

Nothing unsettles a lunch break like Furlough scampering underfoot while one is digging into a plate of takeout shrimp scampi.

I could be a suspect. Perhaps I should be a suspect.

Maybe I slipped past security on his boat slip and bopped O'Riley on the head with a fungo bat and tossed him overboard into a waiting Boston Whaler piloted by an accomplice and then we sped upriver − (or should that be downriver? - to the Gulf of Mexico? Some miles offshore maybe we secured an anchor to the CEO's pudgy ankles and pitched him into the salty deep.

Maybe. I had and still have the motives, and perhaps opportunity as well.

Maybe one of the 40,000 people O'Riley had laid off in the past four years grabbed him between the dock and his waiting limousine. They have motive.

Maybe one of the other 50,000 people still with the company who have been ill-treated were involved. Or lots of them.

It's been several days now since the CEO was last seen. The slight and unusually cool spell is over and daytime temperatures are back in the seventies.

Before O'Riley somehow disappeared between the Never Enough and the Tropical-Times offices a few blocks away on a bedraggled corner on the edge of downtown of this city on Florida's west coast, we learned a great deal.

We learned that the yacht, contrary to rumors, was not a Roman slave galley and that the young women did not row the boat upriver, or downriver, as a burly, sweaty guy banged on a very large drum.

There were, alas, no oars sticking out of the boat's sides when O'Riley sat topside with his little captain's yachting cap perched on his head and his latest Lapp babe serving him Frappuccinos.

The cops haven't learned much about what may have happened to O'Riley. Oh, they've learned about his fondness for sweet and cold coffee drinks and obsession with Irish and Lapp girls.

But what had become of him that day?

Oh, they have their theories, suppositions they don't want to discuss. It's tough to publicly float ideas with tens of thousands of suspects from pressmen in Portland to outraged fathers in Reykjavik and an ex-boyfriend of Katie from County Cork.

So, what did we know and when did we know it?

Yes, we know more about Citizen O'Riley, the fourth Chesterfield Ebenezer O'Riley to head Grabmore. And, yes, again, his middle name is really Ebenezer. Charles Dickens will work his way back into this story in a few more pages. That's getting ahead of our story, though, and O'Riley's initials are, implausibly, CEO.

Getting back to what we know. …

We know, and the cops know, O'Riley traveled to Fort Myers from corporate headquarters in Buffalo every winter, usually mid-January. Everybody at the paper knew about the tours, about how the local managers flipped out Jan. 2 every year to get ready.

The actual newspaper had to be a little thicker on those days when O'Riley was in town. Hand-picked employees, generally the biggest weasels on the premises, were granted an audience with the great one, where they praised O'Riley much as Russian careerists once sucked up to Stalin and blamed all their country's ills on Trotsky or imperialistic, capitalistic Yankee spies.

Every employee every January was ordered to tidy up his or her desk. The linoleum floors were waxed. The 40-year-old newsroom carpets were vacuumed. The only time all year that happened. All this manic running around and fretting and worrying were all part of the annual dog-and-pony show the Tropical-Times staged for O'Riley's forty-minute visit to this Potemkin village near the river.

To keep the analogies in Russia but mixing historical eras and despotic regimes, he was our Czar, floating into town and expecting to see a glitzy, shiny, sparkling palace with happy, shiny people.

And that, by gum, is what he saw.

No discouraging words. No hint of low morale. Not that he cared, of course.

Nothing was left to chance, usually, from having a limousine pick him up to the dinner at The Lanai, a restaurant favored by local elites. Nothing was left to chance until his most recent and perhaps final Fort Myers visit.

Copy editors were always ordered to wear sneakers instead of flip-flops. The spittoons for the old tobacco-chewing and tobacco-spitting sports editor, sadly now retired, were hidden somewhere. And the spittoons magically returned to sports after O'Riley's visit.

Middle managers broke out their best, and likely only, suits for the visits.

That's the why, such as it is, behind the visits. It's been a company tradition since O'Riley's grandfather purchased the paper in 1961 for $4 million.

Get out of Buffalo. Go to Florida. Bring along a few of those hand-picked and plucked maidens from foreign lands, typically in northern Europe. Have the company pay for everything, from the flight on the company plane to the trip on the O'Riley yacht to the foi gras at The Lanai.

Sweep into the office and hold a meeting with the local managers. Remind them that times are tough. More furloughs are needed. So are layoffs.

Why are there so many reporters? What do these people with the cameras do? Do we need to pay for bottled water? Can we trim the mileage to employees from 32 cents to 30 cents per mile?

Think of the company-wide savings! Why, it could be enough for another trip to Reykjavik and meeting contestants in the next Miss Iceland pageant.

That's a brief introduction to our company and CEO, the man nicknamed, O'Really?

When employees refer to O'Riley it's always with a question mark – O'Really?

Never a period. Or exclamation mark. The emphasis was always on the interrogatory   punctuation mark, a definite accent of despair and dismay and puzzlement that permeated the company.

He did what?

He said what?

Now what?

O'Really?

His memo on work ethic: "Work smarter, not harder."

O'Really?

His memo on saving money: "We must be efficient and trim costs in every way possible at every turn so don't forget those little things add up, so let's save in a big way with little things. Don't forget to turn out lights when you leave a room."

O'Really?

His endless jargon as dispensed by public relations and human resource lackeys: "We have a new Exalted, Extreme, Coordinator of Community Information Technological Services and Entertainment Viability for the Information Nexus. We will endeavor to maximize our custom content viability and supremacy to further make us the market leaders in informational transitional transformation tweeting and Facebooking."

O'Really?

Really!

O'Riley.

Meanwhile, the investigation into his disappearance continued and the cops focused on just about everybody, from the executive editor to the on-line editor to the publisher.

And me, of course.

I happen to own a fungo bat, a convenient, light, whippy and useful tool for swatting fly balls or noggins.

Plenty of folks around here own Boston Whalers and anchors and can find their way to the Gulf of Mexico. It's quite large, as you may have heard.

CHAPTER TWO

This is something new. I've been hit by foul balls at baseball games, yelled at by NFL stars and traipsed all over the Dominican Republic and Venezuela on baseball assignments.

But I've never been termed a "person of interest" and a "likely suspect" in a murder or kidnapping or disappearance before. I'm not alone, of course.

There must be thousands. Must be? There are thousands of suspects. At this point, of course, nobody knows for sure what is being investigated. Murder? Kidnapping? Or nothing? The lascivious wanderings of a spoiled, self-indulgent rich kid well into middle age?

The investigators from the city of Fort Myers Police Department are intrigued by the case and, apparently, by me. They know I've called Grabmore Publications a "loathsome company run by repugnant creatures."

Topping that creature list is our missing CEO, Chesterfield E. O'Riley IV.

The cops also know I've referred to the Tropical-Times online editor as "Nurse Ratchet."

They know that there's another individual in our office I've referred to as the "Queen Bee of a cabal of Machiavellian harpies." This woman has left a trail of fired bodies in her wake over many years and her co-harridans have terrorized unsuspecting co-workers for decades.

The sports editor is a semi-literate, philandering buffoon who somehow keeps his job despite a succession of moral, ethical and intellectual failings.

I could go on and on and I will. Later on.

For now, let's go back to the day O'Riley disappeared, that cool January afternoon.

I had wandered out of the office, disgusted by the behavior of the gaggle of corporate drones whose mewling brown-nosing propelled me out the door before I became ill and added another layer of vomit to the newsroom carpet.

I've done this before. Just walked out the door for fresh air. There were times I vowed never to return but two things pulled me back – a paycheck and, odd as it may seem, I loved my job writing sports. Just hated the infernal company.

Anyhow, on that day the CEO disappeared, I wandered down to the yacht basin, where the Never Enough was moored.

I've seen the boat before. Never been on it, of course. Lowly riff-raff such as sports writers never will be invited on the CEO's yacht.

It gleamed in the thin winter sun, sparkling and making one blink because of its blindingly white paint. No security was apparent as I wandered by that day. No over-stuffed, steroid-addled goons carrying truncheons and glaring at anybody who ventured within spitting distance. That was usually the case.

J. P. Hooper, the city of Fort Myers Police Department detective assigned to the case, wanted to know more about my walk that day. About why I left the office. About the timing. About the route I walked.

Normally, to escape the "Pit of Despair," as I call the Tropical-Times newsroom, I just wandered into the parking lot for fresh air. Others have derisively called the place the House of Mirth.

Anyhow, it was such a glorious winter afternoon I decided to head a few blocks north, to the yacht basin.

"Why, on this day of all days," Hooper asked, "did you go all the way to the river, all the way to the Royalty Supreme Yacht Club?"

I tried explaining the need to get away, to remind myself there is life outside this corporation.

I told Lt. Hooper about Nurse Ratchet, whose real name is Mabel Borgia.

About how when she noticed our executive editor, who we will discuss later, was back in the office after a week's vacation, she said with all the cloying, phony-baloney brown-nosing suckling she could summon, "Oh, Col. Longstreet, we missed you so much!"

Then, a few minutes later, she took an unsuspecting potential intern into an empty office next to where I sit. Mabel always left the door open so I heard it all.

"Now," she began, "I know everybody hates me. I don't care. I'm going to get ahead. I don't care who I step on to do it. It could be you. I don't care who I squash. It could be you.

"I don't care who I stab in the back. It could be you. I don't care about anything except getting ahead, except advancing my career, except making sure Col. Longstreet likes me and protects me and promotes me.

"I don't care about you. I don't know your name. I don't care where you go to school or even if you go to school."

At this point, the intern, a shy young woman, started to speak.

"My name is Ashley. …"

Borgia cut her off.

"I don't care. All I care about is if you come to work when we tell you. All I care about is you parroting everything I say. All I care about is you using the Grabspeak Grabmore language. Grabspeak is how we communicate.

"Don't listen to the geezers who call this place the newsroom. It's the Information Nexus. Don't call me the online editor. I'm the Custom Content Curator of Online Dispensation and Orientation and Video Uploading and Downloading Command. Got that?"

Ashley managed to squeak out a meek, "Yes, ma'am."

"I'm not ma'am," Borgia barked. "I'm the Custom Content Curator of Online Dispensation and Orientation and Video Uploading and Downloading Command. Got that?"

Ashley simply nodded this time. Smart kid.

Mabel continued.

"Sometimes you'll hear truckloads of bullcrap from some of the oldtimers. Some of these galoots use words like class and grace and dignity and honor. What a load of bullcrap. What's that got to do with Grabmore? What's that got to do with advancing your career? What's that got to do with the Internet?

"Holy crap! What losers! Listen to me, kid. Avoid those people. If you want a job here and want to get promoted, follow my example."

Just then, Col. Longstreet walked by the open office door.

"Oh, Col. Longstreet, suh, that lavender tie with the topless hula girl painted on it really matches your pale blue shirt. It's quite striking. It shows you're a leader and a genius, suh, and one with impeccable taste."

Meanwhile, I couldn't focus on my profile of a new bullpen catcher the Boston Red Sox had just hired and I had interviewed that morning at their training complex in Fort Myers.

Borgia continued lecturing the intern.

"Don't listen to the morons around here. They're the past. I'm the future. They care about precision and language and storytelling and accuracy. What quaint nonsense. We want and we will get videos of the Daughters of the Confederacy Gardenia Club's annual dahlia showcase up first. Before the television stations. Before anybody. Got that? And don't ask why the Gardenia Club is having a dahlia festival."

That's when I couldn't take anymore. As I explained to the cop, that's when I had to get air and that's when I wandered down to the yacht basin and may or may not have seen O'Riley.

And, of course, may have had a hand or fungo bat in his disappearance. Meanwhile, I'm sure, as I wandered the sunny, palm tree lined streets of downtown Fort Myers, Mabel continued doing what Mabel does. No matter how often she belittled and hectored and harangued young reporters, no matter how rude she was to callers, no matter what, she was one of the golden staffers, one of those anointed by the shiny, golden corporate scepter of promotion, protected from on high by unseen mentors, one of those absolutely bulletproof corporate creatures who fail at everything except getting ahead.

Try complaining to the publisher, executive editor or managing editor and the response was the same.

But…

"She's charming," the publisher invariably said.

"She's talented," the executive editor invariably said.

"She's lovely," the managing editor invariably said.

We called her, behind her massive back, "Charming Talented, Lovely."

As charming as Furlough, the office rat. As talented as a pile of compost. As lovely as one of Yogi Berra's sun-withered and dusty catcher's mitts from the 1950s.

Yet, now to quote the final line of my namesake's The Great Gatsby, "we beat on, boats against the current, borne back ceaselessly into the past."

I'm not smart enough to know what that means but I found myself that day, as I explained to the police, near another boat, one large enough to have suited Gatsby, one grand enough to look at home in West Egg.

Was it mere happenstance that I wandered by the Never Enough the day the CEO vanished?

Or was it part of a plot, a plot against our CEO, against the fourth Chesterfield Ebenezer O'Riley?

The man we call "O'Really?"

CHAPTER THREE

The newsroom boss was a son of the old South, the very old South, a direct descendant of a Confederate general, bearing the name of another and the initials of a famous silent film director. His name: Nathan Bedford D.W. Forrest Longstreet.

He was informal. Or so he claimed. He asked that we not call him Mr. Longstreet. In his best Foghorn Leghorn voice, he often said, "Suh, you may call me Colonel Longstreet." He never served in the real military but enjoyed participating in Civil War reenactments as a Confederate general. Always a Confederate and always a general. But we called him Colonel.

We never figured that out.

Although his family raised soybeans and peanuts on a Georgia plantation, he somehow left the family business for journalism after a stint as a sports writer for his college paper.

The Colonel's favorite movie is the silent epic, The Birth of a Nation, which was directed by D. W. Griffith. That's where the D.W. in his name comes from. When President Woodrow Wilson, not to be confused with former Mets outfielder Mookie Wilson, watched the movie, he found it so mesmerizing he supposedly described it as "…like writing history with lightning and my only regret is that it is all so terribly true."

The film was even more racist than Gone with the Wind. The Griffith epic glorified the Ku Klux Klan, for God's sake. But, suh, you got to give the Colonel credit for trying to overcome his racist heritage.

He spouted the company line about diversity but often referred to black people as "Nigras." That's as in "we got to get more "'Nigra faces' in the paper."

It was astonishing and appalling, but then the Longstreet family also owned forests, forests where Grabmore purchased trees that were made into pulp and then into newsprint and eventually newspapers. And, of course, profits. So, Longstreet, despite his racially insensitive language, remained executive editor and remained a friend of O'Riley.

O'Really? Yes.

Was Longstreet a suspect? Do the cops suspect that O'Riley might want to edge him out of Grabmore despite his family's forests? Did Longstreet's unfortunate racial comments make him a company embarrassment? Well, clearly he was, but had it reached a point where he had to go?

Did the potential of a huge civil rights lawsuit make Longstreet more of a liability than asset, despite all those trees in Canada? Did Longtreet know that and take some sort of preemptive action to save his $320,000 a year job, a job where he could bully more than 100 newsroom people at will, a job where he was a minor public figure with a Sunday column, a job where minions such as Mabel Borgia treated him as some sort of demi-god? It was a formula that fed his ego and his appetite for power.

On the other hand, O'Riley and Longstreet have been known in previous years to meet at the Hooters on Cleveland Avenue for beer and chicken wings and appeared to be friends of sorts.

Longstreet obviously knew O'Riley. Maybe still knows him. If the CEO is still alive, of course. O'Riley would have invited him on board the yacht if the colonel popped by the yacht club. He would have trusted Longstreet. So, maybe it was the executive editor who killed or kidnapped the CEO.

Could be. ...

Longstreet usually took him to the Lanai, an old-time downtown restaurant, where O'Riley would bring Ingrid or Lolita or Irma or whoever his girlfriend of the month happened to be and Longstreet brought his wife, Jezebel. They may have met on the yacht and gone to Hooters for beer and ogling and leering.

Then what? Did Longstreet return to the office and remind the lifestyles editor – er, I mean the Custom Entertainment and Thespian Related Coordinator of Movies, Plays, Museums and Party Coverage and Photo Galleries – to publicize the monthly showing of The Birth of a Nation?

When I think of this company I'm often reminded of a quote about Russia attributed to Winston Churchill: "A riddle wrapped in a mystery wrapped inside an enigma."

Grabmore is an insular society, a cult-like organization as enigmatic to outsiders as Scientology or Russia.

Most employees are decent human beings trying to do a good job and be good people. That's been my experience with the rank and file, the folks who do the reporting and take the photos and write the headlines and operate the presses and fix the computers.

But within the Grabmore cult such an approach is viewed as odd, mystifying to the point of subversive.

Hence, the atmosphere that permeates the corporation and the Tropical-Times, from O'Riley to Col. Longstreet and lower level managers eager to preserve their current positions and also connive and scheme to get newer and better and higher-paid ones.

Meanwhile, I really should get to work on that feature on the Red Sox new bullpen catcher. ...

And then there's the mysterious matter of the whereabouts of a certain CEO, which I find more compelling than the catcher.

CHAPTER FOUR

To get to the bottom of this mystifying company mess, we need to go to the top, to the CEO. First, though, we need to start with the first Chesterfield Ebenezer O'Riley, an Irish immigrant. It's been more than a century since O'Riley No. 1 took steerage on the good ship City of Cheaters that sailed out of Liverpool.

How O'Riley got from County Donegal to Liverpool and that ship is lost to history. But once, somehow, he made it on the ship and across the ocean in the bowels of the City of Cheaters and made it through Ellis Island, there is a paper trail, one that leads to a newspaper empire.

The first O'Riley was 17 when the City of Cheaters reached Ellis Island. He was 5-foot-9 and weighed a sturdy 178 pounds. It was 1908. New York City was crowded but not too crowded for a young, ambitious man who had a gift for language. He was familiar with James Joyce, Oscar Wilde and the poetry of W.B. Yeats.

He was also handy with his fists and with numbers. He could brawl with stevedores and teamsters and pressman and figure out the cost per ton of newsprint and the cost of transporting it from a pulp mill in New Brunswick and into to a pressroom anywhere in North America.

He came to America literate, nearly literary. He was fearless and would go anywhere and do anything. That led him through the front door of the Brooklyn Daily Eagle the day after leaving Ellis Island and landing a job as a copy boy and a figurative as well as literal foot in the door of American journalism.

That story used to be part of Grabmore lore before the bean counters and suck-ups and backstabbers took over.

The story goes that O'Riley, still reeking of the ship, of salt water and urine and stale beer, walked in the Daily Eagle newsroom. He didn't know anybody there. They didn't know him. This may include some hokum but it's what Grabmore people used to hear about how the founder started his empire.

"Hi," O'Riley said, according to the old tale. "My name is Chesterfield O'Riley. I'm from County Donegal in the old country. I can write and I can fight. I can beat up anybody who can write better than me and I can write better than any over-sized, ham-handed galoot who could knock me out of the ring.

"Now, I haven't had a bath in two weeks and I'm poor as the poorest church mouse in the poorest parish church on the Emerald Isle. I need a job. Some soap would be nice, too.

"I'm smart. I'm quick with my fists and my brains."

Fortunately, the right person was listening. Editor Perry Kent liked the lad.

"I appreciate your spunk and vim and vinegar, young man," Kent supposedly told him. "Here's a $5 advance on your first week's salary. Go get some soap and clean clothes and come back here tomorrow morning at 8."

"I'll be here at 7," O'Riley said.

"That's fine," Kent said. "I'll be here at 8. And we'll find something for you to do."

That's how it started. That's how an empire was born and an American legend was created. With $5 and a bar of Ivory soap.

As the first O'Riley built the empire, cobbling together first a weekly in Poughkeepsie and then a daily in Hoboken, as he worked and schemed and hired first-rate journalists and top-notch production people, the company grew.

Another paper here. Then one there. There was the Scranton Screamer. And the Hartford Bugle. Then more, many more.

At first his empire was called O'Riley Newspapers. Simple. Precise. Accurate. Then as his wealth grew, and he built mansions and ordered yachts and acquired a bevy of Broadway concubines, the criticism grew.

He was acquiring too much, too fast for his critics. He was characterized as an immigrant who didn't know his place. And Irish and a Catholic on top of that. He was pilloried for grabbing too much. Grab this. Grab that. Grab more and more.

Finally, the first O'Riley, who was never bothered by critics, changed the company name.

He went hungry as a young man in Ireland. He endured two weeks on that ship without decent sanitation or food. He arrived at Ellis Island with nothing and didn't know a soul in North America. He was smarter and tougher than anybody he encountered.

The critics? The hell with them, he thought.

In 1947, after the Depression and World War II, his empire seemed invulnerable. He owned 47 newspapers. He also owned 21 radio stations and was looking into investments in Hollywood studios and TV stations. Too much?

"There is never too much," he famously bellowed during congressional hearings.

When is enough enough? he was asked in that hearing broadcast nationally on black and white television.

"Never," he barked.

Will you just continue grabbing more and more? More newspapers? More radio stations? More money and power?

"You bet," he snapped.

Shortly after the hearing is when he changed the name of the company to Grabmore Publications. O'Riley the first didn't care about political correctness or public perception. It was about forgetting the City of Cheaters and walking into the Daily Eagle stinking of the ship. It was about power and prestige and doing some good in the process.

Then....

We'll get to the details of his career later, but first, a quick review of the family tree, post-Ellis Island. It's evident as the generations moved on that the O'Riley clan did not evolve.

There was Chesterfield E. O'Riley Jr, who was sometimes called simply the Second. He was the son of the founder. It was said when he died in 1996 at the age of 76 that the cause of death was of a carbuncle of the soul. That was the company rumor. The doctors, however, said it was congestive heart disease. What do they know?

His son, Chesterfield E. O'Riley III, died when he gave his chauffer a night off in Monaco and the CEO attempted to drive his Rolls Royce Silver Shadow on a mountain road on a dark and rainy night. He was with his 19-year-year-old girlfriend, Princess Bambi of Lichtenstein , or so she claimed to be, at his side.

It was 2007. He was 65. She walked away. He was carted away. Upon further review, it turned out the princess was actually Agnes Albritton, daughter of Abe Albritton, a butcher. And she was from Youngstown, Ohio. Not Lichtenstein. Never been there.

It's as if this corporation, this Grabmore, was a medieval fiefdom ruled by primogeniture, the ancient practice of passing along land to the first-born son.

CEO No. 4, the current and missing one, didn't cross the Atlantic Ocean in steerage, living on weevil-infested biscuits and sharing a urine-stained bunk far below decks with other desperate, dirty and hungry folks escaping Europe.

When No. 4 traveled it was in a company jet, in a company limousine or on the Never Enough, where the refrigerators are stocked with Frappucinos and there is always a fetching young lady to fetch yet another cold coffee drink. Where his great-grandfather could quote Yeats and Keats and mix it up on the Brooklyn and Hoboken docks with the toughest brawlers, O'Riley the Fourth had the soft hands of a big-city dandy, never hardened with any labor or even yard work.

Where great-grandpa could fix a Model T and win amateur boxing bouts, the fourth didn't know how to gas up a car at a self-serve pump. He didn't know Yeats and Keats from the Three Stooges.

Great-grandpa built an empire. Although he never established a beachhead in the vibrant Chicago newspaper market, he was the Robert Frost poem Chicago come alive.

"Hog Butcher for the World

"Toolmaker, Stacker of Wheat

"Player with Railroads and the Nation's Freight Handler

"Stormy, husky, Brawling."

Later in the poem Frost wrote, "Building, Breaking, Rebuilding."

That was the first O'Riley, the builder of the Grabmore empire. By time the Fourth O'Riley was running the empire, it was a company of little men and little women, mean, petty, scheming. Instead of quoting poets, they cited memos. Instead of mixing it up on the docks and in the pressroom, they conspired in board rooms and meeting rooms.

Instead of shaking hands and taking pressmen and stevedores out for beers after donnybrooks and shoving matches, they typed scathing annual reviews and fired people.

Times have changed.

The fourth O'Riley wouldn't know Robert Frost from Jack Frost or Vanilla Ice. He never shook hands with a press operator, man or woman, and certainly never had a beer with one. He didn't know any of their names but they all knew his. Thanks to a company blog run by a former Grabmore reporter, everybody in the company with a computer and Internet connection could keep up with company information and rumors.

Although the company remained in O'Riley hands it was also publicly traded. That meant many of the sweetheart, you-rub-my-back, I'll-fill your-wallet shenanigans were widely known. The reporters and pressmen and accounting clerks throughout the empire knew about O'Riley and the way he profited off the layoffs, the furloughs and all the rest. They knew the suffocating corporate environment made many people just walk out the door without sticking around for any sort of severance package.

All the better for O'Riley. Really. Every week of furlough for a $32,000 a year reporter meant a bonus. Every laid off press operator in Portland, both Portlands as it turned out, meant another bonus. So the suspects piled up. …

And the meanness continued and the employee rolls and payroll and circulation figures shrank and shrank and the Internet sucked away readers and advertisers in some sort of death spiral of bad news. O'Riley's solution was always the same. Cut the size of the newspaper, making it physically smaller. Cut the number of reporters and photographers. Give people fewer and fewer reasons to buy the paper.

Repeat the process and earn another bonus.

Meanwhile, the rest of us, those of us with some ink in our blood, along with, no doubt plenty of cheap beer or wine that was little more than swill, plugged away.

We put up with the pettiness and the viciousness because we loved what we did and because, frankly, we couldn't imagine doing anything else.

For me, for most of my career, the sports department was a bit of a sanctuary. Not a full-fledged refuge from Mother Grabmore but a bit removed, just enough to make it tolerable.

When I think of O'Riley, though, I'm often reminded of something from the Bhagavad Gita.

"Now I am become death. The destroyer of worlds."

O'Riley was destroying this world. Really. Other factors were involved, of course, but he was a destroyer of worlds.

That was the Grabmore empire.

Never was that puzzlement more apparent than in the person (and I use that term reluctantly) of the sports editor at the time O'Riley vanished. He was and is the embodiment of the vexing and puzzling Grabmore culture. Let me tell you about this fellow.

CHAPTER FIVE

Every Grabmore employee knows where he or she was the day they heard about O'Riley's disappearance.

The dozen unfortunate members of the Tropical-Times sports department recall the day for another reason. It was the second anniversary of the infamous date Col. Longstreet brought in our new sports editor – Bo Lowe. First name was Beauregard. Shortened to Bo. It was said he wanted it to be Beau but couldn't spell that so went with Bo instead.

Last name Lowe. Not shortened to anything. Which was good because Lowe came up short in so many ways. Mentally, morally, ethically, journalistically.

We learned that in detail in the roughly two years between his first day on the job and the day O'Riley walked off his yacht and into some misty mystery, like some 21st century Judge Crater or Amelia Earhart.

It didn't take long to take the measure of Lowe. We sized him up on his first day.

Col. Longstreet escorted Lowe into a sports department meeting. The sports staff sat at a round table in a square room. The previous sports editor, a former stripper named Bertha Borman, moved on to another paper, a larger paper, in the Grabmore empire. We watched Lowe lurch into the room. He was about 5-foot-6, wearing khaki slacks, a polo shirt with some sort of golf logo and eyeglasses that might have seemed right for Clark Kent.

This guy wasn't Clark Kent, and certainly not Superman.

Longstreet introduced his new sports editor and left the room and Lowe took over. Using some techniques he likely picked up in a management seminar at the country club where he acquired the polo shirt, he began by asking the staffers to introduce themselves.

To my left, sat Tess Stanton, our boating writer. Lowe was curious about her first name.

"It's Tess as in Tess of the d'Urbervilles," Tess explained.

Lowe's empty brown eyes didn't register anything. Not a glimmer of recognition crossed his sweaty little face. His beady eyes were as blank and lifeless as the screen of an old television tucked away in grandma's garage.

"The Darbeyvilles?" Lowe asked. "Is that a WNBA team?"

Tess chuckled, thinking Lowe was jesting.

"No," Tess said, "that's Tess as in Tess of the Thomas Hardy novel."

"Yes," Lowe said blankly.

"My parents were English teachers," she tried explaining. "Especially English lit."

Lowe stared. Nothing registered. His expression remained as blank as that TV still tucked away out of sight in grandma's garage.

"Yes," he said.

"Tess," Tess said.

"Righty-roo," Lowe said, eager to move on. "I have a video at home. It's called Tess and Sweet Bess from Ole Miss Find the Right Mister. Anybody know it?"

The title didn't register. Lowe looked around the room. We were silent, as silent as a D.W. Griffith movie. So, Lowe moved on. As he no doubt was instructed to in one of those management seminars Grabmore loves.

"We'll get around to the rest of you later," Lowe said.

He eyeballed the room. Me. Tess. Cecil, the golf writer. Basil, who covered fishing and hunting. Anna Lee, who covered high school sports. Jimmy Golson, the sports clerk who answered the phones and was our first line of defense against paranoid and angry sports moms who are convinced their son would be an NFL quarterback if only we covered his Pop Warner games. We were exiling her son to a life of crime and degradation all because we don't like his team. When he becomes a serial killer it will be our fault because we didn't send a photographer to take pictures of the boy's games.

Our fault. All our fault. Always. Perpetually. Junior, who stood 5-foot-8 as a high school senior and ran a 5.2 40 and wasn't named our All-Area quarterback, which cost him a scholarship to Florida or Florida State.

Jimmy – God bless him – somehow was able to keep these calls down to 10 minutes or so. How he didn't develop a drug problem is a testament to his, well, to his something. I'm not sure what.

Anyhow, Tess and the rest of the sports staff sported degrees from actual universities. Me? I barely made it through a college of dubious accreditation.

The pause from Lowe continued. No doubt something else a fancy consultant taught the pipsqueak sports editor at one of those seminars.

"Now," Lowe said, the pause over. "One thing I don't cotton to in my sports section is starting stories with the word "it.""

He was twiddling a Grabmore No. 2 pencil in his fingers.

"What?" I asked.

A brilliant question, if I don't mind saying.

"No, it," Lowe said.

I blurted out "It was the best of time. It was the worst of times. It was the epoch of incredulity."

I couldn't recall the entire opening paragraph of A Tale of Two Cities but got those three sentences out.

Lowe's face remained impassive as ever. No glimmer of recognition. No life. No light. The eyes remained as dull as pond water on a still day.

This wasn't going well. Well, few things were in the newspaper business. The economy wasn't doing well. The Internet was sucking away readers and advertisers. And, somehow, newspaper chains kept promoting and protecting empty suits like Col. Longstreet and empty Polo shirts like Lowe.

"You know, Dickens," I pointed out, thinking the reference to Charles Dickens, one of the most famous writers in world history might jog his addled memory.

Still, those beady eyes didn't register anything.

"What paper does he write for?" Lowe asked.

"Ah, one of them London papers," I said.

"Well, if he was any good he'd work for a Grabmore paper like the Tropical-Fish," Lowe said.

"You mean Times," I pointed out, helpfully. "Tropical-Times."

"I still don't like starting a story with it," Lowe said, again. "Where is this Dickens guy? You got an email address for him?"

"Ah," I said, another example of my quick wit. "He's, ah, dead."

"Good," Lowe said.

A painful pause filled the room as we wondered, yet again, how people such as Lowe not only survive but thrive in Grabmore. The rest of us, the ones with IQs in the more or less normal range, refer to them as Grabmorons.

More silence. More seconds passed as we sat there in shocked awe.

Finally, I, ah, asked Lowe what changes if any he planned to keep our section vibrant. He asked why I asked. I said it's obvious. The newspaper industry is imperiled.

He asked if I was afraid.

Well, I replied, like "Franklin Roosevelt said, there's nothing to fear but fear itself."

He said, "who?" I said Roosevelt, he was a president a long time ago.

"Oh, year," Lowe said, nodding his head. "Wasn't he the president who went up Bunker Hill in a wheelchair during the Civil War?"

I just nodded numbly and said, "something like that."

Lowe wanted us to get to work right away on a big story. He said Col. Longstreet had told him that a famous football coach with local ties had just been diagnosed with "prostrate" cancer. We had to do a local story.

"You got to find out," Lowe said, scanning the department," how many women get prostrate cancer."

There was nothing to say or do. We slouched out the door and began researching our assignment: How many women get prostrate cancer? That's what the man said. The way he conflated prostate and prostrate and had us researching the incidence of women with the disease soon became a newsroom joke and eventually made its way to the Grabmore Blog. No wonder the company has such a dismal reputation.

Thus began the Lowe Era in the sports department. Morale continued its death spiral. O'Riley continued pocketing millions thanks to layoffs, furloughs and no pay raises.

The resentment and anger mounted. People like Lowe and Mabel Borgia and Col. Longstreet thrived.

Each sample of Orwellian corporate mumbo-jumbo created more dismay and despair. The Grabmore blog was filled with more details of O'Riley's compensation. The free country club membership. The new cars provided. Free, of course. The corporate chef conjuring up gourmet lunches. Free. For O'Riley.

So, maybe all the factors propelled me to conspire and scheme to someday dispose of O'Riley.

Maybe.

Maybe not.

Meanwhile, the Fort Myers P.D. was on the case. The lead detective was somebody I knew and feared. ...

CHAPTER SIX

The detective assigned to the case was Lt. J.P. Hooper, who I knew from the local old coot recreational baseball league where we both played. Its official name is Roy Hobbs baseball, as in Roy Hobbs of The Natural fame.

He - that's Hooper, not Hobbs - was the catcher for one of the teams. I played shortstop for another. I wasn't, alas, a baseball natural.

Hooper is a hard-nosed former minor-leaguer who had dabbled in rodeo and boxing and seemed tough enough to catch without a facemask, chest protector or cup. I was a light-hitting shortstop who was sent packing from my college team on the first day of cuts and liked to read novels.

Hooper liked to hunt big game. I think with his bare hands. I liked to watch old movies on TCM. I majored in American lit. He majored on the mean streets of Fort Myers in capturing killers, rapists and kidnappers. Again, with his bare hands, it seemed.

When I came to bat in games, I heard him growl some sort of guttural greeting from his crouch as the catcher. It wasn't a word, near as I could tell. Maybe it was hello, or a version of it he learned as a boy hunting alligators in the Everglades. Probably with his bare hands.

Maybe the greeting was his version of that Clint Eastwood line from Gran Torino –"Get off my lawn." Or "Get out of my batter's box."

His team was sponsored by a local store – Bartley's Sporting Goods. Ours was sponsored by a consignment shop specializing in baby wear – Babykins Second Chance Is Your First Choice. It was hard to fit all that on our jerseys so our name, the one on the front of our jerseys, was Babykins.

So when we played it was Babykins vs. Bartley's, which had nothing to do with Bartleby, the Scrivener. Bartley's is an old-time sporting goods store, a fixture in town for more than a century.

I'm sure Hooper called knockdown pitches. Even on me. Even on a light-hitting sportswriter. It seemed whenever I was down 0-2 in the count against Bartley's, which occurred often, the next pitch was an 84 mph fastball near my chin. I'd hear Hooper growl and chuckle as I fell to the dirt.

Yet, somehow, I think he respected me. I wasn't as talented or tough as Hooper but I was out there, I was stepping up to the plate. I sort of stood in front of skittering, speeding ground balls. I hung in there at second base as tough guys such as Hooper barreled in to break up double plays.

Yes, they did that even in the geezer rec baseball league.

My mantra, one popular with those lacking real skills, is that it doesn't take talent to hustle. So I hustled. I ran on and off the field. I ran hard if not fast to first on every weak ground ball I hit. I dived for balls and slid hard into bases, even into Hooper's shin guards at home plate, which was like sliding into a parked Sherman tank.

Despite his better judgment and the typical police aversion to the media he, sort of, kind of respected me. So as Hooper began investigating O'Riley's disappearance, I became his source, his mole within the lower ranks of the mystifying Grabmore empire.

He sensed that I wasn't a corporate flunkey and that I would tell him either what I knew or what I thought I knew or merely suspected. He heard me talk during post-game beers at local sports bars about the wretched corporate culture. That's how he knew I felt deep disdain and even contempt for the folks running the company.

I was his window into the perverse Grabmore corporate culture. We started meeting informally to talk. He shared - very much off the record – what he was finding out.

The first thing he had to figure out was basic - was our CEO dead? Or, had our CEO been kidnapped? Or, third option, was he shacked up with some floozy, overdosing on Frappucino and Viagra and expense account dinners at some nearby or faraway love nest of a bungalow?

The cop and the sportswriter began by meeting on a cool winter morning near the yacht basin to try re-constructing where O'Riley may have gone. It was, as I recall, a Thursday, three days after O'Riley vanished. This was an unofficial meeting for both of us. Heck, I never covered crime or the cop beat so I had no window into the uneasy relationship of reporter and police.

We talked baseball and football and O'Riley and Grabmore and the astounding despair of its employees. Our first chat was at the downtown Starbucks, tucked into a corner near the Fort Myers federal courthouse, where if things went poorly some Grabmore employees, including your storyteller, might find themselves on trial and facing years in prison. That thought more than crossed my mind, it parked itself right there, that I might one day not be able to stroll into Starbucks but would leave the adjacent building manacled and shipped far away for a very long time. ...

CHAPTER SEVEN

He ordered coffee. Black. He growled thanks at the barista with the rings in her nose and lips. I averted my gaze from all that pierced skin and meekly ordered a grande, skinny, no-whip mocha. Hooper growled a deep growl of displeasure. I know what he was thinking. What the hell is a grande, skinny, no-whip mocha? Who the hell drinks this sissified fancy stuff?

He spit a disapproving juicy wad of tobacco in a trashcan and we walked down a short hallway to a seating area in the back. I had promised to tell him everything I know. I lied. I couldn't do that. I'd tell him about the suffocating corporate atmosphere and the mendacious managers and the hypocrisy. I'd tell him about the Orwellian, amoral corporate lingo. I freely explained the low morale and the self-righteous, phony-baloney, sanctimonious prattling about ethics. I had no trouble telling him that for all the blather about journalistic ethics the key word missing from all that bloviating was the adjective situational.

As in situational ethics. As in the ethics depended on the situation and the person involved. If the person was an editor such as Lowe and had been anointed with a bullet proof corporate shield by an unseen golden scepter of some murky, mystifying power, all was well and almost anything went.

Go on a free fishing junket? That was fine. Have affairs with reporters? That was fine. Lie and dissemble and scheme and backstab and brown nose? That was fine. For weasels such as Lowe.

If, on the other hand, the county government reporter accepted a small Coke from a county commissioner's receptionist, that was worth a suspension without pay and a stern reprimand in the reporter's file. No freebies. We must remain beyond reproach.

That was the Grabmore way. A double standard of shifting ethics and retroactive rules. Do something yesterday and a rule is announced against it today and you will be punished tomorrow.

Like I said, I lied to Hooper, who I respected. I didn't want to do it but I had to. I had too many people to protect, including myself. I knew what happened to O'Riley. Really.

I promised to help Hooper. And I would. Up to a point. I couldn't tell him about the conspiracy of reporters, press operators and sports department colleagues.

I couldn't tell him about the folks from Portland. Both Portlands. I couldn't tell him about the janitor from corporate headquarters. Or the sports writer in St. Paul. Or the veteran pressman in Boise. Or the sportscaster in Jackson.

So many were in on this or at were least aware of the secret operation, which had no nifty code name like, say, Operation Nitwit.

One of the advantages of working in Florida, in places such as Fort Myers and nearby places such as Naples, Sanibel, Useppa and many others is that they were winter vacation destinations.

So Grabmore employees came here on vacation. From all those places. All those people. Everybody in the Grabmore empire knew about O'Riley's annual visit. There is nothing suspicious about other folks, the lowly workers, Grabmore's peasant class, visiting here in the winter.

That's how we got together. That's how we planned what we planned, how we fooled Hooper and the FBI and the Grabmore security gunsels. That's how we did what we did.

First, though, I had to meet with Hooper and we would unofficially re-construct the day of the disappearance. So, keeping my eyes averted from the pierced barista, I grabbed my grande, skinny, no-whip mocha and we walked to the back, sat down and talked.

Maybe I should mention the day we, ah, borrowed, O'Riley. We don't like the words kidnapped or abducted or hijacked or shanghaied.

Those words all have such, well, criminal connotations. We don't consider ourselves criminals. We're merely desperate people trying to save our newspapers and our souls and journalism and decency and.
. . .

Well, you get it. And we got O'Riley. But would Hooper get us?

CHAPTER EIGHT

One of the surprising things about getting close to Chesterfield Ebenezer O'Riley was finding out he talked like Jay Gatsby. Even dressed a bit like the iconic literary figure created by the man my parents named me after. We learned his Gatsby-like ways the day we pulled that Chevy suburban up to the curb near the yacht club and strong-armed him into the back of the van.

"Say, old, sport, what is this all about?" a startled O'Riley said to me.

We plopped O'Riley down on the carpeted floor and offered him a Starbucks Frappucino and a bottle of Evian water. We were borrowing him but we're not thugs. OK, borrowing is a euphemism. Not to put too fine a point on it but it was, well, a kidnapping.

We're still civilized folks. Not kidnappers. At least in our minds. Or murderers. Or maybe we are. Or were about to become killers. Although, of course, he didn't know that, which worked to our advantage. Yet, as one might imagine, he was frightened. We tried putting him at ease, which under the circumstances probably wasn't possible.

Up front was our driver, Monique Bunyan, a lumberjack from the Grabmore forests of New Brunswick. I was in the back with three other Grabmore employees, all far more menacing than me.

There was Nigel Claymore, a former IRA operative trained as a sharpshooter, bomb maker and polemicist. Nigel wore khaki slacks, a blue Grabmore polo shirt and a snappy black beret that made him look vaguely French.

Next to him was Sal Hotdog, a distant cousin of mine from Jersey City. I was never clear on where Sal got that last name. But I knew a little about his past, about his days in the north Jersey mob, where he may or may not have broken kneecaps and run crystal meth labs in Bergen County.

O'Riley sat dazed on the floor, looking at the galoots in the van. Plunked down there on the floor, back to the locked rear doors of the van, was the final member of our little group. I don't want to use the word gang because it has such a, well, criminal connotation. Sure, we technically committed a crime by snatching O'Riley off the palm-lined streets of Fort Myers on a sunny winter afternoon. But we felt justified.

Oh, yeah, the final member of the group was Ahmad Mohammad Mamoud, the one sitting on the floor, glaring at O'Riley. Ahmad had trained with Al Qaeda, was taught how to make car bombs and suicide vests. It was how he grew up in Yemen, the son of Afghan immigrants to that country. His parents had escaped Afghanistan just as the Soviets invaded. Ahmad, however, was a gentle soul and didn't subscribe to the barbarous 12th century version of Islam practiced by Islamists.

As soon as he could, he left Yemen, found his way to America and got a pressroom job at the Bergen County Bugle, another Grabmore paper, the same paper where Nigel worked as a sportswriter. As the van smoothly pulled away from the docks and headed off to McGregor Boulevard, O'Riley nervously glanced around. He was wearing white slacks, brown Docksiders, a polo shirt from Burning Tree Country Club outside Washington D.C. and his omnipresent little captain's cap. He's about 5-foot-9, 190 pounds with a round face, pointy nose and pale complexion.

"Say, old sport," he said, eyeballing me from under the beak of the cap. "If you want money, I got money. Plenty. What do you want? Polo ponies? Cars? Yachts? A Swiss bank account? I can arrange for any of those. I got them. Just name it, old sport."

I didn't answer. Neither did anybody else. We sat in silence for a few moments as Monique edged the van past the Lee County Justice Center. As O'Riley cowered and shook and glanced at the menacing and muscle-bound Grabmore employees, he knew he was not in a good position. He couldn't downsize his way out of this predicament. He couldn't decree furloughs from the back of the van and find himself dropped off at a fancy restaurant on tony 5th Avenue South in Naples.

As he sat there, Nigel told me a little of his story and how he followed the same geographic and career arc in his life as the Grabmore founder, the great-grandfather of the pudgy, weak little man in the back of the van. Nigel, like Ahmad, wasn't a violent man. He was a throwback to previous centuries. Sure, he grew up around violent people but he harbored a gentle soul.

Yes, he was a rough defender on the soccer pitch and a hard-hitting welterweight boxer with a chin of granite, able to give and take punches and good enough in the ring to fight a few pro bouts in Ireland. At the same time, he was a big reader, sort of like the Grabmore founder. Nigel was a fan of Tom Wolfe, both his journalism and literature. He grew up on Hunter Thompson and read Ernie Pyle's World War II journalism. He knew the tales of Ernest Hemingway during World War I and World War II. He was a fan of Martha Gellhorn, one of Hemingway's wives and a remarkable war correspondent. He wanted to be like them. He also loved sports and journalism history.

Nigel followed his dream to America, to Bergen County and the Bugle. That's where he came to know the Grabmore corporate culture and the pettiness, backstabbing and brownnosing that O'Riley No. 4 encouraged, which was so different from the way the company started.

Now, he had the CEO who was helping destroy the company. We all had him and now that we had him what were we going to do with him?

Well, the first thing was getting out of town. Fast. Get away from the yacht club and hope nobody noticed O'Riley tossed into the back of that van by three nervous looking guys glancing around as they tossed their human cargo in the van, which moved as soon as the doors closed.

CHAPTER NINE

Nigel told me about a book he found in a Dublin library as a child. It was the first-person tale of an impoverished Irish lad who left for America long ago on a boat called the City of Cheaters. This young man in the book had many of the same interests as Nigel. He was an athlete and lover of literature and poetry and journalism. The young man had ambition and dreams and was fearless.

The book was a memoir entitled Poet, Pugilist and Pressman. It was by the first Chesterfield O'Riley in America, the great-grandfather of the corporate bureaucrat sitting and trembling in stunned and scared silence in the back of the van hurtling along McGregor Boulevard to some secret destination. At least secret to O'Riley.

We knew where we headed.

Nigel had told me before of how he dreamed about America and going to work for the Grabmore empire. Of how he viewed the first O'Riley as a role model. Of how he wanted to be like the first O'Riley. He wanted to box. He wanted to be tough but fair. He wanted to write poems and novels and work in journalism. He wanted to succeed but not in the way that O'Riley No 4 and his puke-scented minions did it. The life of a sycophant was not for him. No mewling brown-nosing for Nigel.

When he left Ireland for America and came to the Bergen County Bugle in 1993 to cover soccer and boxing for the Grabmore paper in north Jersey he wanted to succeed in the same way as O'Riley the First.

The van rattled along and Nigel pulled from a backpack a worn copy of Poet, Pugilist and Pressman. It turns out he had several copies and handed one to Sal and Ahmad and told Monique he had one for her as well. She was busy driving at the moment.

Nigel pushed his black beret back on his head, eased down on the floor and glared at the current O'Riley, the money-sucking leech and lecher who was destroying Grabmore and shattering the lives of thousands of its current and former employees. O'Riley was silent. And relatively still. Except for the incessant trembling. Nigel asked him if he had read his great-grandfather's memoir. O'Riley mumbled that he never reads books. Nigel glared at him and said, "That figures."

Nigel held up the book as if it were holy text. He looked at O'Riley. O'Riley shivered and quaked and croaked out, "What are you going to do with me?"

"Funny you should ask that," Nigel said. "We haven't quite figured that part out. The abduction was the easy part. Some people want to kill you. Some want to keep you hidden away like a monk. No more Frappucinos. No more Irish or Lapp girls you've borrowed for your pleasure."

Nigel glanced around. At Sal and Ahmad and up front at Monique. And started talking again.

"You know the movie Casablanca? Probably not. Anyhow, as that movie was being made, the writers didn't have the ending figured out. That's sort of like this situation. Except you won't be spending time with Ingrid Bergman and we'll never have Paris. And this isn't the beginning of a beautiful friendship. The end? What we're going to do with you? We've been discussing it, haven't we, Ahmad?" Nigel said.

Ahmad paused and glared at O'Riley.

"When I was a boy in Yemen I learned how to make suicide vests," Ahmad said. "Do you know what happens when a suicide vest wrapped around the chest explodes? Do you know how far the body parts fly when the vest explodes? Do you know how many parts fly through the air and end up on tree branches and in coffee cups? It's not a pretty sight. We haven't decided what we're going do with you. Isn't that right, Sal?"

Sal, a beefy man wearing beige cargo shorts and a blue New York Giants jersey, nodded.

"Mr. O'Riley,," said Sal, ever polite. "Before I went to work delivering your Panama City paper - that's the Panama City in Florida, by the way, not the one in Panama - I worked on the other side of the law. I never did what some people call wet work. That means killing people. But I heard things. I know how these things go.

"You ever heard of somebody being shot in the head three times and the case being ruled a suicide? Well, where I come from, that was a pretty common event. It would be a shame if you turned up in a ditch or a crack house with a suicide note in your fancy, Nancy-boy yacht club blazer jacket and three .38 slugs in your head."

O'Riley continued trembling.

CHAPTER TEN

Nigel decided it was time to get back to the book. The van rolled along and Nigel spoke: "This is how your great-grandfather started his American career and his empire, the one crumbling while you're chasing teenage Irish lasses and drinking your fancy coffee and using Grabmore as a personal ATM machine. This is how he started Chapter 1 of Poet, Pugilist and Pressman:"

I reeked of urine and beer and sweat and oil and stale, weevil-infested biscuits that day I walked in the front door of the Brooklyn Daily Eagle. I was 17. The last time I had been in a schoolroom was when I was 9. I hadn't eaten anything in 24 hours. I hadn't bathed or even washed in three weeks or so. I was wearing the same clothes I wore when I left Dublin three weeks earlier. I had nothing. No job. No friends. No future. Hardly any past. I spoke with an accent.

I had nothing but books and dreams and ambitions. I wanted to write and learn. I wanted to be like Oscar Wilde, except without the sodomy. I wanted to be like Yeats. I wanted to be like journalistic heroes such as Richard Harding Davis and Ida Tarbell and Lincoln Steffens. I later became disillusioned with Steffens for his myopic and implausibly rosy view of the Soviet Union. But that's getting ahead of the story.

But how could that happen? How could I become a journalistic success? I had no education. No mentors. No hope. I came through Ellis Island and now what?

America beckoned. A vast continent of opportunities and newspapers and hope. Sure, I didn't have a formal education but I had always read. Dickens and Twain. Hardy and Poe. James Fenimore Cooper and Thackery.

I knew I could write. Certainly, not like a great novelist but I could tell stories. I could report and write with clarity. I knew that at 17. I wanted to spend my life working with words and using my fists for recreation and competition.

So, I left Ellis Island and found my way to Brooklyn and still smelling like the belly of a ship reeking with unwashed refugees from Europe, walked in the front door. My suit was grimy and stained and speckled with holes. I heard the rumble of presses running somewhere in the bowels of the great building. I saw reporters walk through the lobby. They didn't know me. I didn't know them. I was hungry and desperate but somehow I felt at home. These men were like me in some ways.

For the moment, they were different. They had money in their pockets. They had jobs. They had used soap in recent weeks. Their suits were clean. They had friends and family on this continent. But I felt at home that day. Felt some peace. I knew good things would happen.

So, once I walked in the door and I glanced around I knew, even then, even at 17, that I had found my future. I didn't know I would become one of the richest men in America. I didn't know I would someday own more than 90 newspapers. I didn't know I would own dozens of radio stations. Well, that would have been impossible to know then because commercial radio was still years in the future.

I didn't know I would become nearly as rich and powerful as Hearst and Pulitzer. I didn't know I would someday advise a young man named Orson Welles as he worked on a movie called 'Citizen Kane.' Mr. Welles assured me the movie wasn't about me. Mr. Welles, the young genius whippersnapper, said he respected me even if he sometimes disagreed with some things I did. All that was in the future. All that was unimaginable the day I walked into the Brooklyn Daily Eagle in 1908.

Nigel stopped reading aloud. ...

It was then that the van pulled into a parking lot between a Starbucks and Mr. Ho's Chinese restaurant, a few miles from the yacht club and the Tropical-Times office.

The rest of our kidnapping gang was on vacation, spending free time committing a federal crime. I had to get back to work and keep my alibi airtight.

Waiting for me in the parking lot in her Honda was Tess from the sports department. As arranged earlier, she met us there between the mochas and General Tso's chicken. Good thing O'Riley didn't know we were so close to a Starbucks. O'Riley would remain in the van, would remain in the custody and care of my colleagues, my confederates.

I had to get back to work, get back to that feature on the new Red Sox bullpen catcher. Had to prove I was working and not part of a conspiracy to, ah, borrow the CEO of Grabmore Publications.

I sidled past the trembling O'Riley and out the van's rear door. Before slamming it shut, I told him, "Have a nice day. Your new friends are going to hang on to you a while."

O'Riley mumbled, "Where are they taking me? What are they going to do to me?"

"Honestly," I told him, "I don't know, old sport."

All the details of our little plot had yet to be worked out. More and better planning would have been prudent. We never actually thought our hare-brained, half-baked scheme to kidnap the CEO would work. But we seen our chances and took 'em. As well as Chesterfield Ebenezer O'Riley IV.

The van rumbled out of the parking lot, away from Chinese food and cappuccinos, its cargo tucked away. I sat next to Tess and told her the plan, such as it was, was going well.

We had the CEO. We were taking him somewhere remote and hidden. Then what? We still didn't know.

Would we leave him somewhere deep in the Ten Thousand Islands? Or miles out in the Gulf in the Mexico? Or some muddy grave in the Everglades? Or demand a ransom?

There would be time to figure that out later. I had that sports feature to write and an alibi to secure by being seen in the office on the day Chesterfield Ebenezer O'Riley IV disappeared from the yacht called Never Enough and the palm-lined streets of downtown Fort Myers, a few blocks from the Tropical-Times offices.

CHAPTER ELEVEN

Tess didn't drive me all the way back to the office. She dropped me off a couple blocks away so I could casually stroll back as if I had just been gone a few minutes. First, though, we chatted. I updated her on how smoothly we abducted the CEO and how terrified O'Riley was as he sat trembling in the back of the van.

Tess was nearly as scared as I was. Not to mention O'Riley, of course. None of us had ever been part of what could quite likely be termed a criminal conspiracy. What else could it be called? We had conspired. Quite clearly. We had, I must admit, committed a crime. Technically. And in every other way.

We snatched an American citizen off the streets of a placid little downtown. We bundled him in the back of a van. It probably wouldn't help to point out the van was American made, a Chevy Suburban.

We rationalized the act. Like nearly every decent human being, we viewed O'Riley as a heartless, soulless, amoral, greedy, lecherous corporate villain. All true. Certainly. But that wouldn't make us innocent in the eyes of the law. We were guilty. No doubt.

And now that we had him, what was next?

The van by now was heading south on U.S. 41. Through San Carlos Park and on through Estero and Bonita Springs and on to

Naples and points beyond. Where was he being taken and what were we going to do with our prize captive?

As Tess drove me back downtown in her Honda, she expressed fear. Make that terror. She wasn't involved in the abduction. But she was clearly an accessory. She and her husband, Cliff, have three children. She was aiding and abetting one of the ringleaders. That would be me.

By time Tess dropped me off and I walked back in the newsroom, back to the puke, tobacco and ketchup-stained carpet, the kidnapping wasn't news. It was too soon. Nobody knew O'Riley was missing. Not yet. Maybe he had stopped by Hooters for some wings and beer and leering. That was typically part of his annual winter visit. I had to, meanwhile, get cracking on my feature on the Red Sox new bullpen catcher.

Even more than usual, I struggled with this story. Not because it was a challenging story. It was a harmless little feature on Pepper Martino, who has knocked around the fringes of pro baseball for years.

I typed up ledes, newspaper jargon for the start of stories.

Everything was straight from the dustbin of the worst ledes in sports writing history:

A funny thing happened to Pepper Martino on his way to the major leagues.

What a difference a year makes for Pepper Martino.

It was a dark and stormy night the day Pepper Martino was injured at high noon in a Gulf Coast League game.

Geez. ...

I needed to clear my head and focus. Using any of those ledes would banish me forevermore to typing up Little League scores and high school volleyball agate. Or get me promoted to executive editor.

Still, it was difficult focusing on Pepper and his three-year career as a back-up catcher in the low minors and his heart-warming tale of overcoming a childhood in a gated community as the son of two orthodontists who ferried him to youth baseball games all over Florida.

In the car on the way back downtown, I rehashed to Tess how we plucked O'Riley off the street. He came bopping down the dock, his little captain's cap perched on his head, his polo shirt with the golf club logo proclaiming his wealth as loud as a quartet of steel drummers at a third-rate beach resort and his white slacks, his white socks and brown Docksiders.

He wasn't accompanied by any of those steroid-addled louts who usually worked his security detail. He had that usual Grabmore vacant stare, the beady-eyed gaze that betrayed no sense of humanity or knowledge or interest in anything besides money and career advancement.

Nigel and the gang were parked nearby. I had walked from the office and the timing was, frankly, implausibly fortuitous. As I strolled down West First Street, there was O'Riley and the van. We all converged. ....

I said hello. I didn't address him by name. I lied. Said I was a tourist and was looking for the Lanai restaurant. He looked annoyed. O'Riley wasn't used to dealing with the peasant classes on the streets of an American town. He usually was ferried from his gated home, the one with the moats on all sides, to his exclusive country club or to his corner office at Grabmore Towers. Crossing paths with somebody other than valets and chauffeurs and corporate lackeys made him uncomfortable. There was no layer of security or brownnosing weasels protecting him. Not this time, not this moment.

I said, "Sir, I just came down from Poughkeepsie and I'm looking for this fancy restaurant called the Back Porch or Balcony or Rear Door or something."

He tipped his little captain's cap back on his head, looked left and right and he was startled into silence and stared at me for a moment.

"Ah, sir, maybe you don't know the place," I said.

He began mumbling. It's as if a busboy at the country club had asked for stock tips. His little mind was racing. He was likely thinking why did I want to walk to the Lanai? Now I got this unwashed idiot from Poughkeepsie asking questions.

Finally, evidently figuring the best way out of this encounter was providing a straight answer, he said, "You mean the Lanai."

I asked for directions. He began pointing and I asked him to step closer to the curb. That's when we pounced, when my colleagues leapt from the van and tossed him roughly into the back and slammed the door.

It took somewhere between one and two seconds. The door was locked. O'Riley was too scared to say anything. He was ours. We were on our way. But on our way where? And what were we going to do with him? And once we did what we did, whatever it was, how were we going to get out of this mess?

If we killed him, how did we dispose of the body? Were we capable of murder? Oh, yeah. Maybe not me but some of my friends in that Chevy Suburban.

If it were a kidnapping, would we ask for ransom? If so, how much? And ask who? Stockholders? Readers?

Were we going to hold him indefinitely? How long would we hold on to him? And where? How would we feed him? Who would pay for it? How long could we take time away from jobs and family to monitor this corporate criminal? Could we ship him somewhere? Mali? Somalia? Siberia?

Well, we'd figure that out. If only we were as smart and resourceful as O'Riley's great-grandfather.

The story of how Chesterfield Ebenezer O'Riley came to call his company Grabmore is all there in his book, Poet, Pugilist and Pressman. Too bad his great-grandson doesn't read books.

Speaking of our CEO…

Nigel and the rest of my other new best friends still had O'Riley someplace south of Naples. At least I think they're south of Naples, that's where they're supposed to be, according to our plans.

There's not much land south of Naples. It's water and the Ten Thousand Islands and then more water and Marco Island and more water and then the Florida Keys and more water and Cuba.

Back at the Tropical-Times, it was business as usual that afternoon. Mabel was brownnosing and bullying her way up the corporate ladder. Or at least trying to get up that ladder crowded with others sharing her ambition and lack of scruples. That ladder must be a grimy, slippery thing.

I was struggling with my feature and typing up a bio box on the uneventful career of the new Red Sox bullpen catcher. Photo editor Polly Schwartz was juggling the assignments of 10 photographers and answering questions from 12 editors and 40 reporters, all of who thought their assignments and photos were the most important of the day, if not in all journalism history.

The storm was about to hit, though. I knew it. Tess knew it. Not others. Soon, Col. Longstreet and Mabel and the police will realize that O'Riley isn't just on another bender at Hooters or his favorite Fort Myers strip club, Strumpets on the Strand. That's, by the way, a local place that is part of a regional chain of strip clubs. There are others called Strumpets on the Bay, Strumpets by the Sea, Strumpets Lakeside and so on and so forth. …

I quietly filed my feature story on the catcher, packed up my laptop and walked out the door and headed home. By morning, it would all be clear – O'Riley was nowhere to be found. Not all would be clear. He was clearly gone. But the where and the how would be mysteries.

For now, I drove home and sat on my porch and read parts of Poet, Pugilist and Pressman, from the copy Nigel had so graciously provided.

Opening at random, I read the portion where O'Riley testified in 1947 before the House Un-American Activities Committee, which was investigating his empire. How did, congressmen such as Martin Dies of Texas demanded, a penniless and dirty Irish boy – a Catholic one at that! – own all those newspapers and radio stations and amass all that power and wealth?

They smelled part of a vast communist conspiracy. They were sure Karl Marx himself or perhaps Leon Trotsky, not to be confused with baseball player Hal Trosky, personally walked O'Riley to the Liverpool docks, purchased his ticket for New York, bade him farewell with kisses on both cheeks and wished him good luck in his quest to destroy America from within. Marx or Trotsky wouldn't have said, of course, Godspeed because they were, well, Godless commies.

CHAPTER TWELVE

Here from the first O'Riley's book, is part of Chapter 9, titled, Land of Opportunity, My Land:

I seen my opportunities and took 'em. That was the slogan of an old-time New York City politician named George Washington Plunkitt.

He's not remembered that much here some years past the mid-point of the 20th century, even here in Gotham, more than 50 years after I walked off the City of Cheaters and through Ellis Island and in the front door of the Brooklyn Daily Eagle.

Now, I'm more powerful and famous than Plunkitt ever was. Maybe more powerful than Boss Tweed ever was back in the last century and nearly as powerful as William Randolph Hearst and Charles Foster Kane.

Of course, Kane was make-believe, a creation of that young whippersnapper Orson Welles. I remember when the kid came to me. He wanted to make a movie about a powerful newspaper tycoon. He wanted to base the fictional tycoon on Hearst, whom I had no use for.

So we talked. This was back in '38. He wanted to know how I built my empire. It wasn't anything like Hearst or Kane. Both were blessed with enormous fortunes and started out with every advantage.

I started out that day in 1908 in the lobby of the Brooklyn Daily Eagle with $5 and a request to spend some of it on soap. Now, I may go out and buy Palmolive or Lifebouy. Not a bar of soap. But the companies. Both. If the mood strikes me to do so.

Would that be un-American? That slimy Texas congressman Martin Dies seemed to think so.

That's why he summoned me to that infernal committee he created in Congress to investigate anybody who dared to criticize Jim Crow or lynching or thought my friend Franklin Roosevelt wasn't a commie and his wife Eleanor wasn't a lesbian hellhound from Moscow operating under direct orders of Joseph Stalin. That's how the loons on that committee thought.

How, this Dies character wanted to know, did I – a penniless, Catholic immigrant boy with dirty clothes reeking of the bowels of the City of Cheaters – build this empire? We used to call my modest outfit O'Riley Publications and Communications. As some of you oldtimers may recall.

Until that day when I sat at that table in front of those microphones and photographers and that Texas nitwit who saw commies under every bed and behind every newsroom and Hollywood typewriter. Well, there were a few, I have to admit. Behind the typewriters, that is. Commies. I don't know about under any beds.

So, I tried explaining how I came to own all those newspapers and radio stations and even a few Canadian forests.

My first day of work at the Eagle I arrived at 7 a.m. for my 8 a.m. meeting with the top editor. Mr. Perry Kent. I had read the paper front to back and then back to front. I knew what was in the paper and what he wanted and I learned as much as I could about the place called Brooklyn.

I had also stopped the night before at a public library and read some of the other New York papers. I was new in town and new in the country. I needed to learn fast about this place and the newspapers.

When Mr. Kent showed up at 8:03 a.m., I was standing there, scrubbed and wearing a new jacket and clean slacks and a smile. He nodded gruffly and said he could spend five minutes with me. That was it. He had a paper to run. Dozens of stories and reporters and editors to deal with and deadlines. We talked for an hour.

I told him about leaving Ireland, about spending two weeks in the stinking, pestilential, steerage of the City of Cheaters and how I read Yeats and Wilde and Thackery and "The Adventures of Huckleberry Finn" as the boat bounced and lurched and bounced yet again. I told him about the urine-stained mattress and the weevil-infested biscuits.

He sent out for breakfast, a breakfast I'll never forget. Eggs. Sunny-side up, which was sort of an omen of things to come. Bacon. Great coffee. Coffee like I had never tasted. An orange. A banana. Not a weevil in sight. And blueberries. I had never seen blueberries before.

Mr. Kent told me, basically, "Kid, you don't have any experience. You're too young. Your accent needs the edges taken off. You need directions to the front door and don't know a home run from a nickelodeon. But I like your moxie, gumption, vim and vinegar. Also, now that you've been introduced to soap you don't stink like the infernal steerage of that ship. What's it called – City of Louses?

"Well, whatever, here's what I'm going to do. Go find a room at the YMCA. Here's another $5. Buy some more clothes and stock up on soap. Come back tomorrow morning at 8, not 7. We'll find something for you to do."

So that's how it started. I came back the next day and the day after that and the day after that. I was always early. Mr. Kent always found something for me to do. Sharpen pencils. Clean out trashcans. Run errands. Pick up donuts and cigarettes. Learn telegraphy. Tag along with reporters on assignments. Learn how to edit and to write headlines. Spend time in the pressroom and with sales reps. I learned as much as I could as swiftly as I could.

A year later, at 18, Mr. Kent assigned me to help cover city hall and I'd venture across the famous bridge into Manhattan where I soon hobnobbed with the likes of Bat Masterson, the former western gunslinger turned sportswriter. That same year, a young writer named Damon Runyan came to town. I got to know him as well. There were dinners at Delmonico's. I learned to write and write fast. The importance of accuracy was drummed into me.

When I was 19, Mr. Kent named me assistant sports editor and boxing columnist. He quintupled my salary and said he planned to buy a paper in Poughkeepsie. Would I like to buy in?

Well, I had a little money. Enough for my room. Occasional dinners at Delmonico's. where I was usually the guest of Bat or Damon. Soap. That was about it. He'd loan me the money. That's what he said.

So, briefly, that's how it started. A loan from Mr. Kent and I was on my way. Oh, don't forget the soap. Couldn't have done it without the soap.

That's where I stopped reading for the night. I didn't get to the part where the company is re-named Grabmore. I think that's in Chapter 10.

First thing in the morning, the day after the kidnapping, that Tuesday I planned to see the latest O'Riley, to talk to the corpulent CEO. Where? Where we planned to stash him, in that house in Chokoloskee, a fishing village and tourist town south of Naples, near the water and on the fringe of that hopeless maze, the Ten Thousand Islands.

People have gotten lost back in there, wandering the waterways between all those islands. .... I wonder how Chesterfield would fare if we took him back there in a Boston Whaler some dark, moonless night and left him alone. Alone with the alligators and snakes and mosquitoes and the dark and the quiet and that infernal maze of islands that provide no geographic sense of where you are or where you're going or where you've been. ...

Are we the sort of people who would do something like that?

CHAPTER THIRTEEN

I left Fort Myers behind, driving south on I-75 as far as it goes south. Past the shopping centers and trailer parks, past the golf courses and gated communities, south and east to the past, paid the $3 toll where the Interstate turns east. Then toward the Everglades, taking a right turn at an interchange and heading south down S.R. 29 to an outpost on the fringe of the Everglades.

S.R. 29 slices through a remote corner of urban Southwest Florida. The two-lane road is bordered much of the way by chain link fences in the hope of keeping Florida panthers from venturing onto the highway. Cars zip through the "towns" of Jerome and Copeland, which each seem to consist of a few lonely houses. One must then brave the flashing light at the intersection of 29 and U.S. 41, where the east-west traffic of 41 barrels along seemingly heedless that somebody may be going north or south.

Then down the final stretch of 29 and into Everglades City, a town once known as simply Everglade, a fishing and tourist retreat many miles in distance and attitude from the central Florida glut of tourist destinations and the glitz of Miami Beach. Then, the journey still isn't done. Keep going, drive down a causeway to where the road runs out of land, to a place called Chokoloskee.

That's where we hid O'Riley. My late uncle Orville owned one of the biggest houses in town, one he left to me. It's a big yellow house with a wrap-around porch shielded from neighboring homes by trees and shrubs. It has a hurricane-proof annex without windows and doors that lock from the outside. Our gang - I hate that word - of rookie kidnappers could access it from the kitchen or through the two-car garage.

That's where we stashed the CEO. It should be noted, he was stashed in comfort, nearly in style. With air conditioning and a flat-screen television and a refrigerator stocked with frappucinos and beer. There was plenty of food and a microwave. But no windows. No fresh air. No sunshine.

As windowless prisons go it's not bad. At least we like to think so. We may be kidnappers but we're not thugs. Well, technically, some of us have thug on our resumes what with the mafia and terrorist connections. Anyhow, O'Riley wasn't tied or gagged or beaten. Just locked in that annex, which included a sparklingly clean bathroom with a shower, bars of Irish Spring soap and stacks of wash clothes and towels from Bed, Bath & Beyond, all recently purchased at the Bell Tower Shops in Fort Myers.

As I drove that lonely stretch of S.R. 29 I imagined the frenzied reaction at corporate headquarters in Buffalo and in the Tropical-Times newsroom. Where is O'Riley? Why isn't he on his yacht? Or in his limo? Did he wander off? Where is he?

I knew. A few other folks knew. I zipped on down to Uncle Orville's house to check with Nigel and Ahmed, Monique and Sal. And our guest. How is our prize? Now that we have him, what will we do with him? Bundle him onto a boat and take him deep into the Ted Thousand Islands and just drop him on some random isle on Lostman's River? No, we're not the type to do that. That's a death sentence and would qualify as cruel and unusual punishment.

We had our plans. Or at least some vague ideas of what might be next, a whisper of a plan. Technically, I guess, that's not a real plan.

I walked in and Nigel was drinking coffee and eating a blueberry muffin. He filled me in. O'Riley was scared and puzzled. Why did we kidnap him? How much ransom did we want? Nigel told me O'Riley was informed that no ransom demand had been made or would be made.

Let's make this clear right now. I'm not in charge. Nobody was really in charge. I just happened to have a rich uncle who died and left me a large house tucked away down in Chokoloskee, one with plenty of frozen food in freezers, a microwave and four bedrooms and that annex built to withstand a Category 4 hurricane or Category 4 CEO.

Nigel and the rest of the out of town folks were spending part of their precious vacation time engaged in this kidnapping and hiding out of O'Riley, who was, at the moment, guzzling frappucinos and watching the E network.

We were wondering what was known about O'Riley. Was he considered missing yet? Had anything been reported? We figured we'd start at the Tropical-Times website, tsquared.com. Really, that's what the website is called, tsquared.com, as in the T in Tropical and the T in Times.

Yep, there was the news with a banner headline and a photo of O'Riley, posted a few minutes earlier on this Tuesday morning.

Beloved CEO Missing

Chesterfield E. O'Riley, the CEO of Grabmore Publications, the parent company of the Tropical-Times, has not been seen since early Monday afternoon.

O'Riley was scheduled to inspect the Tropical-Times building and operations today but company officials haven't been able to locate him. His cell phone was discovered late Tuesday afternoon on a seawall near the Royalty Supreme Yacht Club.

"We're not sure what we have here," Fort Myers Police Department chief Bubba Tippins said. "When we know more we'll announce more. Heck, when we know anything we'll announce that."

Grabmore Publications issued a statement this morning: "Thousands of Grabmore employees across the country are distressed that our Dear Leader is missing. We all pray fervently that our magnanimous, benevolent, brilliant CEO is returned unharmed so he can continue to lead Grabmore in its relentless quest of journalistic excellence."

That was it. It was time to check the Grabmore Blog. The blog was started by Brad Beeswax, a former business reporter at the St. Louis Republican-Democrat. It was intended as a forum for intelligent discussion about the company and the industry. Well, not so much.

Folks were already commenting on the O'Riley disappearance on the blog.

Here's a sampler:

• From anonymous: "Hope the stoopid rat basterd rots in heel."

• From mickeyminniemouse: "He didn't go anywhere. He wasn't kidnapped. No ways. It's all part of the master plan. The ATF and Al Queddah and Mexican drug lords are all in this. I know. Right now I bet he's in some haciendah in Saudia Arabiyah banging some Arab missy. And U.S. taxpayers are footin the bill. Believe you me. That's what happened."

• From Marv Throneberry: "Who?"

Well, that, sadly, despite the best intentions of Brad Beeswax, is much of the blog. But then there was this item from what employees call the Puzzle Palace, the purple 13-story corporate headquarters in Buffalo:

• From udontknowme: "I work in the P. Palace, as we sometimes call it. I don't know where O'Riley is now. I just heard he's missing.

"But folks out there in blog-land should know more about O'Riley's sweetheart deal. Every time an employee is laid off it means a $7,100 bonus. Do the math. 40,000 laid off times $7,100. I think it comes to something like $280 million. His golden parachute guarantees him $19 million as a parting gift. If he leaves because of ill health – which is not defined – the parting gift jumps to $43 million. How many jobs could have been saved if not for this unpardonable largesse by his friends on the board of directors?

"How can the personal chefs and the limo and free country club memberships and the two months paid vacation, how can any of it be justified morally, ethically, financially or intellectually? Well, got to go. Got to get to work. Really."

So much for the blog. We'll check it again later.

It was time Nigel, Monique, Ahmad and I check on our new best friend, the CEO of our company, the missing executive. He's not missing to us. We know exactly where to find O'Riley.

CHAPTER FOURTEEN

Sal Hotdog, wearing an Eli Manning New York Giants jersey and tan cargo shorts, cracked open the door between the kitchen and the annex, the new home of Chesterfield Ebenezer O'Riley IV.

O'Riley had changed into clothes we provided for him, shorts and a green T-shirt with the words Fort Myers Beach on the front. We had stocked up on clean clothes and towels for our guest. He still wore the Docksiders from yesterday, from the time less than 24 hours ago when everything changed. For him. For us. For many others.

O'Riley was taking a sip of a cold Frappucino when the door opened. He grabbed the remote and muted the E Network's re-run of an episode of Keeping up with the Kardashians.

"You know," O'Riley said, "you're not going to get away with this. You just can't kidnap one of America's richest and most beloved people and hold him ransom and expect to get millions of dollars."

We didn't say anything for several seconds. Sal, who stands 6-foot-4 and looks beefy enough to play offensive line for the Giants, stepped closer to O'Riley.

"Who said anything about a ransom? And who is this beloved person? It couldn't be a money-grubbing, scumbag like you."

O'Riley didn't know what to say. He sank back a bit deeper into the red velvet couch, the gaudy thing one of Uncle Orville's wives had purchased for him in the '70s.

The CEO stared up. At Sal. At Nigel, wearing his black beret at a rakish angle. At Ahmad, holding his prayer rug. At Monique, flexing her biceps and triceps, which rippled ominously and impressively.

At me.

Nigel, holding a copy of Poet, Pugilist and Pressman, tried explaining.

"Well, old sport, it's this way," Nigel told him. "We're not after money. Well, a 4 percent annual raise would be nice. Instead of no raises. For three years. And increasing our mileage to 39 cents per mile. And for you to stop gutting the company to indulge your every perverse and perverted whim.

"There is a difference, old sport, between perverse and perverted. There's a dictionary on the table over there. I don't know if you know how to use one. Just open up the cover and leaf through the pages. The words are in alphabetical order. So you should be able the find the P words."

"I'm not an idiot," O'Riley said, sputtering and nervous, spittle popping out of his mouth. "I'm the CEO of a major company. I'm in charge of dozens and dozens of newspapers and TV stations and radio stations."

I then told him the story of Edgar Watson, who was murdered in 1910 a short walk from where Uncle Orville's house now stands. Watson was a pioneer Florida businessman who built an empire and a home here in the Ten Thousand Islands. He was a feared and fearsome man, one who reputedly killed his employees on payday instead of paying them.

That idea seemed to appeal to O'Riley. I then told him about the October day more than a century ago when Watson came puttering up to the shore there in Chokoloskee in a little power boat to find a group of townsfolk waiting.

They were all armed. They were tired of Watson's bullying and power. Before Watson could take a step on shore, every man in the group fired his long gun. Watson was dead before he plopped to the sand.

There's a sign in the Smallwood Store in Chokoloskee, which still stands and was open then, with these words on it: "Killing Mr. Watson was a community project."

I didn't compare O'Riley to Watson or our little gang to the Chokoloskee shooters but an implication hung there in the air-conditioned room with the muted Kardashians on the flat screen TV. The implication was that our kidnapping was also a community project. One that might end poorly for the victim.

Silence followed.

I looked at O'Riley and told him one line I had memorized from Killing Mr. Watson, Peter Mathiessen's brilliant novel about the case.

From memory, I told what it was like coming down to this neck of the Florida woods, as written by Mathiessen.

"Who else would come to these overflowed rain-rotted islands with not high enough ground to build a outhouse and so many skeeters plaguing you in summer you'd thought you'd took the wrong turn to hell."

I let that sink in for a while and told O'Riley "We might just keep you here until summer and then take you out in the Ten Thousand Islands."

I paused for a moment and shared this nugget with him: "And you don't want to go wandering off around here. Just recently a veteran fishing and tour guide from these parts had a group of tourists out for a boat ride. The captain stuck a hand in the water and an alligator bit it off. So be careful."

That seemed to focus his attention but O'Riley tried pointing out yet again how rich and powerful he is.

"You know," I said, "The Ten Thousand Islands are 2,000 square miles of mangrove islands and wilderness. One island looks like another. One island is like 10,000 other islands. If we drop you off out there, even if we left you on a boat, you'd never find your way out. Some day in a year or two, your sun-bleached bones may be found by somebody smuggling illegal aliens in from Guatemala or some place and they sure as heck won't tell anybody what they found."

"What about all my money?" he asked.

"Try bribing an alligator or snake with a fistful of hundred dollar bills," Nigel said.

"But I got all this money," O'Riley bleated.

Now it was Ahmad's turn.

"We know that. That's why we kidnapped you. Or part of the reason."

Another several moments of quiet followed. O'Riley clutched his Frappucino, which was still cool.

I glanced around the room. Now what? We had him? What's next? If not a ransom, then what?

Again, Sal talked.

"I probably shouldn't say this. In fact, I've been advised not to. I'm in the Witness Protection Program. I squealed on some old friends. If I get caught for this, it's out of the program and into jail for me."

O'Riley took this in and didn't say anything. Sal continued.

"So, we all have something to gain if we work together. You, Mr. O'Riley – and I don't know why I just called you as Mr. O'Riley – are in a sort of prison here. In this room. But as prisons go, it's pretty nice. Flat screen TV, fluffy towels from Bed, Bath & Beyond. All the frappucino you'd like. Better than Leavenworth, which some of my friends now call home. Or the bottom of the Atlantic Ocean, about 34 miles due east of Asbury Park. That's where you might find some more of my old friends.

"This is better. On the other hand, spending every day all day in this 900-square foot room – that includes the bathroom – will get old. No fresh air. I'm sorry. We just can't let you out. But we do have a deal in mind. A deal that will get you out of here. A deal that will allow you to see blue skies again. And maybe even visit Iceland again to ogle the Miss Iceland contestants.

"It's too soon to get into details now. But enjoy the Frappucinos and the Kardashians. We'll be back later to talk some more."

O'Riley unmuted the TV as we closed the door.

Now what? We had him? But what to do with him? Sal mentioned a deal in mind but we had no deal in mind. That was a lie, just something to calm down O'Riley. We couldn't tell anybody outside our little band of conspirators that we had him but we had to come up with some sort of tentative plan. We double checked the locks and headed up the road for lunch at the Rod & Gun Club in Everglades City.

Monique stayed behind. We decided it would be prudent to always have somebody at the house.

So it was Sal and Nigel and Ahmad joining me in my Toyota Camry, the one with 160,000 miles on it. Just a short drive away to the historic inn that has been around since the 1860s, since before even Mr. Watson found his way here.

We sat at a round glass top table on the veranda overlooking a canal. We heard a waitress on her cell phone talking to somebody who had to be a husband or boyfriend. "Now, Hank, when you coming home from the gun show?"

We didn't hear the answer. Ceiling fans whirred around slowly above us and the clatter of shoes could be heard on the wood floor.

We were looking over the menu when a blond woman wearing flip-flops, pink shorts and an orange tank top with a flamingo on the front stopped at our table. She was 40 or so but trim and fit looking with blue eyes and she wore a baseball cap with a Tampa Bay Rays logo. Her pale bond hair tumbled out the back of the cap.

"Hi, guys," she said.

I responded with my usual brilliant wit.

"Ah, hi."

"What are you guys doing?"

"About to order lunch," I explained.

"Anything else?"

Picking up my Corona, I said, "I believe we're also going to drink some beer. Maybe a lot. But not our friend here, the one with the water glass. His religious convictions don't permit alcohol. I, on the other hand, have no convictions. Religious or otherwise."

My attempt at humor eluded this meddlesome woman, this intruder who reminded me of Judy Holliday in the classic 1950 film Born Yesterday.

"What else you guys doing?"

I tried explaining this was a business meeting.

"What kind of business you fellows in?" she asked.

I didn't think it wise to say kidnapping was now our business and business was booming. So, she sensed an opening, grabbed a chair and slid it over by the end of our table. What are your names?

I introduced the fellows. Sal was introduced as Lee Child. Nigel became Dennis Lehane and Ahmad was dubbed Elmore Leonard.

"Funny," the woman said, "You don't look like an Elmore."

"Well," Ahmad said. "I'm Elmore. Very Elmore. Almost Elmore to a fault."

She let that sink in for a moment.

"Hi, my name is Troxie," she said.

"Roxie?" I said. "Like Roxie Hart in Chicago?"

"No, Troxie."

I still didn't get it.

"Trixie?" I asked.

"No, Troxie. T-R-O-X-I-E."

"Oh, that's an unusual name."

"Well, I'm an unusual person," she said.

There was no disputing that.

"So, what are you guys having for lunch? I recommend the captain's platter. $19.95. You get fish and shrimp and oysters and scallops and more. I think a Kendall Jackson pinot grigio goes really well with this. Two of those pinot grigios go even better. So I'll have two.

"Oh, do you guys mind if I join you? Thanks. Don't mind if I do."

She turned to me. What's your name? I told her it was Dashiell. Dashiell Hammett.

"You know, Dashiell, your friends are kind of cute," Troxie said.

"What about me?" I asked.

"You know, you seem pretty smart," she said.

I've always come up short in the looks department. But this wasn't about me. We had a captured CEO stashed away down the street and needed to make that our focus. We were, frankly, flummoxed by Troxie's intrusion. Instead of more planning on our criminal enterprise that risked long jail terms for all of us and deportation for Nigel and Ahmad, we had the company of this woman who struck us, unfairly to be sure, as a floozie. Or bimbo. I'm not sure of the difference.

We didn't have the nerve to ask Troxie to leave. She kept jabbering away and told us more about how she ended up in Everglades City. She came from her hometown of St. Petersburg, way up Florida's west coast, for a shuffleboard tournament at the Rod and Gun Club. St. Pete, she explained, housed the Shuffleboard Hall of Fame.

Her goal was to someday be enshrined in the Shuffleboard Hall of Fame alongside legends of the sport such as Mae Hall. She then pulled out of her purse a photocopy of a 1964 Sports Illustrated feature on Mae Hall, an all-time shuffleboard great. This Troxie person explained she signed up for any shuffleboard tournament near the seashore or anywhere so she could shuffle into shuffleboard immortality.

I asked Troxie for her last name and again wasn't sure what she said.

"Trotsky?" I asked. "Like the Russian revolutionary Stalin had tracked down to Mexico and murdered? Like that Trotsky?"

"No, silly, not like that Trotsky," Troxie said. "It's Trosky, like an old-time baseball player."

I recalled the name.

"Hal Trosky," I said. "Played for the Indians back in the '30s. Power-hitting first baseman. Had some big home-run years."

Troxie was impressed and asked how I knew that. I explained I was a sports writer with a particular interest in baseball history. She told me about Trosky's six seasons with 25 or more homers and how in 1936 his 42 homers were second in the American League, behind only the great Lou Gehrig. And, she added, he was her great-grandfather.

"Have you ever covered shuffleboard?" Troxie asked.

I had to admit that shuffleboard was one of the few sports I never covered.

"You never heard of Mae Hall?" Troxie asked, dismayed. "The greatest shuffler of them all. Enshrined in the hall, right there in downtown St. Pete."

The lunch talk went on and on. And so did the beer and wine. Troxie did most of the talking. She asked Elmore/Ahmad where he was from.

"Yemen," he said.

"You don't have to say yes ma'am, to me," she said. "You can call me Troxie."

"No, that's where I'm from," Ahmad explained.

"There's a country called yes ma'am?" Troxie asked.

Ahmad then explained the geographic peculiarities of his home and how to spell it and it finally sank in.

Little did we know that afternoon as we sat on the veranda under those fans that we had not seen the last of this meddlesome, intrusive, shuffleboard-obsessed, pinot-grigio drinking woman. And Chesterfield Ebenezer O'Riley IV had yet to see the first of her.

CHAPTER FIFTEEN

We returned to Uncle Orville's house. Sal had picked up a grilled grouper sandwich on a Kaiser roll for Monique and we apologized that she had to stay at the house. Heck, we even brought back a grilled grouper sandwich with a side order of fruit for O'Riley. Ahmad delivered it and held the door open as he handed over lunch. O'Riley preferred fried sandwiches with Lay's potato chips but Ahmad said something in Arabic. Whatever it was didn't sound nice.

We left O'Riley to his grouper sandwich – grilled! _ and we presume another episode of Keeping up With the Kardashians.

I was a little drowsy from three beers at the Rod and Gun Club, wanted to read more of Poet, Pugilist and Pressman and also let the effects of the beer seep away before driving 84 miles back to Fort Myers. I wanted to find out more about how O'Riley Publications became "Grabmore Publications."

So I trudged upstairs to what used to be Uncle Orville's bedroom and stepped out on his balcony, where a hammock was slung in the shade. Pelicans and seagulls swooped through the balmy air, snook splashed in the water and palm fronds rustled as I climbed in and curled up with the book, with Chapter 10, titled, Grab This, Congressman.

From Poet, Pugilist and Pressman:

People often ask me why I changed the company's name to Grabmore. Well, it was testifying before Congress in front of that festering pack of half-wits, nitwits, dimbulbs, dolts and dullards on the House Un-American Activities Committee.

It was those semi-literate, knuckle dragging, beetle-browed congressmen from places such as Dogpatch that pushed me to it. Lil' Abner is smarter than some of these poltroons, jackanapes, guttersnipes and ninnyhammers. Let me tell you.

They dared to question my patriotism. This country gave me the opportunity to build an empire and employ tens of thousands of Americans. During the war I was one of FDR's $1 a year men. That means I worked for a year for $1. To help America win the war. For America. For $1 a year. That's less than a penny a day.

Me, they call un-American?

I worked with folks like Frank Capra and John Ford to explain why America was fighting the war and what was at stake. All I did was review some scripts for movies they made. I didn't know anything about making films but I was flattered they asked for my input.

I was by then too old to fight but not too old to help. Any way I could. Writing scripts and pamphlets and organizing and speaking. And these politicians questioned my loyalty and patriotism?

I think it was a congressman named T. Herman Zweibel, or something like that, who accused me of just grabbing more and more. Grabbing more money. Grabbing more newspapers and radio stations and power. Grabbing, grabbing, grabbing. More power. More yachts. More mansions. More this. More that.

So what. ...

I sat there at that table in front of those photographers and took it for a few minutes. Took about as much as I could and then told them my plans. I took a sip of water and leaned forward to the microphone and spoke.

"You guys win. You're right. I am going to keep on grabbing and building and grabbing and building. I'm going to buy more papers. And more radio stations. And maybe a congressman or two. They should come a lot cheaper than a decent newspaper or even a fledgling radio station in Keokuk.

"The thought just occurred to me that I'm going to change the name of the company. No more O'Riley Publications. From now on it's going to be Grabmore. Grabmore Publications. So every time I buy another paper or hire another 100 Americans and pay them a livable wage they'll be working for Grabmore.

"It will say Grabmore on their paycheck. On the masthead of all those papers the name Grabmore will be there on the front page. In 90 American cities. Before tens of millions of Americans every day.

"When they listen to my radio stations they'll hear that W-whatever or K-whatever is part of the Grabmore Radio Network. So, Mr. Zweibel and Mr. Dies and all you other rapscallions, I take pride in grabbing more. And more. And more.

"I did it the old-fashioned way. I came to this country with no money. No soap or clean clothes. I worked hard and fought hard but clean. I hired good people and paid them well. A livable wage. Decent hours and benefits.

"Sure, I had an occasional union dispute here and there, but ask any union boss. We had some flaps. Even some fisticuffs on the press decks in Hoboken and Tacoma and Dayton. But what's a few bloody noses and black eyes among friends? We fought and then shook hands. I gave a little more and they gave up on some of their demands and we moved forward.

"They did well. I did great. I'd hate to see the day my company is run by mealy-mouthed, weak-kneed, jargon-spouting bureaucrats. That's not the case now.

"It hasn't been the case since the day Mr. Kent of the Brooklyn Daily Eagle gave me an equity stake in the Poughkeepsie Potato Peeler, a weekly and my first paper. It's been the case since we turned the Peeler into a moneymaker and folks in Poughkeepsie wanted to spend 2 cents on it. I made money. Then some more. Then started buying more papers and followed the same formula. Give folks a reason to buy the paper. Give them interesting stories and try to be fair and accurate.

"Yep, it worked. Turned a penniless lad, one who used to dine on weevil-infested biscuits on the steerage on a ship called the City of Cheaters and I became one of the richest men in America.

"I like the ring of it – Grabmore. So forevermore, that will be the name of my company – Grabmore.

"And with that, gentleman, I bid you good day. I have an empire to run. Americans to inform. Americans to hire. Americans to pay.

"You can do with me as you will but I'm going out for a beer. Maybe two. Good day."

With that, I folded up a stack of papers, buttoned my bespoke, pinstriped suit, pushed my chair back and walked out of the hearing room.

That's where I stopped reading. Closed the book and my eyes. And dozed off for perhaps 20 minutes in that hammock on my late Uncle Orville's balcony there in Chokoloskee, as the breeze rustled the palm fronds and the seagulls and pelicans swooped over the water. I woke a bit later and flopped out of the hammock and staggered down stairs, rubbing the sleep out of my eyes.

Monique was on the back porch, pumping iron, doing biceps curls with 35-pound dumbbells. Sal had dozed off on the couch watching ESPN. Nigel was somewhere in the house. Ahmad was in the kitchen, puttering around and doing something with hummus and oatmeal and wheat germ and kale. Whatever it was, I didn't want to know about it or taste it.

Then came the knock at the front door.....

CHAPTER SIXTEEN

The knocking wasn't insistent or harsh. It was almost tentative, a tapping rather than a rapping.

Ahmad forgot about his kale, though, and stepped out of the kitchen. Sal woke up with a start from his nap. Monique dropped with an authoritative thump the 35-pound dumbbell she was using for concentration curls. Nigel was on the back porch reading a Randy Wayne White novel and didn't hear the knocks at first.

I nearly tripped over a piece of lint at the noise.

The cops? Already? How could they? It had been only about 24 hours or so since we bundled O'Riley into the back of that Chevy Suburban in downtown Fort Myers.

Then it came again. That tapping.

Sal peered outside and didn't see any cop cars. We exchanged glances. Worried glances.

Then the tapping. Again.

I walked to the door and gently opened it. No cops with search warrants and no SWAT team rappelling down the side of the house.

It was Troxie.

"Hi, again," she said.

"Hi, again," I said.

She looked inside the house.

"This place is nice," Troxie said. "I love the orange shag carpeting. Haven't seen anything like it since I looked through my Aunt Gertrude's photo album of her house in the '70s. She lives in Dunedin. It's up north of St. Pete."

"I know where Dunedin is," I told Troxie, a bit more brusquely than I intended.

"You lied to me, Mr. Hammett," Troxie said to me. "The Rod and Gun Club manager told me the names you gave me are of famous writers and not your real names. That's so wrong."

I then re-introduced everybody – Sal and Nigel and Ahmad. And also Monique, who wasn't at the Rod and Gun Club. I told her my name is Scott, not Dashiell. Sadly. Dashiell is such a cool name. Sal walked over and asked how she found us and what she was doing at the front door.

"Well, Mr. Offensive Lineman, you guys aren't hard to find, especially in a place like this," Troxie said. "Let's see, we got a guy big enough to block for Eli Manning and looks like he could work for Tony Soprano.

"We got some Irish dude with an Irish accent who likes to wear berets like some French artist from the '50s. Then, there's Ahmad, who most folks around here probably thinks is Osama Bin Laden's No. 1 son. He's lucky somebody hasn't crawled out of the Everglades to shoot you and ask questions later. And then there's you."

She looked at Monique, fit and muscular as an Olympic weightlifter. Troxie hadn't met Monique yet.

"Oh, hi, there," she said to Monique. "I don't believe we've met."

"You're right," Monique said. "We haven't met."

"Well, you certainly stick out here, too," Troxie said. "They don't see too many black lesbian weightlifters here in Chokoloskee."

Monique took it in good humor.

"That's not all. A black lesbian weightlifter lumberjack from Canada," she said with a smile.

Then came silence. Troxie looked over at Sal. Nigel looked at me. Monique looked around the room. Then Troxie looked at me.

"Scott, no offense, but you sure don't help this gang blend into the background here," Troxie said. "People in Chokolosloskee and Everglades City don't go around reciting from memory the opening day lineups for the 1962 Mets and 1936 Indians on bar bets. Plus, I saw you guys get in that Camry and head south. The road ends right here. Unless the Camry is some sort of James Bond car it couldn't go any farther south. And the Camry is out front. In front of the third-biggest house in Chokoloskee."

"Well, congratulations," I said.

Now what?

"Troxie, what brings you here?" I asked.

She then walked in and found a seat in the beige La-Z-Boy recliner, another gift from one of my late Uncle Orville's wives. I think it was wife No. 3, aunt RuthAnne. One word, please, she always reminded us about the correct spelling of her name.

"Hey, this is pretty comfortable," Troxie said, leaning back. "A girl could get right comfortable here."

We had underestimated the meddlesome pinot grigio woman.

"Ah, Troxie," I asked, "what brings you all the way down here?"

"There isn't much money on the shuffleboard circuit," she said. "And what do you mean all the way? It's only a few miles from Everglades City. I'm kind of tapped out. I've rented a trailer in Everglades City. I need work. Thanks again for lunch, by the way. I don't know how much longer I can hang on to the trailer.

"I've been cleaning houses and waiting tables part-time at City Fishhouse. You guys are up to something other than playing baseball trivia games with drunken fishermen and crabbers and tourists from Rhode Island. I can tell.

"Whatever your secret is, it's safe with me. You need help here? I've worked as a maid and domestic. I'm not gonna give up shuffleboard, though. That's long term. The Shuffleboard Hall of Fame is my long-term goal. Short-term, I need more than a couple lunch shifts a week and getting by cleaning a few houses around Everglades City and Chokoloskee."

Nigel had come in from the back porch and walked over, the Randy Wayne White novel under his arm.

"You're a bonnie lass, as they used to say where I come from," Nigel said. "We really don't know you. We just met. How can we trust you? Can you really cook and clean? Can you keep a secret? Leave your contact info. We'll talk about it and get back to you."

Troxie leaned forward in the Lazy Boy, pushed herself up and said, "That seems fair."

She gave us her phone number and email address and walked out the door, only a few minutes after arriving. Her desire for work was something else to talk about.

And we needed to check on O'Riley again. That came first

This time we all went into the back room, where O'Riley was watching a Tivo'd episode of Dancing with the Stars.

"I really like this Tom Bergeron," he told us, referring to the show's host.

"That's wonderful," Sal said. "I used to be a ballroom dancer. Before I became an astronaut and after I was hairdresser in Key West."

"Really!?" O'Riley said.

That's the Grabmore CEO for you. The intellectual firepower and curiosity of a kumquat. The depth of a bowl of wonton soup. The wide-ranging interest of a napping house cat.

To think his great-grandfather could quote Yeats and Shelly and Shakespeare. ...

Sal, in all his bulkiness and immensity and menacing size, walked over to the CEO and reminded him by his mere presence how much his world had changed in 24 hours.

O'Riley became silent for a moment. He glanced at each of us in turn. We didn't say a word. He glanced at the front door. It was unlocked but he had no chance to escape.

Not from this crowd. Not even from me. I may not have been a great baseball player but I was still quick and strong from regular track workouts and visits to the gym.

Then, there were the others. Two trained terrorists. The former mafia strongboy. Monique the strongest female lumberjack on the planet, a distaff Paul Bunyan, if you will.

He smartened up quick.

"Now what?" he said, forgetting all about Dancing with the Stars. "Are you going to kill me?"

His eyes misted over. He wobbled and stepped back and collapsed on to the couch. It was Ahmad who spoke.

"You know," he said, "I probably shouldn't tell you this but we don't intend to kill you. Not unless you annoy us so much you push us to it."

"I won't annoy," O'Riley said. "I promise."

Then Nigel, still clutching that Randy Wayne White novel, spoke.

"O'Riley, you're going be our guest for a while," he said. "It's kind of open-ended. We got food and drinks and money to keep you tucked away here indefinitely. There will be no ransom note. No demands made to corporate headquarters. The freezer is stocked with frozen meals. We'll give you some fresh fruits and vegetables as well.

"But you're not going anywhere. Somebody will always be on the other side of that locked door. And it will always be locked.

"We're not sure what we're doing next but you're not leaving. And we're not going to kill you."

O'Riley didn't say a word. Just sat there. Dazed. A glazed, stupefied look on his round little face.

"Have a nice evening," Sal said as he closed the door.

O'Riley was locked away for his second night of captivity.

It was time for me to head home. I had to get back to Fort Myers and go to work the next day. Our annual staff meeting to plan spring training coverage was set for the next morning.

CHAPTER SEVENTEEN

The long drive home gave me time to recall how we got to this point.

How a sportswriter in Fort Myers and all the rest got together and wound up kidnapping a CEO. How a former Mafia enforcer now delivering newspapers in Florida's panhandle got involved. How an IRA-trained immigrant turned boxing writer in New Jersey got involved. How a trained Al Qaeda operative who never used those skills turned pressroom operator in Bergen County got involved. How a lumberjack and mill forclady from Canada got involved.

How we all ended up in Uncle Orville's house there in Chokoloskee, a long way from Fort Myers, not to mention Yemen. Blame it on Facebook. ....

I was on Facebook. As was virtually everybody I knew. At some point many Grabmore employees vacation in Florida.

Sal, Nigel, Monique and Ahmad had all "friended" me on Facebook to get vacation tips for Southwest Florida.

I suggested the Pink Shell Resort on Fort Myers Beach. We didn't know each other ahead of time but they all ended up staying there the same time. Each had sought my vacation advice separately.

I agreed to meet them for a beer at the Pink Shell. It turned out they were all there the same week, the same evening. So we gathered one evening just to talk about our jobs, lives and watch the sunset and drink beer and grouse about Grabmore.

Monique grabbed a Molson and talked about the time O'Riley visited the New Brunswick mill where she worked. She was introduced to the CEO as a top lumberjack.

"Don't you mean lumberjill?" O'Riley blurted out, apparently thinking that was the epitome of wit.

Like something Oscar Wilde or Dorothy Parker might have said. Of course, O'Riley had never heard of Oscar Wilde or Dorothy Parker. Monique didn't like that lumberjill crack. She didn't like the tidbit I told her about Col. Longstreet, the Fort Myers executive editor, using the word "Nigra."

She talked about her family, about how several generations back they had been slaves on a Georgia plantation and how they somehow, miraculously, through the Underground Railroad, reached Canada just before the Civil War. The family had prospered in Canada but family lore was passed along about the violent masters from the antebellum days.

She sensed O'Riley was a sexist pig and from what little I told her about Longstreet she sensed he was a racist careerist. Grabmore and the Longstreet family owned the forests and mills where she worked.

Resentment, seething resentment, had been building inside her for years.

"I bet lots of people have ancestors who owned slaves," Monique said. "I'm not mad at them. I'm sure most of them are fine people. It's not their fault bad things were done by great-great-great-grandpa to some poor, defenseless teenage black girl in Georgia or Alabama or Florida in 1849.

"Heck, shake my family tree and a criminal or two will likely fall out. But this Longstreet creep, he doesn't seem much different than his ancestors. The typical Grabmore asshole. No class, no grace. Where do they all come from? Why do they thrive in this company? Can't something be done?"

Sal sat there nursing a Budweiser. Apparently, it was his turn to talk.

"I knew some bad people back in the day, back when I was in the rackets in Jersey, in places like Parsippany and Whippany and Atlantic Highlands," Sal said. "They did some bad things. Beat up people. Even killed people. But there was a code. They had some sense of honor. They didn't pick on random people going about their lives.

"If you didn't try to muscle in on our territory or sell drugs to our customers, we left you alone. But these Grabmore executives, they're another breed altogether. No honor. No code. It's all about power and getting ahead.

"When I got into the witness protection program and they told me my job would be delivering papers in the Florida panhandle, I thought that was cool. I like most of the people I work with. It's those management weasels I don't get. The rules change every day to suit their needs. They got this special lingo instead of just talkin', you know, like real people. Back in my previous life, everybody talked plain. You knew what they meant. They said what they meant and meant what they said.

"These Grabmore people. … I remember the time O'Riley came to Panama City. All the managers put on their suits and lined up out on the loading dock. They wore their Grabmore ballcaps and when O'Riley's limousine drove by the dock they grabbed their caps and bowed and held the caps over the hearts and yelled "Hip-hip, hoo-ray for Grabmore the best company in all the land! Hip-hip-hooray for Mr. O'Riley, the best CEO in all the land.'

"I nearly threw up and thought about getting out of Witness Protection and going straight to prison. Anything to get away from these Grabmore suckups."

So it went that night, the night that changed everything.

Nigel talked about his boyhood in Northern Ireland, how he was weaned on IRA politics but preferred soccer and boxing and hanging out in the public library. His uncles, he said, were active in the IRA and insisted he follow their examples. He learned to shoot and build bombs.

But he didn't want to really hurt anybody. Oh, the occasional bloody nose in the ring or bruised shin on the football pitch were one thing. Killing, well, he didn't want part of that. He told about coming across a copy of Poet, Pugilist and Pressman in a corner of a Belfast library. It ignited an ambition. To move to America and become a journalist and then a novelist.

He knew Chesterfield Ebenezer O'Riley's family still owned all those papers. He figured his descendants and top managers must be like the company founder – athletic and intellectual, tough but fair, resourceful and interesting.

Nigel landed that job at the Bugle in Bergen County and soon discovered how the company had changed.

"It wasn't about righting wrongs or crafting a finely-written profile," Nigel said that night. "It was about office politics."

He recalled the day O'Riley popped into the Bugle office.

"The managing editor, a blond-haired woman named Olympia Killjoy, greeted him at the door," Nigel said. "She was literally jumping up and down and clapping her hands. 'Oh,' she said, 'Mr. O'Riley, this is the greatest day ever for the Bugle. All the employees are lined up here to meet you. We weren't sure how to line them up so we did it by size, shortest to tallest. Is that OK, Mr. O'Riley? We could change. We could line them up alphabetically. Or by salary.'"

Here Nigel paused. He looked around the tiki bar and took a swig of Budweiser.

"You know what he said then?" Nigel said. "Let them line up by levels of desperation, from those least afraid of losing their job to those most afraid. I'll check back in five minute once you get it sorted out. Meanwhile, I need an ice cold frappucino.' That's our CEO."

We all had stories. Well, every Grabmore employee had stories.

Ahmad also worked in Bergen County. He said when O'Riley walked into the press room, he asked, "Hey, Mohammad, where's your IUD?"

Ahmad even grinned before he said, "Not only is he a racist, he's a moron. The buffoon doesn't know the difference between an IED and an IUD. And he's running our company. No wonder people keep losing their jobs and we don't get raises and the worst people thrive. If we could only get rid of O'Riley. ...."

That's when we looked at each other and started the planning. Memories of that night distracted me as I drove home from Chokoloskee.

The next morning, I would return to the Tropical-Times offices, to our sports department meeting about spring training. But I was also eager to hear what people in the office and on the Grabmore blog were saying about Chesterfield Ebenezer O'Riley IV, the missing and possibly dead CEO.

CHAPTER EIGHTEEN

At least the flag out on front of the Tropical-Times building wasn't at half staff. That told me management didn't think O'Riley was dead. But the managers certainly were atwitter with anxiety.

Over my morning bowl of whole grain cereal with raisins and fat-free milk, I had read the print coverage of the story. Although perhaps 5 percent of the paper's readers could tell you the Tropical-Times was owned by Grabmore and no more than 1 percent could identify the company's CEO, the story was plastered across the front page. This was the banner headline in 48 point type: "Is CEO OK?"

This was the sub-headline: "Grabmore top boss O'Riley missing; foul play possible"

Ace cops reporter Ace Hamill, who has covered Florida crime for 32 years, was assigned the O'Riley story. There were front-page photos of O'Riley, one of him on his yacht, another at his polo club and yet another of him gambling in a Monaco casino with movie director Quinton Tarantino, who later was asked about the guy next to him.

"Never seen him before," Tarantino told TMZ. "Struck me as a doofus. But somebody gave me a book called Poet, Pugilist and Pressman. It's by this idiot's great-grandfather. I may do a movie on his great-grandfather. His great-grand-father was not a doofus.

Maybe Leonardo DiCaprio in the title role. We'll see. Gotta go. Let me cash in my winnings

"Keep me away from that moron and those jabbering teenage girls he's got with him."

This is what was on the front page of the Tropical-Times that Wednesday under the Ace Hamill byline:

Chesterfield Ebenezer O'Riley IV, scion of one of America's most powerful families, vanished from downtown Fort Myers on Monday afternoon.

The CEO of Grabmore Publications, the parent company of the Tropical-Times, was last seen on his yacht the Never Enough around noon, sipping a Frappuccino and giving career advice to a young female employee.

The employee, whom authorities are not identifying, was seen eating lunch early Monday afternoon at the Oasis Restaurant in downtown Fort Myers and is not a suspect.

O'Riley was in Fort Myers to visit the Tropical-Times and did not leave a message with other company officials saying that he would not make his appointment. He is usually fairly punctual, newspaper management indicated.

Tropical-Times officials realized O'Riley was missing by about 3 p.m. Monday when he did not step off his yacht and into a waiting limousine that was going to drive him to the paper's offices a few blocks away.

"This is very distressing," Tropical-Times executive editor Col. Nate Longtreet said. "Chet, as I call him, is one of America's foremost journalists, public intellectuals and business leaders. I can't imagine this company moving forward without his powerhouse IQ and uncanny wisdom guiding the ship of Grabmore through these turbulent waters of these tumultuous times."

By Tuesday afternoon, more than 24 hours since he was last seen, the Fort Myers Police Department was investigating.

"If he was kidnapped, the FBI will be taking over the case," Fort Myers police chief Bubba Tippins said. "But we don't know if

O'Riley was kidnapped or got drunk and passed out in some floozie's Cape Coral condo and is still sleeping it off."

Grabmore officials tried calling O'Riley. His cell phone was spotted and heard on a seawall near the Royalty Supreme Yacht Club early Monday afternoon when its old car horn ringtone awoke a homeless man sleeping on a bench. The man's startled screech alerted officers to the telephone.

Longstreet said O'Riley has no known enemies or even bitter business rivals.

"We call him our Dear Leader," Longstreet said. "He's universally beloved and respected within the company. I know all Grabmore employees share my worries about our Dear Leader's welfare and hope he returns once more to pilot the Grabmore ship of state."

Continued Page 4A

See Also, Page 4A: A legend in pictures, an O'Riley photo gallery.

On Tsquared.com: More on O'Riley including photos, a timeline of the Grabmore empire and comments from community and national leaders.

Well, it's out there. The story is definitely out there. I walked in the Tropical-Times side door and went about my job. I had ideas typed up for our spring training coverage I wanted to print out prior to our 11 a.m. sports department meeting.

I nodded hello to Tess, my sports department confidante. She walked over to the printer and I whispered that all is well, that O'Riley is stashed away in a secret hiding place. I never told her where because the less she knew about specifics the better protected she would be.

Meanwhile, Mabel was in full-blown Mabel mode from her command post.

"Oh, this is the worst thing ever," she said, loud enough for everybody in the newsroom to hear, even Longstreet in his office with the doors closed. "Our dear Dear Leader. I hope he's safe. I saw him once when he visited. So handsome. So smart. So brilliant.

"He's like a combination of that actor George O'Clooney and that real smart science guy from long ago with the frizzy hair.

101

Eisenfeld? Eisenstadt? Whoever. Mr. O'Riley, our dear Dear Leader, he's like that smart. Only smarter. And better looking than George O'Clooney."

O'Clooney? Nobody bothered pointing out Mabel mangled the actor's name.

With that she glanced at Longstreet's office, clearly hoping he heard her worshipful lamentations. What good are worshipful lamentations if the right person, the person to boost your career, doesn't hear them?

What a day.

There was time, before our 11 a.m. meeting with sports editor Bo Lowe, to check the Grabmore Blog to see what my fellow employees were saying.

Grabmore Blog comments:

From Triple-Xfoxxyladie: "What a pig this guy is. He should be emasculated, the sleazie ceo skum. I've seen the girls he brings on that yacht of his. He should be ashmed of hissself. I hope them kidnappers kill the creep."

From editordude: "Can't people spell any mores. Why is this blog so filled with such typos all the time? What's wrong with people. And O'Riley? I met him once. Sort of. He walked through our newsroom clutching a cold bottle of Starbucks Frappucino and wearing that riduclous captain's cap.

"He asked me, 'What do you do, old sport?' I said, 'Well, Mr. Gatsby, my name is Nick Carraway and I live in that little house near your mansion.' He had no idea what I was talking about. Just nodded blankly and walked away.' I got a scowl from our managing editor for that wisecrack. But she later admitted she kind of liked it because she had no use either for this idiot sucking money out of our paper to pay for his trips to Iceland and Lapland and wherever."

And this from Corporatedrone123: "I work at corporate HQ. Most of us know what sort of person we're dealing with here. We know he lives in some alternative universe lacking any sort of accountability for his actions. As long as he owns 54 point something percent of the company, the board can't do anything. But even if there were folks with common sense on the board, they wouldn't do anything.

"All they care about is the next quarter. They don't want to invest in making our newspapers and TV and radio stations better in the long term. It's all about making money now.

"I'm not a violent person but if O'Riley turns up dead on a Florida beach or flop house not many tears will be shed here in Buffalo."

Finally, this again from anonymous: "Hope the stoopid rat basterd rots in heel."

So the blog was singing. …

The folks still employed at the Tropical-Times had a website to update and a paper to put out. The sports department had to plan spring training coverage. I had to remind the sports editor again and again that there were two Major League Baseball teams holding spring training in the county.

He knew about the Boston Red Sox but always seemed to forget the Minnesota Twins were also in town. But my attention kept drifting away from discussions about starting rotations and bullpens to my Uncle Orville's house down in Chokoloskee, to where my friends Sal, Nigel, Monique and Ahmad were babysitting America's most famous missing CEO.

Maybe we should just kill him. It was something we would have to discuss. It would make things easier for all of us, assuming, of course, we were not caught.

A dead CEO whose body is never found would make it easier for all of us. From Chokoloskee we were on the fringe of the Ten Thousand Islands, 10,000 places to stash a body that would rot fast in the Florida heat.

Or we could just run out to the Gulf of Mexico, wrap O'Riley up in some of the extra orange shag carpeting in Uncle Orville's garage, attach some dumbbells to the dumbbell and pitch him overboard. But could we actually murder a quasi-human being? It was something to discuss the next day.

CHAPTER NINETEEN

While driving my old but reliable Camry to Chokoloskee I received a call from Lt. J. P. Hooper of the Fort Myers Police Department. The catcher from my rec baseball league didn't call about our big game this weekend at Terry Park. His team, as usual, was in first place and had signed up an ex-pro pitcher who would start against us. An ex-pro who actually was good enough to pitch in a few big-league games.

Wonderful. We had no chance against guys like that. Our team was near the bottom of the league standings. Their team, their first-place team, got an ex-pro who would make quick work of my team, Babykins.

But Hooper wanted to talk about O'Riley's disappearance not old guy amateur baseball. I told him I was on my way to my late uncle's house to unwind on a day off, sprawl in a hammock, read and perhaps play some shuffleboard.

He said our chat could wait a day, that I wasn't going to be arrested but he had some questions, serious questions, pointed questions about my conduct and whereabouts the afternoon O'Riley disappeared. That was just more to worry about. Was I now officially a suspect in whatever happened to O'Riley? Or merely a person of interest?

Sal, Nigel, Monique and Ahmad and I had all agreed that we would not exchange phone calls, emails or texts, that to do so would leave electronic trails that even Inspector Clouseau could track.

So, what was going on there at the house? What happened the day before while I was in the office discussing Red Sox and Twins relief pitchers with our befuddled sports editor?

I parked, walked up the three steps to the front porch and opened the door. Sal, as usual, was half-asleep on the couch with ESPN's "SportsCenter" on the TV. Ahmad was in the kitchen making a concoction in a blender. Monique was pumping iron on the back porch, focusing on lat pulldowns on some sort of multi-purpose weight training gizmo one of Uncle Orville's wives bought him. Can't remember which wife.

Nigel was just about finished reading that Randy Wayne White novel I saw him reading a couple of days ago.

"So," I said, "how's our favorite missing and perhaps kidnapped and possibly dead CEO doing this morning?"

Sal stumbled to his feet, muted the TV and said, "Let's go see."

Nigel placed the book on the coffee table. Monique flexed her back and neck. Ahmad came out of the kitchen and we walked to the door. Sal pulled out his key and opened the door.

O'Riley was ready this time. He brandished a plastic knife from the takeout box from the Rod & Gun Club grilled grouper sandwich lunch.

"Don't make me hurt you," he bellowed with false bravado, causing Sal to laugh with a rumbling cackle.

Monique said, "O'Riley, put that thing down before we put you down face first on the couch and tie you hands behind you with baling wire and fishing line."

O'Riley quickly dropped the plastic knife on the floor. I picked it up and told him, "This was my uncle's house. Please don't throw trash on the floor."

He nodded and began weeping, his shoulders shaking, his gaze darting fearfully across each person in the room. They all could make quick work of O'Riley in any sort of altercation. Even I could.

"What are you going to do with me?" O'Riley asked. "I don't want to die. I don't want you to take me out to the 100,000 islands or dump me into the Gulf of New Mexico."

"Ah, Chesty," I said, deciding to use the informal version of his first name, "it's the Ten Thousand Islands and the Gulf of Mexico. If there's a Gulf of New Mexico the western U.S. is in big trouble."

"I don't want geography lessons from you ruffians," he said, sinking back into the couch that now doubled as his bed. "I want to go back to my yacht. I never hurt anybody."

"You never hurt anybody?" Nigel said.

He stepped closer and was brandishing the Randy Wayne White novel as a weapon. I now saw the title, "The Heat Islands."

"You going to hit me with that thing?" O'Riley asked, referring to the book.

"It's not a thing," O'Riley said. "It's a novel. Something you clearly know nothing about and care nothing about. And you never hurt anybody?"

Nigel walked across the room and sat in a wicker chair by the little round table where O'Riley could eat his meals.

Now Sal, wearing a New York Yankees jersey, spoke.

"Never hurt nobody?" Sal said with snorting disdain. "Never hurt nobody? All those layoffs. All those firings? No pay raises. Most Grabmore employees struggle to make mortgage payments and buy groceries and get their kids decent clothes for school.

"Meanwhile, you go jetting off to Lapland, wherever the hell that is. You get a bonus every time somebody gets laid off. Oh, we know about that. We know about your personal chef at corporate headquarters. We know about the company buying you a new BMW every six months. We know. Oh, boy, do we know.

"Our initial thought was just to keep you here for a while. It probably didn't include murder. Now, though, we're having second thoughts. Isn't that right, Monique?

Monique nodded.

"Do you remember me, Chet, old sport?" she asked.

He shook his head.

"I figured," she said. "Thousands of employees. But I thought you might remember me because it's probably not every day you call an employee a 'Lumberjill.'"

"Is that what this is about?" O'Riley asked. "That I made a bad joke?"

"No, old sport, that's not it," I said. "Here, I brought you a bag of spring mix salad stuff from Publix."

I tossed the bag on the coffee table.

"There's some salad dressing and toppings in that little fridge. Make yourself a salad and go back to your TV. We got some things to talk about. That we doesn't include you. We're going to lock the door now. Have a nice afternoon."

So we went back into the house. Ahmad locked the door. It was time for another Rod and Gun Club lunch. This time it was my turn to stay at the house.

They took the Chevy Suburban, another bequest from Uncle Orville, and went for lunch. I asked them to bring me back a captain's platter and no horseradish. Hate that stuff. And maybe another grouper sandwich for O'Riley.

I caught a few minutes of SportsCenter, hit the off button on the remote and picked up a copy of Poet, Pugilist and Pressman.

It was quiet in the house and, indeed, in all of Chokoloskee. It was one of those splendid Florida winter afternoons – mid 70s, low humidity and just the slightest hint of a breeze.

Uncle Orville was big into fishing and he left me all that gear in his will but I never caught the fishing bug. I don't know a rod from a reel, bait from tackle and can barely tell the difference between a minnow and a tarpon. I'd rather play baseball or basketball, ride my bicycle or read a book.

While my fellow Grabmore sufferers were at lunch, I planned to sit on the front verandah with a cool glass of lemonade and read more about and by the first O'Riley, the one who built Grabmore and named it.

That was my plan until a pink mini-Cooper turned into the driveway and came to a stop a few steps away.

Now what? The driver side door opened and I could see blond hair.

It was my favorite pinot-grigio drinking, shuffleboard obsessed resident of St. Pete, still down in this part of the state, a long way from the Shuffleboard Hall of Fame.

"Hello, Dashiell," she said as she closed the door. "And how is Mr. Dashiell Hammett today?"

"Well, Troxie, you know my name's not Dashiell. And my friends' names aren't Lee Child, Dennis Lehane and Elmore Leonard."

"Actually, once I found out those are the names of, like, famous writers, I thought it was kind of funny. What are you doing? Mind if I come on the porch?"

By this point, of course, she was on the porch.

"Just going to relax, read a little bit and sip some lemonade," I told her.

"Lemonade? You don't happen to have any pinot grigio, by any chance?" she asked.

"Sorry, plumb out of pinot grigio. I think we have a nice malbec. Will that do?"

She nodded and I said "Sit right there and I'll get you a glass of malbec."

"As long as you're up, why don't you make it two glasses."

"I'm not in a wine mood right now."

"I didn't mean one glass for you. I meant two for me."

I sighed, ducked inside the front door and brought the bottle and one glass and told Troxie it was all hers, an entire bottle of malbec. All for Troxie Trosky.

She started talking about Mae Hall, the St. Pete shuffleboard legend and the 1964 Sports Illustrated story about her.

"You know, when this story came out, Mrs. Hall had won 46 of the 76 tournaments she had entered over 14 years," Troxie said.

"You don't say?"

"I just said that," Troxie said. "Not only that, she was second in another 18 tournaments."

"That's fascinating, Troxie, but what do you want?"

She didn't ask me to go buy a bottle of pinot grigio. Troxie Trosky, the shuffleboard playing great-granddaughter of a slugging Cleveland Indians first baseman, was looking for a job and a place to stay.

A job working for the kidnapping firm of Hammett, Child, Lehane and Leonard. Although, of course, she didn't know we had a kidnapped CEO locked up a few steps away. She was looking for a spare room of her own in Uncle Orville's big house in the tiny town.

She also mentioned that in driving around town the day before she had noticed a shuffleboard court out back. That court was put in by another of Uncle Orville's wives, this one named Ruth Ann, not to be confused with RuthAnne, another one of his wives.

Uncle Orville somehow married two women with the same name and each insisted her way of spelling it was the only proper way to spell it. RuthAnne and Ruth Ann.

"Well, Dashiell, or Scott, or whatever the hell your name is, what do you think?" Troxie asked. "I can take care of this place, clean and do yard work and practice shuffleboard and I heard your friends don't live around here and there's something going on here that I haven't quite figured out. Give me enough pinot grigio, though, I can figure out anything. So, what do you say?"

"I don't know what to say," I told her. "But I think it's time to switch from lemonade to malbec. Let me get another glass. And I think we have a couple more bottles of malbec in the kitchen."

CHAPTER TWENTY

"Hey, this malbec stuff ain't bad," Troxie said, sitting on a wicker couch on the front porch, a few feet away from me and my malbec.

"It comes from Argentina," I said, virtually exhausting my knowledge of malbec. "That's about all I know."

A moment of silence followed as we each sipped and savored the cheap malbec. The cheap stuff was all I could afford. I work for Grabmore, after all. Not even Uncle Orville's generous will leaving me the paid-off house, a Chevy Suburban and, well a few thousand dollars, would bump me into the expensive malbec income bracket.

I could be laid off or fired or even jailed any day now. I always kept that in mind.

"So, Dashiell, I mean, Scott, what do you know about shuffleboard?" Troxie said.

"Probably even less than I know about malbec," I said, thinking I'll soon need another bottle or two of the stuff.

Troxie tipped back the Rays baseball cap on her head, leaned forward and started telling me all sorts of things about shuffleboard.

"Nobody knows how old shuffleboard is," Troxie said. "Really. Nobody knows where it was first played. Or who played it first. It's like a gift from the gods. Or maybe aliens. I don't know.

"People in Europe have played it for, like, 500 years. You know that English king, the fat one who killed some of his wives? He played shuffleboard."

"I think that was Henry VIII," I helpfully pointed out, just about exhausting my knowledge of British royal history and malbec in one afternoon.

"Right, that guy," Troxie said, clearly on a roll. "Do you know what a tang is?"

"At the moment, I prefer the malbec," I said. "You mean Tang, the stuff astronauts supposedly drink in space?"

"No, a tang is what the stick is called in shuffleboard," Troxie said. "The thing you use to push the biscuits."

"Biscuits?"

"Those," she explained, "are those things shuffleboard players push on the surface."

I'm convinced as of that moment I knew more about shuffleboard than any sportswriter in America. My education continued.

"You should feel lucky being on Florida's west coast. The St. Petersburg Shuffleboard Club is right up the road. Sixty-five courts. Masonry courts, no less. A grandstand that seats, oh, I don't know 250 or 300 fans."

Troxie was having a good time sharing shuffleboard knowledge.

"A shuffleboard champ could almost give up pinot grigo for this malbec," Troxie said, taking another sip. "What a great day. A great day for shuffleboard. And malbec. Where's everybody else?"

I explained they went to Everglades City for lunch.

"Why are they all here? You guys don't seem to have anything in common. You got that big Italian guy from New Jersey. Sal Hamburger or whatever his name is. You got that Irish guy who always wears a beret and is always walking around with a book. Then you got that Muslim dude. And the black chick weightlifter from Canada.

"And then you. You're about as white they come. Something's going on here. I can tell. Don't know what it is."

I took another sip of malbec and watched a pelican swoop down into the water across the street.

"Nothing's going on," I said. "We all work for the same company. They're here on vacation. I told them they could stay a few days at my house. I still can't get used to that – calling this place my house. It was left to me by my uncle Orville."

"Orville? Like Orville Redenbacher? Like Orville Wright?"

"Yes, Troxie, like the popcorn guy and the airplane guy. But not like Orval Overall, who pitched for the Cubs more than a century ago."

"Orval Overall?"

"Yep, that was his name. Won 20 games in a couple of seasons for the Cubs."

"Orval? You're sure."

"Absolutely. His nickname was the Big Groundhog because his birthday was Feb. 2 and he was about 6-2 and 220 pounds. He won the clinching game for the Cubs in the 1908 World Series. They didn't win another 2016."

"I gotta say you are chock full of the most useless information of anybody I think I've ever met. Orval? You sure?"

"Yep. And thanks. And yes. I did not make up that name. And I take pride in being useless. Can't change the oil in my Camry or boil a pot of water or bait a hook, but I do know my baseball trivia."

"I'm sure that impresses the girls."

"You can't imagine. My only pickup line from the days when I tried using pickup lines was asking women if they knew who the third baseman was in the famous Tinkers to Evers to Chance infield for the Cubs."

"And how did that work out?"

"Not so well."

"Well, who was the third baseman?"

"Harry Steinfeldt."

"I'm sure women swooned when they heard Harry Steinfeldt played third base for the Cubs."

"Not so much. So anyhow, how do you like that malbec?"

"It's quite smooth. Something different about it."

"It's sort of a dry red and has a higher alcohol content that most wines. Got some hints, I'm told, of plums and black cherry. I don't know about that but it's quite a mixture. That high alcohol content is definitely an attraction."

"Yep."

Troxie then pretended to fall out of her wicker chair.

"Seriously, this house was left to you by a rich uncle? I thought that happened only in bad movies."

"Well, it happened to me. I'm not sure Uncle Orville was rich. I'd say prosperous."

"He didn't have any kids."

"Nope. Four wives. No kids."

"What were his wives like?"

"Well, there was RuthAnne and Ruth Ann and Carrie Ann and Anne-Marie."

"Ann?"

"And what?"

"No, Ann. He had quite a thing for women named Ann."

"That he did."

"So, Scott, you were saying you and your house guests all work for the same company."

"Yep, an outfit named Grabmore. Owns dozens of newspapers and radio stations and TV stations and advertising agencies and forests."

"So, you all work together at the same place?"

"No, I work in Fort Myers but the others work other places and just came down here on vacation."

"Vacation? At your house? At Uncle Orville's house? Why are they here? What are you doing together?"

"Oh, just hanging out."

"I don't see that. Something's going on. I can sense these things. This is more than a vacation. More than fishing and kayaking and drinking."

"What makes you say that? The malbec?"

"I'm not as ditzy or stupid as some people think, Scott. I've been to college. I was an honor roll student in high school. People think blonds are dizzy. I haven't been hit in the head with too many biscuits on the shuffleboard circuit. Something's going on here. Something more than fishing for snook off that dock out back."

I tried changing the subject.

"Tell me more about shuffleboard. I'm a sports writer for the Tropical-Times. That's the Fort Myers paper. Maybe I'll pitch a story on shuffleboard to the sports editor. It may be a tough pitch because it has so many letters. Anything more than two syllables and he's in trouble."

"You'd do that? A story on shuffleboard?"

"Maybe."

"Have you ever played?"

"Not really."

"I see you got a shuffleboard court out back. Wanna learn?"

"Sure. I'll get the tangs and biscuits out of the storage shed. They were a gift from one of Uncle Orville's wives. Not sure which one but I'm pretty sure Ann or Anne was part of her name."

So would soon continue my shuffleboard education, on the court behind the category 4 hurricane shelter where a certain category 4 CEO was locked away, possibly watching once again another episode of Keeping up with the Kardashians.

Unless there was an episode of The Real Wives of Chokoloskee on one of those networks the CEO likes to watch in his hurricane bunker.

I opened the storage shed and removed the dust-covered tangs and biscuits.

"Now, the goal is to knock your opponent's biscuits into the kitchen," Troxie told me.

She didn't mean the room in the house where the cooking is done. Or in my case the microwaving. The kitchen is when a disk enters the 10-off area, which is a very big deal in the shuffleboard world.

"Boy, I wish we could have seen Mae Hall in her prime," Troxie said, going on again about the St. Pete shuffleboard legend.

"In that Sports Illustrated story I told you about, the one from 1964, Mae talked about an epic victory over Mary Scalise, her archrival. I memorized what Mae said: 'From past experience, I knew the court had a drift that would make my disk curve after it slowed it down. So I shot around the block, got rid of her 7 and took it into the kitchen.'

"So, is that cool or what?"

I admitted it was very cool indeed.

"You know what her husband Herbert told Sports Illustrated in 1964 about that shot?"

I had to admit I had no idea what Herbert Hall said to Sports Illustrated in 1964 about his wife's great shuffleboard shot. Troxie paused, like a great actor waiting to deliver a line.

"This is what Herbert Hall said: 'One of the best shots of the year. The crowd went wild, and a lot of people waved Mae Hall dolls.' Now, do you see why I want to be the next Mae Hall?"

"I promise, when the Troxie Trosky shuffleboard dolls come out I'll be the first to buy one," I told her. "And I'll wave my Troxie Trosky doll when you win a big tournament in St. Pete."

Troxie liked that and gave me a kiss on the cheek.

"Now, Scott, there is a beauty and geometry to this game," she said, holding a tang. "At each end of the court is a triangle. The goal is to knock your opponent's biscuits out of zones – see the numbers on the court? – with a positive value and then you increase your own points by landing disks in areas of high point value. Got that?"

"I think so."

Then we heard the sound of a vehicle pulling into the driveway.

"That sounds like Uncle Orville's Suburban," I said. "We'll have to play some other time."

So we walked by the category 4 storm shelter where we had locked away our category 4 CEO and around to the front porch.

CHAPTER TWENTY-ONE

Troxie and I walked around the house, each with a tang in one hand and a glass of malbec in the other. Just as we turned the corner, the Suburban's four doors opened and each of my four pals paused for a moment as they eyeballed us. Monique walked up and whispered in my ear, "What is she doing here?"

"She stopped by for a visit," I said.

"Is that all?"

"Yes, that's all. Well, plus we drank some malbec and were about to start playing shuffleboard when we heard you pull up."

"I thought she was a pinot-grigio girl."

"Alas and alack, not a drop of pinot grigio is in the house, not a drop of pinot grigio to be found in all of Chokoloskee," I said.

"Don't alas and alack me, you smart-ass, smart-aleck, two-bit, small-time, small-town sportswriter," Monique said.

Nigel, holding a to-go bag, walked over and patted Monique on a shoulder.

"Settle down," Nigel said.

Then he turned to me and he said, "Scott, we're all a little stressed. And Miss Trosky, nice to see you again."

He then took off his beret and did an exaggerated bow and swept the beret in front of him.

"Gee, for people on vacation, you folks sure seem stressed out," Troxie said. "What's the deal here? Were your fries cold and beer warm at lunch?"

Then Sal stepped over, amiable as usual.

"It's a Grabmore thing," Sal said. "We all work for this big company and it, well, it sucks the life out of people."

"Management seems intent on crushing people's souls and spirits," I said, taking another sip of malbec.

"Sounds awful," Troxie said.

"You can't imagine," Ahmad said.

"Gee, Ahmad, you know your English is really good for somebody from Yes Ma'am," Troxie said. "What language do you Yemeners talk?"

"Arabic is the official language but I also know Pashto," Ahmad said. "But I started learning English when I was 8. And now I'm 38. So I've had lots of practice."

"Well, you, like, you know, talk English really good, Ahmad," Troxie said. "When Scott introduced you as Elmore Leonard it just didn't seem right. I didn't know Elmore Leonard was like this legendary crime writer dude. You just don't look like somebody named Elmore."

"Oh, I'm very Elmore," he said.

"He's too Elmore for his own good," I said.

A moment of silence followed. Nobody, including me, knew for sure what that meant.

"Why," I said, "are we standing out here in the sun? Let's go up in the shade of the porch. And you got my lunch?"

"Got it right here," Nigel said, holding up a bag.

I reached in and pulled out a Styrofoam package, opened it and it contained a grouper sandwich. Not what I ordered.

"Ahh, guys. ...." I said. "I didn't ask for a grouper sandwich."

"The other box is for you," Sal said.

Indeed it was. Troxie noticed two takeout boxes and one was for me. Who had ordered the grouper sandwich? My four friends ate at the Rod & Gun Club. Why that sandwich? There wasn't anybody else in the house. As far as she knew. They didn't bring it back for Troxie because they didn't know she'd be here.

I could see her surprisingly agile mind working.

Sal quickly said he would take the other box inside and I ate my captain's platter on the porch.

"Something is definitely going on here," Troxie said. "I remember reading a Sherlock Holmes book once. He had some line in there about the game is afoot. Something is afoot."

Obviously, the game was afoot. We had kidnapped a multi-millionaire CEO, the CEO of our company, a spoiled, obtuse, borderline obese, middle-aged rich kid brat, who we had stashed away on this property.

How long could we keep him? The hurricane shelter was stocked with food and water and Frappucinos enough to last six weeks. At least. And we could always buy more. It had its own generator, so if power were lost to the house, the lights and air conditioning would continue working. O'Riley could stay comfortable and well fed alone for weeks or months or maybe even years.

But, frankly, despite all his manifest transgressions, we didn't have the heart to keep him locked away in solitary confinement indefinitely in a room without windows. We hadn't thought this through as thoroughly as we should have. I guess, on some level, we never really thought we could just pluck a CEO off the streets of Fort Myers and hide him away and not get caught. Even the plucking part seemed very unlikely. But it all came together seamlessly and implausibly on the streets of downtown Fort Myers. We had the CEO. We hadn't been caught, at least not yet. But we had him. That's for sure.

Now what?

I picked up one of those little white plastic forks and dug into the seafood platter.

Monique was inside, not wanting to be around Troxie. The guys stayed on the porch with me. Or more precisely, with Troxie, who is a comely woman, nearly fetching, what with that blond hair tumbling out the back of the Rays baseball cap, blue eyes and trim physique.

"So, what makes this Grubmore place so bad?" she asked.

"It's Grabmore," I pointed out.

"Oh, yeah."

I packed a forkful of rice into my mouth and then waved the fork, indicating to wait just a moment.

"Well, we all have our stories," I started. "All Grabmore employees have their stories. Stories about management crushing people's souls. Pettiness. Meanness. Let me tell you my doubles tennis story.

"I was playing doubles tennis. Me and a sports writer against another writer and the guy who was sports editor at the time. Now I wasn't an experienced tennis player but enjoyed the game. I was at the net when the sports editor's partner tried a lob over my head. It was terrible. One of the worst lobs in the history of tennis.

"It seemed to pause, just hang there in the air above my head with a flashing sign that said, 'Hit me!' I did. An overhead smash. I hit it square, flush. Everything behind the smash and crushed that little yellow ball.

"The ball smashed into the forehead of the sports editor, who was maybe five feet away on the other side of the net. It bounced off his forehead, over the net, over my head, beyond the back line, over the chain link fence behind the court and then over some trees and into a lake.

"I didn't mean to do that. It was an accident. The next day when a staff meeting began I was tied up on a telephone interview with a high school football coach. I continued with the interview instead of cutting it off to attend yet another time-wasting meeting filled with corporate drivel.

"The sports editor didn't think anything was more important than one of these corporate brain-washing sessions. He stormed out of the meeting, told me to go home while he thought what he was going to do with me. That he hoped to fire me. He was serious. I was sent home.

"A couple of hours later, the assistant sports editor called and said he had saved my job. That even at Grabmore, one usually didn't get fired for doing your job instead of going to a meeting.

"But I was being demoted from covering professional sports to covering youth sports. All for, essentially, a poorly aimed overhead smash off a typical Grabmore editor's forehead.

"That, Troxie, is Grabmore."

Troxie poured herself some more malbec.

"Why do you keep working there?"

"It's not easy but I need a job and I love my job, believe it or not. Every Grabmore employee has his or her stories."

"Why don't you do something?"

"Like what?"

"I don't know. Maybe kidnap the company president and hold him hostage or something."

I took a big gulp of malbec and exchanged looks with Ahmad, Nigel and Sal.

Sal said, "Troxie, that's not a bad idea. The guy who runs the place is actually the CEO and not the president. Not a bad idea, at all. We'll think about it."

She beamed.

"Really?"

"Well," Nigel said, "not bad isn't the same as good. How would you make it a good idea?"

Troxie shrugged, indicating she didn't know.

I started speaking, thinking to give her a simple Cliff's notes picture of our CEO.

"Maybe you need to know more about our CEO. Let's see. His name is O'Riley. Every time he fires an employee he gets a $7,100 bonus. That would be at least tip money if he ever tipped waiters and waitresses and bartenders.

"No pay raises for employees while he has a company jet and a company yacht and company cars and country club membership. He brings teenage girls back from places like Iceland to work on his yacht. You get the picture?"

Troxie was no longer smiling. She had worked as a waitress. She knew the importance of tips. Once, she had been a teenage girl and sympathized with the naive girls O'Riley lured to his yacht. She had, apparently, an innate sense of decency and fair play, something she could tell from my capsule CEO description that O'Riley lacked.

"I hate people like that," Troxie said. "Well, if you ever decide to kidnap the creep, let me know. I'll help."

Again, the four of us exchanged glances.

"I'll do whatever I could to help," Troxie continued, looking at me. "Especially if you let me stay in your cool house and play shuffleboard out back."

"We'll be sure to keep you in mind if we need a kidnapping accomplice," I told her with a grin. "Send over your kidnapping resume and kidnapping references."

She found that mildly amusing and said it was time to go. She wanted to go back to her trailer and rest up before working a night shift at the City Fishhouse. She needed that tip money.

I wanted to go upstairs in my post-malbec stupor, collapse into the hammock on the upstairs balcony, read a bit more of Poet, Pugilist and Pressman and take a nap.

Then it would be back to Fort Myers. I promised Lt. Hooper we would talk the next day about the missing Grabmore CEO. And players in the Fort Myers Roy Hobbs Geezer Rec Baseball League always keep promises to one another.

Catcher to shortstop, member of Bartley's to member of Babykin's. It's a sacred bond. Or in my case a sacred Bond.

CHAPTER TWENTY-TWO

I staggered upstairs, feeling the effects of all that malbec, grabbed my copy of Poet, Pugilist and Pressman and stumbled, nearly falling into that swaying hammock on the balcony. Palm fronds waved in the gentle afternoon breeze. That combination of swaying hammock and waving palm fronds and malbec nearly made me spin and tumble right out of the hammock.

Fortunately, I had a safe and soft landing in the hammock, the book clutched to my chest.

The first Chesterfield Ebenezer O'Riley was becoming something of a hero to me, even a role model, the antithesis of his great-grandson, who was locked away downstairs. .O'Riley No. 4 was likely sipping a Frappucino and watching the Kardashians do whatever it is Kardashians do on that reality show that is apparently aimed at very stupid people.

O'Riley No. 1 had no use for such fluff. He was a man of substance.

I decided to read the chapter on his early days as a sports writer in New York, in the years before World War 1.

The chapter's title was Jocks, Poets, Playwrights and Some Ink-Stained Pals.

I settled down deeper into the hammock and started reading what Mr. O'Riley wrote more than a half-century earlier. I have no trouble referring to him as Mr. O'Riley. He earned that Mister in front of his name. Not so O'Riley No. 4, our houseguest, to use a euphemism that sounds like Grabspeak.

Here, then, some more of what is becoming one of my favorite books:

Most people, I know, just think of me as this old coot rattling around inside one of his mansions or puttering on one of his yachts.

They probably think I'm now like Charles Foster Kane, the newspaper tycoon in "Citizen Kane." About the only thing that fictional tycoon has in common with me is that we're both rich. And old. And don't ask me about Rosebud.

But I was young once. That's what I want to write about in this chapter, being a young sportswriter in New York City in the years before World War I and then branching out and becoming a newspaper tycoon.

Here we are in 1961. We have an Irish boy in the White House as president. I met his father, Joseph P. Kennedy, in the '20s. Didn't really care for him but Jack seems like a nice kid.

So much has changed in the more than half a century since I first walked in the Brooklyn Daily Eagle front door, stinking of the City of Cheaters. Hungry. Dirty. Poor. Smelling like steerage and all those other desperate immigrants.

For starters, as I think I've said before, I can afford plenty of soap now. Before going on I want to share something from one of my favorite poets, William Wordsworth:

"Though nothing can bring back the hour

Of splendor in the grass, of glory in the flower;

We will grieve not, rather find strength in what remains behind."

That comes from a poem called "Ode on Intimations of Immortality from Recollections of Early Childhood." I don't want to get all pretentious and maudlin on anybody who might read this. I just like the ring and tenor of those lines, the beauty and lyricism of Wordsworth's words.

But I do have a larger point.

A few, actually.

I always thought a strong sports section was vital to a good newspaper. And I didn't want some stereotypical sports dolts running the sports section. There are, among many others, two types of people I find irksome to the point of distracting madness.

One is the sports fan or writer who doesn't know anything about anything outside sports, who wouldn't know Wordsworth from a Woolworth's sale on hosiery. I wanted people writing and editing my sports sections with an understanding of the world, who realized sports is part of the rich tapestry of life. I can't imagine a life without sports just like I can't imagine life without literature and poetry.

The other irksome types are those dad-blasted, snooty, pseudo-intellectual snobs who believe sport is beneath their notice, that in their self-absorbed, aren't I so-smart smugness only semi-literate mouth-breathers care about sports. Well, a pox on both their houses.

Where was I?

Oh, yeah, sports section.

My ideal sports editor was Stanley Woodward, who worked for the New York Herald Tribune in the 1930s. He assembled great writers and let them write. I recall the advice he gave the best of them, Red Smith. He told Red, "Don't God up the ballplayers."

In other words, no hero worship. No ass-kissing. I hate that stuff and would hate to see it in the people working in my company. Anybody who tried it with me usually got fired.

I wanted to hire Woodward and Smith away from the Herald-Tribune to work for any of my papers anywhere but they wouldn't leave.

One of the first writers I met in New York was Bat Masterson. People nowadays know him from his days as Wild West gunfighter and the TV show starring Gene Barry as Bat.

I remember Bat telling me once in Stillman's Gym as we watched middleweight champ Stanley Ketchel sparring that his motto out west in his younger days was "Shoot first, and never miss."

126

He let that sink in for a moment and then said, "Don't forget that, kid."

I never had to shoot anybody but I never forgot what Bat told me.

Ketchel, by the way, meant an unfortunate and early death a few months later out in Missouri. It was 1910 and he was shot in the back by, as the story goes, the common-law husband of a woman Ketchel knew quite well. A woman who was cooking his breakfast at the time of the shooting.

Somebody said shortly after the fatal shooting, "Tell 'em to start counting 10, and he'll get up."

Stanley Ketchel didn't get up. Hasn't got up since.

I promised Bat that I would not forget his advice about shooting first and never missing. Like I said I never got around to shooting anybody, though. Boy, there were times I was tempted to shoot a few people.

Damon Runyon, who's probably best known now for "Guys and Dolls," told me Bat wasn't much of a writer. In fact, Damon said, "he has no literary style, but he has plenty of moxie."

I like moxie. Moxie is what got me hired at the Brooklyn Daily Eagle. Moxie is what convinced Mr. Kent to invite me in as a partner with my first newspaper, that weekly in Poughkeepsie.

I love moxie. As I was saying, way back when, I got to know writers such as Lincoln Steffens and Damon Runyon and Rex Lardner.

Now, to be clear, I'm not claiming to be pals of any of these folks. I was on the periphery, a young guy awed to be around them. Some of them were young, like me. Others were established such as journalism legend Ida Tarbell, whose work brought down Standard Oil.

Although I'd run up to Poughkeepsie in those days to check on the weekly and I was investing what little money I had in some other papers, I was still working fulltime for the Brooklyn Daily Eagle. I was a sports writer who also dabbled in covering theater and the fledgling movie industry.

The people I met were a who's who of sports and entertainment at the time. You'd be surprised who I met. Boxers such as the great Jack Johnson, the black heavyweight champion. I think he was better than Jack Dempsey, Joe Louis and Rocky Marciano or that young fellow Cassius Clay but most people nowadays don't even know anything about Johnson.

When I heard about how many white people hated Johnson and prayed for a white champ, I thought back to my time on the City of Cheaters and reading Huck Finn as the ship plowed through the Atlantic Ocean. The runaway slave, Jim, is the best person in the book. He had nobility about him that the white characters in the story didn't.

I had never met a Negro as a boy in Ireland. But as I read the book on the deck of that ship, I vowed to treat any black people I met in America with dignity. It troubled me that the great author Jack London called for a Great White Hope to reclaim the heavyweight crown for the white race by beating Johnson. I'm getting off track now.

Readers of this book may want to know more about how I became a tycoon than for my thoughts on Wordsworth and Jack London and my brief encounters with the famous.

Did I ever tell you about the time I met silent movie star Clara Bow? She was known as the It Girl. One of the prettiest girls I ever met. And I met quite a few.

As John Keats, another one of my favorite poets, wrote, "A thing of beauty is a joy forever."

Clara Bow wasn't a beauty forever but I hope Grabmore, the company I built, remains one.

W. B. Yeats is another poet I like and it's not just because he was Irish.

Here's part of his poem "The Second Coming:"
"The falcon cannot hear the falconer
Things fall apart; the center cannot hold
Mere anarchy is loosed upon the world.
The ceremony of innocence is drowned

The best lack all conviction while the worst
Are full of passionate intensity."
I hope that never happens to Grabmore.

Here's my final poetry quote of this chapter and maybe the book, something else from Yeats, from the poem "A Drinking Song:"
"Wine comes in at the mouth
And love comes in at the eye
That's all we know for truth
Before we grow old and die
I lift the glass to my mouth,
I look at you, and sigh."

That in my post-malbec daze is where I stopped reading, put the book down and dozed off once again in that hammock on Uncle Orville's second-floor balcony. The malbec and the stress were getting to me. I helped kidnap a CEO. We had this colorful shuffleboard fanatic nosing around the house. The cops were asking more questions. Would they come down to Chokoloskee in a fleet of Crown Victoria Interceptors and start nosing around Uncle Orville's house?

First, I had to drive back again to Fort Myers. Lt. Hooper wanted to talk once more.

CHAPTER TWENTY-THREE

It was back to the Starbucks in downtown Fort Myers, the coffee shop on the ground floor in the old three-story brick Kress Building, one of the oldest structures in town. It was built in 1928, when the Grabmore founder already owned a couple dozen newspapers.

James Taylor was singing Fire and Rain on the in-house sound system. Taylor crooned that, "I've seen lonely times when I could not find a friend."

Would I need to find a friend, a criminal defense lawyer type of friend, after meeting Lt. Hooper of the Fort Myers Police Department, the gruff-talking and gruff-acting detective?

He is a no-nonsense sort of guy. I, on the other hand, love nonsense. We met outside on the street corner on a pleasant morning several days after the CEO vanished.

We chatted briefly about our upcoming game in the geezer baseball league. I'm sure, as was often the case, his team, the one loaded with ex-minor-leaguers and college players, would quickly dispatch our team, the one named Babykins and filled with guys who were mostly adequate high school players. Like me.

He told me about the latest addition for his team, a 6-foot-5, 40-year-old guy who was all-state football and baseball at Sarasota High, was a backup quarterback for the Gators, drafted in baseball by the

Tigers and reached the majors for a couple seasons as a pitcher. Still threw about 85 mph, Hooper told me. And could spin 80 mph sliders knee high or buzz fastballs just under your chin.

Great. By contrast, our newest player was a 5-foot-8, 49-year-old who the Tropical-Times named honorable mention all-county when he pitched at Cape Coral High more than 30 years ago. He was cut from the baseball team at some Division III school in Tennessee and on his best day probably couldn't hit 80 on the radar gun.

It looked like Babykins would get waxed again by Bartley's. Of course, I had more things to worry about then striking out three times in a game. Again. And losing to Bartley's. Again.

Kidnapping convictions carry, I'm certain, long prison terms. Do prisons provide rec baseball teams and Starbucks?

Hooper growled something, indicating our baseball chat was over and we walked inside. He barked a request for a large black coffee and said a very gracious thank you and tipped the barista $1. I ordered my usual grande, skinny, no-whip mocha and Hooper growled a sort of sighing guttural exasperating sound of dismay that a grown man, a fellow baseball player no less, didn't drink his coffee black. Just black.

I made sure to leave a $1 tip, as well. And thanked the barista. Hooper softened his growl after my display of good manners and a tip.

That's $2 more in tip money for the barista with the piercings and tattoos would ever get from one Chesterfield Ebenezer O'Riley IV. We got our coffee and walked around the corner of the display case to a back room, one that has a narrow walkway leading to a courtyard facing, fittingly, the federal courthouse. The sort of place, I imagine, kidnapping cases would be tried.

On the side of the walkway were two rust-colored upholstered chairs with wooden armrests and stains from people's oily hair on that upholstery. In between was a round wooden table with a glass top where we set our cups.

"Well, Bond, what do you think happened to O'Riley?" Hooper asked, quite bluntly.

I picked up my cup and took a sip.

"Gee, Hooper, I have no idea," I said. "And I don't really care."

Despite our many differences, Hopper and I shared some things. We loved baseball and believed in good manners and tipping baristas. We also hated rude, rich blowhards who didn't have the decency to leave even a quarter tip.

"You know, Bond, I've heard you talk about Grabmore around the batting cages at Terry Park and after the games at those outside tables at Hooters," Hooper said. "I remember the things you said. I know you have contempt for the company and its leaders. Frankly, I don't blame you.

"I don't have any use for these assholes, either. But kidnapping, not to mention murder, is still illegal. At least I think so. Last I heard. I'm not a lawyer, just a cop. And my job is to try to figure out what happened to your CEO. I think you know something. I'm pretty damn sure you know something.

"I also think it's possible you're involved in whatever happened. It's just too damn suspicious and convenient that when you happened to walk downtown is when O'Riley vanished. It's possible the next time we talk it won't be in Starbucks, but in a room at police headquarters. By the way, Bond, we don't serve – what are those drinks called? Mochas? - And we sure as hell don't play James Taylor during interrogations.

"So, Bond, you want to tell me something now in the comfort of Starbucks while you got your sissy-boy drink?"

Well, he had my attention.

"Are you saying I'm a suspect and should get an attorney?"

"Not so fast, Bond. I'm not saying that. Maybe a person of interest. I just think this thing stinks like that carpet in your newsroom. Why doesn't the company get a carpet-cleaning service in to take care of it? Or rip it out and replace it?"

"If I ever meet O'Riley I'll bring that up," I said, lying to Hooper.

Of course, I had met O'Riley but Hooper didn't know that. He apparently suspected it but had no proof.

"Tell me, again, what did you do that afternoon, the one where the CEO, your so-called Dear Leader, vanished?" Hooper asked.

I pretended to be exasperated, but I was scared. I took another sip of the mocha. It's always something with these "m" drinks. Malbec with Troxie and now mocha with Hooper. What's next? Mojitoes with Kim Kardashian?

I definitely preferred sitting on the front porch with Troxie talking about shuffleboard to sitting here with Hooper dodging questions about kidnapping.

"Geez, Hooper, I told you. It was a great day. One of the few afternoons we have here all year long where it isn't hot and muggy or warm and muggy. I wasn't under a tight deadline on a story and couldn't take any more of Mabel's maundering talk, relentless backstabbing and brownnosing.

"I needed air and to escape the Pit of Despair. Downtown Fort Myers, as you know, is great with its old buildings and palm trees and brick streets and the Caloosahatchee River flowing by.

"I strolled through Centennial Park and by the yacht club. I noticed O'Riley's yacht from a distance but didn't walk near it. Those goons he usually has around for security don't like people walking close to the boat. So I just walked around for 30 or 40 minutes. And went back to the office.

"I didn't see O'Riley and sure didn't see anybody shoot him or stab him or hit him over the head with a Louisville Slugger. So I don't know what else to tell you. He's gone. Maybe he fell off the boat. Did you ever think about that?"

"Yes, we did," Hooper said. "Didn't you see the video of the river being dragged? It was on your website. By the way, what sort of idiot came up with the name tsquared.com?"

"Do I have to answer that?"

"No, forget it."

"Are we done here?"

"Not yet. What do you think happened to O'Riley? You're kind of smart. You somehow got a college degree from some half-baked school. You probably know most of the letters of the alphabet and can get them in the right order most of the time. What do you think happened to your CEO?"

I paused, trying to come up with a plausible scenario that could send Hooper searching other angles for like the next, oh, 40 years.

"Good question. I've given it some thought. You know about the girls he hires to work on the yacht? The eighteen- and nineteen-year-old girls from Iceland and Ireland and Lapland, wherever the hell that is?

"Here's my theory: The father or boyfriend of one of them came all the way here and killed him and disposed of the body. What do you think about that?"

"We're checking into that. Haven't found any evidence of any father or boyfriend of any of the girls from any of those places entering the country. So I don't think that's what happened. Not a bad thought, though, for a guy who struggles to hit .200 in a rec baseball league.

"By the way, your batting average is going to drop even lower after you face our new guy on Sunday. I told you he got to the big leagues for a while?"

I nodded. My chances of getting a hit off a big-league pitcher were about as good as my chances of drinking mojitos with Kim Kardashian.

So I shifted back to Grabmore and asked Hooper if he knew anything about profit margins. He shook his head.

"Well, I don't either," I said. "It's a topic that falls into that MEGO category."

"Me go," Hooper said.

"No," I explained, "that's M-E-G-O. As in My Eyes Glaze Over. That's what happens when the subjects of finance or business come up. My eyes glaze over and my forehead hits the keyboard."

"What's your point?"

"My point is this: You ever noticed the railroad spur that runs behind the Tropical-Times building?"

Hooper nodded that he had.

"Well, that's where they deliver the newsprint that is made into newspapers. The joke for decades has been that when the railroad cars leave after dropping off newsprint they leave packed with cash.

"The Tropical-Times in its heyday had profit margins of more than 40 percent. Think about that. Now, it may be half that, probably a lot less than half. I bet most Fortune 500 companies are happy with 5 or 6 percent.

"Where did all that money go? You've seen O'Riley's yacht. I'm sure some of it went toward that yacht obstructing the view of the Caloosahatchee. And the company jet. We have a monthly newsroom award for good work. It's called the Top Banana. Every month four or five folks win the award, which is a certificate, $25 in cash and a banana. It used to be $50 and two bananas. But management cut the prize booty in half. The cash prize and the banana prize.

"I was happy to win. Don't get me wrong on that score. There's a lot of good people doing good work at the paper. Talented, ethical, honest people who succeed in spite of Grabmore instead of because of Grabmore."

Hooper sat there in silence for a moment.

"Hey, I know Grabmore is an awful place," he said. "That's not the point. And off the record, if I went on a hunting trip with O'Riley deep into the Big Cypress Preserve, I wouldn't shed a tear if he got lost in the woods or met some untimely hunting accident. None of those things are why we're here. It's my job to find out what happened to your CEO.

"Well, I got to get going. The chief wants an update on this case. And good luck Sunday in our game. You're going to need it."

With that, Lt. Hooper walked out the back door of Starbucks and into the courtyard that separates it from the federal courthouse, the place where I may be on trial someday.

Along with Monique and Sal and Ahmad and Nigel.

It was time to go to work, back to the Tropical-Times office.

CHAPTER TWENTY-FOUR

Just when you think the Grabmore culture can't surprise you, guess what? You're surprised. There are always surprises. The only surprise comes when you're not surprised.

After the short drive from Starbucks, I walked in the Tropical-Times side door employee entrance and immediately noticed our online editor, Mabel Borgia. She wore mourning clothes, an all-black dress and black veil, like something a mediocre actress at a funeral in a particularly bad 1950s B movie might have worn.

She still sported her normal black Chuck Taylor Converse high-top sneakers, which didn't go with the dress and veil. At least I didn't think so. But then I don't know anything about fashion. Maybe high top sneakers now go with black mourning clothes. I'm a sports writer, after all, a group notorious for lack of fashion sense. I was wearing gray cargo shorts, a cheap tangerine-colored Hawaiian shirt from Target and white sneakers. Who am I to mock or criticize the way other people dress? Me? With my paisley shirts from thrift stores and threadbare sports coat I bought second hand in 1999?

Anyhow, Mabel had built an O'Riley shrine at her desk. A candle burned. Photos of the CEO adorned her wall. She had a large jar on her desk with a hand-written note taped to it with these words: Save Our Dear Leader.

She was asking Tropical-Times employees to contribute to a fund in case a ransom demand for his return was delivered.

I noticed a few pennies and a twenty-dollar bill in the jar. I had to ask even though I knew the answer. And despite the fact I avoid as much as possible being within 50 feet of Mabel I had to hear her say it.

"Well, Mabel, who was the generous soul who put $20 in the save Chesty fund?"

"I did, of course," she said. "And don't call him Chesty. You should refer to him as our Dear Leader or Mr. O'Riley."

"Yes, Mabel," I said and I then walked away as swiftly as possible over toward the sports department.

The newsroom was quiet. People were going about their duties. Most of the folks aren't Grabmorons and take pride in doing good work despite the suffocating corporate atmosphere. I stopped by Ace Hamill's desk on the way to sports. Ace, as I think I mentioned earlier, is our crackerjack cops reporter, a snarling, sullen veteran of 32 years covering crime and working for the Tropical-Times.

People think Ace is some sort of ironic nickname but it's his actual, real first name. He was named after Ace Adams, who pitched for the New York Giants in the 1940s and that Ace's real first name was, well, Ace. Same as our Ace.

Anyhow, our Ace has seen and heard it all. Every big case in area history for more than 30 years has usually carried the Ace Hamill byline on the Tropical-Times front page.

The plot to steal the downtown Thomas Edison statue? Check.

The rustling by would-be cowboys of llamas at the local alpaca farm? Check.

The crystal meth lab run by a coterie of local clergymen that included a rabbi, priest, minister, imam and led by a Svengali-like charlatan atheist new world guru espousing banging drums and smoking pot? Check.

Ace had also endured three decades of Grabmore pettiness and backstabbing. He makes Lt. Hooper look as sunny as Chuck E. Cheese.

If anybody knew what the cops knew, it would be Ace. They trust Ace for his accuracy, respect for facts, solid reporting, straightforward writing and low tolerance for BS.

I try to avoid Ace. Oh, I certainly respect him but his grumpiness is off-putting. I walked over to his desk, which is decorated with photos of J. Edgar Hoover, Robert Woodward, Carl Bernstein and Carl Hiassan.

"Good morning, Ace," I said tentatively.

"Hrrumph," he explained.

"I was just wondering if you know anything about O'Riley that you haven't been able to report?" I asked.

He knew I didn't mean that he would withhold information but that there might be some information he couldn't pin down. Ace is nothing but professional and careful in his reporting.

"Hrrumph," he further explained.

"OK, got it," I said. "Do the cops have any leads at all?"

"Nope," he said in his typical Ace snarl.

Then he brightened.

"Hey, Bond, have a nice day," he said, nearly smiling. "And nice job on that story about the new Red Sox bullpen catcher. How do you think they'll do this year?"

Like I said, Grabmore is always full of surprises.

I told Ace that the Red Sox should contend, as usual. The farm system invariably produces two or three prospects every year, they have the budget to snag big-ticket free agents and can make a good trade or two. He signaled our chat was over.

"Hrrumph," he said and then went on to analyze the case more by saying, "Errr....."

"Thanks, Ace," I said and sidled my way over to the sports department.

Col. Longstreet starting that day had added a new feature to the top of the paper's front page. It was a box with O'Riley's photo and this headline: Help Find O'Riley.

Beneath that were a few bullet points:

•Chesterfield Ebenzer O'Riley IV, an icon of American business and journalism, disappeared from Fort Myers on Monday.

•A special Website has been established to sift through leads and pay tribute to this gifted leader. Look for dearistleader.com. Note: We wanted to use dearleader.com but somebody else already has that domain name.

•Special hotline to our Information Nexus, manned 10 p.m. to 4 p.m. Monday through Friday. Concerned citizens may call in tips at 555-TIPS. Note: The hotline closes for lunch from noon to 1 p.m.

•Our special email address for tips is savedearleader@yahoo.com.

•Employees are voluntarily raising funds to pay a ransom and so far have raised $20.06.

The Grabmore blog was aflame with comments. I checked it quickly before going out to the Red Sox practice fields to see what was going on now a month before the team reported for spring training,

•From conspiracycoverupdude: I bet O'riley is in Area 54. Or is that 51? Was that famous New York bar called Club 54 or Club 51? I can never remember which is which. Anyhow, I know O'riley was snatched by a secret government program that mates CEOs with alien beauties from the planet Hotbabe in the Orion system. He may be on a spaceship now headed for other stellar systems. I wouldn't worry about our ceo. He's doing more better than any of us here.

•From saveyourjobs: "Who cares about this portly pig? The sooner he's gone the better. But what happens now? Whose gonna take over? There is no Chesterfield Ebenezer O'Riley V. That we know of. Just because he's gone don't mean things are going to get better."

•From anonymous: "I hope the stoopid rat basterd rots in heel."

As always, I felt enlightened and even inspired after spending a minute or two on the blog with such insightful, reasoned and rational people. Oh, and ones who write so brilliantly, as well.

Now, what? Job 1 was, well, my job. I still had it. Still loved it. The priority now was going out to JetBlue Park and poking around for an interesting feature story. The media frenzy that is Red Sox spring training was a month away. Things were informal at the park in January.

The only other sportswriter I might bump into out there would be Jim Renoir, who gave me the impression he might not be suited for this work. That would make two of us. I don't think I'm cut out for it, either.

Jim works for the Naples Gazette-Union-Leader-Press, which acquired its unwieldy name because it was the product of several newspaper mergers over the years. Those mergers left it with the acronym of GULP. Or the Naples Gulp or the Gulp on the Gulf. The Naples paper was owned by another large corporation, Intercontinental Missiles Inc., a large defense contractor, which also owned a couple dozen papers around the country.

Intercontinental began in the 19th century as Jimbob's Livery Stable in St. Joseph, Missouri and made fine scabbards, saddles and canteens. Those were sold to the United States Army. Supposedly, George Custer had a Jimbob's scabbard and canteen that day he rode into battle at the Little Big Horn.

The company grew and changed with the times, branching out into machine guns, grenades, fighter planes, nuclear submarines, drones, aircraft carriers, portable toilets, lingerie, a California winery and newspapers.

That diversified corporate profile also included employees who covered sports, people such as Jim. He pulled into the JetBlue parking lot right behind me.

"Boy, you guys got quite a mystery at your place, don't you?" Jim asked.

I nodded.

"What do you think happened?" Jim asked. "You think somebody killed that O'Riley dude?"

By this point I was getting used to lying.

"I don't know," I told Jim, lying yet again.

"Boy, did you hear 60 Minutes and Dateline are coming down to do stories about the missing CEO?" Jim asked.

Actually, that was news to me.

"Are you sure?" I asked.

"No, but that's the scuttlebutt," Jim said. "You think David Ortiz is here yet?"

Ortiz, of course, was the Red Sox DH, one of the best hitters in Red Sox history. It was unlikely he or any other big-league regulars were at the ballpark yet. Now, the only ballplayers on the premises were usually some minor-leaguers. You never know, though, who might pop in early.

So Jim and I walked around the practice fields. I was there physically but my mind was elsewhere.

Was O'Riley locked up tight and secure?

What would happen when Monique, Sal, Ahmad and Nigel had to leave and go home three days from now?

Was that meddlesome Troxie poking around the Chokoloskee house?

What were Hooper and the Fort Myers P.D. up to?

And who would 60 Minutes and Dateline send down to work on the story? Lester Holt or Chris Hansen for Dateline? Scott Pelley or Lara Logan for 60 Minutes? Logan, I think, looks a bit like Troxie.

So many worries.

How bad were we going to lose Sunday in our rec baseball game?

What is the standard prison term for kidnapping?

What prison would I be sent to?

I don't suppose Lara Logan would be my cellmate.

Could I even get a foul tip off this new pitcher Bartley's has signed up?

Should the other four kidnappers and I include Troxie in our conspiracy?

Could she be trusted?

How long could we keep O'Riley?

My conscience was beginning to nag at me. I was starting to feel sorry for O'Riley, cooped up in that room. Sure, it had air conditioning and a flat screen TV and all those new towels from Bed, Bath and Beyond. The refrigerator was stocked with plenty of food and drink. The bathroom was nice, nicer than the one in my little condo.

But still. …

The guy was locked away in that same room. Every day. All day. Every night. All night. No fresh air. No sunshine. How much longer could we keep him there?

Suddenly, it all became clear.

No, not the O'Riley situation.

My need for a story for the next day's sports section. WBZ radio's Jonny Miller, a legend in the Boston media and always in Fort Myers well before spring training, spotted me and came over and said former Red Sox great Jim Lonborg had stopped by.

Lonborg was on vacation and was curious about the Red Sox spring training home, which is so much grander than Chain O' Lakes Park, the team's home in Winter Haven when it trained there during his heyday in the 1960s. So, we talked to Lonborg and I had a feature for the next day's paper.

But the next day I had to go back to Chokoloskee. Things were coming to a head. My kidnapping colleagues were leaving soon and we all realized something needed to be done. Something needed to be done before we were arrested.

But what?

We'd talk about that when I got to Chokoloskee in the morning.

CHAPTER TWENTY-FIVE

After work, and once in the comfort and comforting disarray of my condo I've dubbed The Hovel, I prepared to call Troxie.

First, though, I sat on the lanai, put my feet up and listened to the birds singing and the leaves of the big oak out back rustling slightly. Would the day come when home was a jail cell? I can't take these little pleasures for granted now that they may be taken away.

For now, The Hovel was still home. To most folks, this place may, indeed, be a hovel. No DVD. No flat screen TV. Furniture that dates back to the '70s, maybe early '80s.

But it's home. I have my library of baseball books such as The Baseball Encyclopedia and biographies of players and novels about the game.

The Hovel also includes my other books. There's something comforting knowing To Kill a Mockingbird and Catch-22 and The Grapes of Wrath and The Great Gatsby and many others are on shelves always within reach.

Maybe, somehow, by osmosis, the talent of Harper Lee and John Steinbeck and F. Scott Fitzgerald and others will seep into my fingertips. Alas, of course, it doesn't works that way.

Anyhow, I wanted to know a few things, things Steinbeck and Fitzgerald couldn't help me with at the moment. Did Troxie stop by the Chokoloskee house during the day? Did she talk with Sal or Monique or Ahmad or Nigel?

In the cool of the evening I sat on the lanai and called Troxie. She said no to all the above. She worked a lunch shift at City Fishhouse, picked up a couple of extra hours in the afternoon thanks to the tourist rush and then returned to her trailer where she napped, watched a little TV and practiced shuffleboard.

Oh, she said, there may have been a glass or two of pinot grigio. Troxie also admitted she's become something of a shuffleboard shark, playing tourists for small bets to supplement her modest income. She always wins. That's what she said and I believed her.

I asked her to meet me at the Chokoloskee house around noon the next day. That would be Saturday, five days since the kidnapping. There were things to discuss, things I didn't want to talk about on the phone. I also promised a bottle of pinot grigio.

"I'm there," she said. "Count on it."

I told her I had picked up a bottle of Kendall Jackson Grand Reserve pinot grigio. I think from 2008.

"Oh, I'm definitely there," Troxie said.

I had the good manners not to mention the bottle cost about $20, which is more than I normally pay for a bottle of anything. But then what we might ask Troxie to do could be worth a lot more. Our freedom. Our peace of mind. And it would also be risky for my all-time favorite shuffleboard player.

I also didn't tell her that I found out pinot grigio comes from what is considered a mutant clone of the pinot noir grape. I didn't want Troxie to think I was calling her a mutant. Or her favorite beverage is a mutant, bastardized spawn of a grape that makes a better wine, a red wine, and not the dainty white one she drinks. Definitely not going to mention any of that.

Besides, I worked with a few mutants over the years at Grabmore and she doesn't fit the classic mutant Grabmoron profile.

I didn't bother calling my Chokoloskee colleagues. To the outside world, they were fellow Grabmore workers I graciously allowed to

148

stay in my vacation getaway. We were trying to keep the electronic chatter between us to zero, if possible.

They knew I'd be there sometime late Saturday morning. That would be soon enough.

I was up early Saturday, got a 20-mile bicycle ride in and then showered and hit the road. The bicycle rides clear my head and I often figure out how I'll write a story while I'm pedaling along.

On this day, I was thinking more about how we'd get out of this mess. We clearly hadn't thought this through. How do we resolve the case of the locked up CEO?

I'd think about it some more on the drive to Chokoloskee and we'd discuss it before Troxie arrived.

The guys and Monique were on the front porch when I pulled in the driveway. Nigel was now reading The Grapes of Wrath. Monique was doing pushups. Sal was reading Sports Illustrated and Ahmad was on his laptop doing something.

They all looked worried. I assume I looked worried as well. I certainly felt worried, worried nearly to the point of all-out arms akimbo and flailing, running-around-in-circles, howling-at-the-moon panic attack. In two days they'd by flying home and O'Riley would still be locked away. He could identify all of us.

"We've been thinking," Monique said.

"Don't you know thinking is against Grabmore corporate policy?" I said. "The Tropical-Times sports editor tells people to type, not think. Seriously."

"That's stupid beyond belief but believe me we've all heard the same sort of bull," Nigel said. "Different places, different departments, same BS."

Sal nodded, took a swig of coffee and asked me, "You think the Giants can win the Super Bowl again?"

"I suppose," I said, not in a mood to discuss the NFL playoffs.

Now it was Ahmad's turn.

"We just can't keep the guy locked up," Ahmad said. "It's not right. He needs fresh air and a little exercise. He's going to have severe psychological problems if he stays in there much longer

149

watching Dancing with the Stars and Wheel of Fortune and Three's Company. We basically got the guy in solitary confinement.

"We can take him out back and let him play shuffleboard or something. But then what? Do we just open the front door and let him walk out and call the police?

"I don't think we want to kill him. Do we?"

There was a general murmuring that killing wasn't our style. Plus, well, it's wrong, a moral absolute. We agreed on that. Killing was out. Just letting him go was also out of the question. Did that mean we had to hold on to him indefinitely? And how long is indefinitely? A week? A month? A year? Ten years? Twenty years?

Our kidnapping scheme hatched over beers on Fort Myers Beach had developed into a quagmire, one without an apparent solution. Monique stopped doing push-ups when I stepped on the porch.

"Scott, we've been talking," she said, leaning back against the railing of the front porch. "We don't want to bring any more employees in on this. We've all talked to a few co-workers, people we really trust, in general terms but we don't want them to risk prison by bringing them here.

"And you can't come down here every day to look after O'Riley. So we've been thinking about asking Troxie to serve as our O'Riley babysitter."

"That reminds me," I said. "I left something in the car."

I walked over and retrieved the bottle of Kendall Jackson pinot grigio.

"Let me guess," Monique said. "You invited Troxie over?"

"Indeed," I said, "and she should be here any minute. Unless a big shuffleboard tournament broke out in Everglades City."

We chatted for a few minutes about what we'd ask from Troxie and what we would do with O'Riley. We even talked about a potential solution.

We watched the pink mini-Cooper come puttering along and then turn into the driveway. Troxie stepped out with a bounce in her step and that blond hair bobbing out the back of her Rays' baseball cap. She was also carrying a bag from Total Wine.

She placed it on the wicker table on the porch and reached in.

"For you, Scott, a bottle of malbec," she said, handing it over.

She reached in again and handed Monique a six-pack of Molson and a Montreal Canadiens T-shirt. For Sal she had a six-pack of Budweiser and a Derek Jeter rookie baseball card. She then handed Ahmad a package of Twining's Earl Grey tea and something else, a smaller package.

"I picked this up in a middle Eastern market in Naples," she told Ahmad, handing him the package.

He opened it and smiled.

"Hawayig!" he said, now beaming. "That's hard to find here."

"Ha-what?" I said.

"It's a national spice back home," Ahmad said. "It's a mixture that includes fennel seeds, ginger, cardamom and aniseed. You ought to try it sometime."

Troxie certainly surprised us. All of us thanked Troxie for her thoughtfulness and generosity. Monique spoke again.

"We told you about the company we work for, right?" Monique said.

"Yeah, Gabmore, or something like that," she said.

"Well, close enough," Monique said. "And you've heard about the company CEO, right?"

"That O'Rourke guy?" Troxie said.

"Close again," Monique said. "It's O'Riley."

"I saw something on the news the other day about him. He's missing. The cops think he might have been kidnapped but there's been no ransom note."

I happened to have that day's Tropical-Times with me and showed her the front page with the box asking readers for help. And also a photo of O'Riley, his little yachting cap on top of his head.

"Remember what you said the other day?" I said. "That somebody should kidnap the guy?"

"Yeah," Troxie said, looking puzzled. "You didn't go out and do something so stupid, did you?"

Nobody said a word. Troxie looked around the porch at each of us.

"You didn't, did you?" she asked. "You couldn't, could you?"

Again, silence.

"It wasn't because of what I said the other day, is it?" she asked again. "I was kidding, sort of."

More silence.

"You did it?" Troxie said.

We all nodded.

"Wow!" Troxie said. "You're all crazier, braver or stupider than I thought. Not that I thought any of those things, of course."

I said, "I think we all need a drink. Ahmad, what about you?"

"Well, I'm tempted but I think I'll have some of this tea," he said.

I went in the kitchen to get the corkscrew and some glasses. Ahmad came in to do whatever it is one does to brew tea. Monique and Sal popped the tops of their beers.

I came back out and opened the wine bottles and poured some pinot grigio for Troxie and some malbec for myself.

She took a sip and asked, "You got him? You really got him?"

We all nodded.

"Where?" she asked.

"Here," Sal said.

"Here?" Troxie asked.

It was my turn.

"Yep," I said. "I'm sure you noticed that hurricane shelter annex sort of thing attached to the house. The part without windows. That's where our CEO is right now."

"What are you gonna do with him?" Troxie asked, taking a gulp instead of a sip of pinot grigio.

"Well," I said, "we haven't figured that part out yet."

"Boy, you guys are some master criminals," Troxie said. "What if I call the cops?"

Ahmad had just returned with his tea, which was steeping, whatever the hell that means.

"We don't think you'll do that because you think he's a corporate weasel and criminal, too," Ahmad said. "Plus, he doesn't tip baristas and waitresses. At least according to what I read on the company blog. If it's on the blog it's got to be right."

"Why are you telling me this?" Troxie asked.

Now it was my turn.

"You like this place, right?" I asked.

"You betcha," she said. "I can't believe it was, what, your Uncle Orville who left you this place? What he was he like?"

"Well, sort of an international man of mystery," I said. "He ran some import/export business out of New York. I would ask what he imported and exported and he would never say. He'd always change the topic to sports. He loved sports and that's how we connected.

"You're probably wondering how some big shot New York City businessman ended up here. So am I. But he came down here in the '70s, back when this place was the Wild West. Drug smuggling was out of control in the area. It was a perfect place to drop off pot in the Gulf or in the Ten Thousand Islands. The locals got involved. Uncle Orville moved down here.

"I remember talking to a guy once who was a smuggler here back then. He said the first night he worked he was handed a paper bag with $5,000 in cash. The next night, another paper bag. This one had $15,000.

"The Colombians and others involved in drugs wanted in on the action here. The good ol' boys here kicked them out of town and told them to never come back. The good times continued. For a while.

"Back in the mid'80s there was a big raid and about 80 percent of the men in town were arrested. This guy I talked to a while back, he said he had $8 million in cash in his house when he was arrested.

"Uncle Orville, though, was conveniently in Hong Kong at the time of the raid. He was working on some deal involving chopsticks and mandarin oranges. He was never implicated or charged with anything. Still…."

Troxie just said, "Wow? Must have been a lot of chop sticks and mandarin oranges to go all the way to Hong Kong."

"Yep," I said. "Guess so. But Uncle Orville always called when he was in the area and if he was here during spring training always came to Fort Myers for games. He died a couple of years ago. Massive heart attack. Now, I got this cool house."

I looked at Troxie.

"You like this house? You like the peace and quiet of Chokoloskee? You like the feeling of old-time Florida, right? You like the shuffleboard court out back? And the tangs and biscuits in the storage shed?"

Troxie nodded and said again, "You betcha."

"How would you like to live here?" I asked. "Rent-free. Take care of the place. Power and utilities will be taken care of for you. I'll stock up on pinot grigio if you agree. Lots of pinot grigio. And you'll have full use of that Suburban in the driveway."

Troxie took another sip.

"So, you want me to be an accessory to your crime?" she asked.

"You betcha," I said. "You want to meet Chesterfield Ebenezer O'Riley IV?"

"You betcha," Troxie said, grinning, apparently thinking this might be fun and a bit of an adventure down here on the fringe of the Ten Thousand Islands, a long way from the St. Petersburg shuffleboard courts.

CHAPTER TWENTY-SIX

Troxie picked up her purse, which had been on the floor of the front porch next to her wicker chair. I hadn't noticed the purse before. How many men notice purses? Not me, that's for sure.

A woman could carry a 30-year-old, dirt-encrusted, blood-stained, lipstick-smeared piece of mud-slathered vinyl with holes in it or a new, fancy, $5,000 purse made of whatever expensive purses are made out of. I wouldn't notice. I'm going to estimate somewhere between 99 and 100 percent of the straight male population wouldn't notice. Or care.

As she opened the purse, she looked around the porch at each of us and said, "I want to show you something."

Sal said hopefully, "You got a Mickey Mantle 1952 rookie card in there?"

Troxie laughed and said, "I don't even have a Hal Trosky rookie card."

A Mickey Mantle rookie card in mint condition could fetch about $40,000 on the collector's market. Or so I've heard. That's a lot of pinot grigio. Or malbec.

Troxie instead pulled something else out of her purse, something imposing and surprising. She placed the item on the table between the bottles of wine.

"A gun?" I said, with the observational insight and powers of a Grabmoron.

Sal was much more precise.

"A .38," he said, eyeballing it the way a baseball card collector might judge a vintage Mickey Mantle card. "A Smith & Wesson .38. The Bodyguard .38. Stainless steel barrel. Rubber grip. Accurate and with little recoil. A fine weapon."

Troxie smiled.

"You know your weapons, big fella," Troxie said.

"In a previous job, before I started delivering newspapers, I often carried one with me," Sal said. "For protection. Just for protection."

I, too, was impressed. A UPS truck drove by on the street and Troxie placed a napkin over the .38.

"My dad was a St. Pete cop," she said. "From the time I was a little girl he wanted me to be able to protect myself. I started karate and ju-jitsu lessons when I was 8. I'm third-degree black belt in both.

"He started taking me to the police pistol range at Woodlawn Park when I was 12. I became a certified marksman at 15 and even competed for a while shooting in national contests. I could out-shoot most of the men on the force. I think that hand-eye coordination needed for shooting translates really well to shuffleboard. So, I can handle just about anything your CEO Boy can throw my way."

Well, this was encouraging. CEO Boy, as she called O'Riley, would have trouble in a fight against a stuffed teddy bear, let alone a sharp-shooting, third-degree black belt karate and ju-jitsu expert who is also likely one of Florida's top shuffleboard sharks.

Troxie not only knows a lot about shuffleboard but apparently a lot about guns, as well.

"My dad always told me this was the best gun for protection a woman can carry," Troxie said, pointing at the .38.

She picked it up and placed it back in her purse, where it easily disappeared from view because of its small size.

"Now that I've had a couple of sips of wine I'm not going to touch the gun again," Troxie said. "That's something else dad always talked about. Gun safety. Anyhow, he told me some women carry smaller caliber weapons, say a .22 or .25 or a .32. He said those don't always stop some 260-pound galoot hopped up on crystal meth or cocaine.

"He said the .38 does the trick. Not only stops 'em but puts 'em down. Remember the scene in Blazing Saddles when Mongo is chained to the jail cell? Somebody talks about shooting him but is told that will just make him mad.

"Well, that's basically what dad said about using a .22 against some over-sized psycho. So it's this snub-nosed .38 for me. Not that I'll need it against your CEO. The .38 will stop anybody. I won't need it against CEO Boy."

I liked the way Troxie referred to O'Riley as CEO Boy and did it with such sneering disdain and withering contempt. Almost like a Grabmore employee.

"When do I get to meet him?" she asked.

"In time," said Nigel, who added, "I'm getting hungry. Anybody for cheese and crackers?"

We all nodded yes and he went in the house to put together a snack platter. We talked about our weekend plans while Nigel was in the house. I said I planned to stay in Chokoloskee overnight and return to Fort Myers in the morning for my baseball game.

Sal, Ahmad, Nigel and Monique said they wanted to take a ride into Naples on Sunday and stroll along Fifth Avenue South, gaze in the fancy shops and restaurants and pretend they could afford to eat or shop in any of the places. Then they planned to walk over to Tin City to find a more affordable lunch place.

Troxie said she was able to pick up another lunch shift on Sunday at the City Fishhouse. She also said she was renting the trailer in Everglades City on a week-to-week basis and could move into the house Sunday. She'd pay for the upcoming week and just load up the mini-Cooper and move in to what used to be Uncle Orville's house.

All she brought with her from St. Pete had been some clothes, a laptop and two or three James W. Hall novels. Troxie is full of surprises. Hall is one of my favorite Florida novelists and one who is also underappreciated. Troxie said a customer at the surf shop where she worked recommended the Hall books.

We both agreed that we liked Hall's Thorn series of books. Thorn is a sort of loner and private detective who lives in the Keys and has a strong sense of right and wrong. Thorn has no first name in the books.

Nigel returned to the porch carrying a large platter holding different types of cheese and crackers and grapes and cut-up apples. He heard the end of our Hall conversation and said he'd like to read a Hall book and I recommended Under Cover of Daylight. Then it was on to business, CEO Boy business.

"OK," Troxie said, "What do you want me to do?"

The rest of us sat there, gaping at one another like Grabmorons waiting for somebody to speak.

"Well, we haven't figured it out exactly," Sal said.

"Boy, you guys are something," Troxie said. "No wonder the newspaper business is in trouble. You kidnap CEO Boy and didn't have any plan besides throwing him in the back of that Suburban over there?"

"It's not that bad," I said. "We planned to bring him down here and put him in the hurricane shelter. Plus we bought a case of Frappucino and new towels and wash clothes at Bed, Bath & Beyond."

"Then what?" Troxie said. "Geez, I remember when my dad got promoted to detective in St. Pete he said some of the stupidest people he met were criminals."

I could see that the Troxie we first met in the Rod & Gun Club was some sort of public persona, a ditzy façade she put on to fool people. Under that blond hair was, as they used to say, a sharp cookie. That Troxie, the Troxie who pretended to be nearly as slow-witted as the Tropical-Times sports editor, could sucker tourists into shuffleboard matches where they likely thought she was just another

Florida airheaded beach bimbo. Soon, after their biscuits were skillfully and artfully knocked into the kitchen, Troxie would be clutching their cash in one hand, holding a tang in the other and the tourists would go back to their rented Caprices a few bucks lighter.

"So, let me get this straight," Troxie said. "Four of you are leaving Monday. Scott here has a fulltime job about 90 miles away. Let's go meet CEO Boy.

"Hold on," Sal said. "We need to set up some ground rules here."

We've tried not using our names around O'Riley but they slipped out. He clearly knows we work for Grabmore. He likely realizes he's somewhere in Florida, not all that far from Fort Myers because when we abducted him we didn't put him on a plane or boat.

But other than that, he probably doesn't have a clue. About a lot of things but more to the point he likely doesn't have a clue about where he is and who has him. Troxie was waiting for somebody to speak.

"Well," Nigel said, "we haven't let him out of that room since we put him there. He doesn't know if we drove him north, south or east. I hope he realizes we couldn't have gone too far west because we would have run into the Gulf of Mexico before long. But then his grasp of geography doesn't seem very strong."

Troxie then asked the question none of us could answer.

"How long are you gonna keep him?" Troxie asked.

There was more sipping of wine, beer and tea and nobody answered for several seconds.

"That's the part we haven't figured out yet," Monique said.

"Well, you just can't keep him locked up in there until he dies," Troxie said. "Unless you plan to make that part of your plan."

"No, no, no," I blurted out. "No killing."

"So," Troxie said, "then what? Keep him until he dies of old age in 30 or 40 years?"

More sipping. More noshing of cheese and crackers. But no answers. More wine. More beer. More tea. But nobody spoke.

"Here are our options," Nigel said. "A: We kill him. B: We decided no killing. C: We return him to the yacht club and pretend

159

like nothing happened. D: That won't work. It's been in the papers and on-line and on the news. E: We drive to the nearest police station, hand him over and plea for mercy."

It was a nice summation. But every one of the options led to the same place - prison.

Plus, it would put O'Riley right back on the CEO throne up in Buffalo, right back to where he was before, looting and pillaging, down-sizing and gutting newspapers, ordering furloughs. And the whole point of our monumentally ill-conceived effort was to get him out of power.

Once he returns to the comfort of the Never Enough and the ministrations of another Lapp babe, he would certainly turn us in to the cops. There had to be another option.

"I got an idea," Troxie said.

CHAPTER TWENTY-SEVEN

Troxie took off her Rays' cap, placed it atop the purse that held the .38 and leaned forward.

"OK, why not make a deal with CEO Boy?" she said, eyeing each of us in turn.

She then took a sip of pinot grigio, grabbed some of that cheap Publix cheddar cheese and a Ritz cracker off the platter and leaned back in the wicker chair.

"What kind of deal?" I asked.

"A deal," she explained, "that works for you guys and for him. You don't go to jail and he gets out of here."

"So, he just goes back to his yacht and then to his office in Buffalo and to all those Miss Iceland pageants and nothing changes?" Monique asked.

"Oh, no, big changes," Troxie said with a sly smile.

And quickly asked, "Yacht?"

Monique explained it's 99-feet long, called the Never Enough and is staffed by 18 and 19-year-old girls from overseas, from places such as Ireland and Iceland and Lapland, wherever the hell that is.

"I see," Troxie said.

Meanwhile, I was intrigued by what Troxie said before she asked about the Never Enough, about a way out of this.

"What sort of changes?" I asked. "And why would he change anything?"

"Because of you guys," she said, pointing her wine glass at each of us.

She paused a moment.

"He knows what tough characters you all are," Troxie said. "Except, of course, you Scott. No offense."

I didn't understand where she was going with this scheme, whatever it was she was dreaming up in what appeared to be a pinot grigio-fueled delusion or cheddar cheese haze.

"Here's how it will work," Troxie said, smiling again. "You tell him he's got two choices. The first choice is he stays in that hurricane shelter until he dies. Which after a couple more weeks cooped up in there watching the Kardashians could be soon.

"I don't care how nice those Bed, Bath & Beyond towels are and how many cases of Starbucks Frappucinos you got stocked up, he'll go batty and become suicidal. "

"That part we understand," Monique said. "What's the other part?"

"You tell him he can walk out, can get some fresh air and sunshine and freedom if he agrees to a few conditions," Troxie said. "It will require some lying but he's a CEO so lying is one of the few skills he has."

Now it was my turn.

"OK, so he lies," I said. "Lie about what and to what end."

"He'll lie about where he's been, for starters," Troxie said. "No kidnapping. Never happened. No disgruntled employees snatched him off a street corner near that yacht, the Neverland Express."

"Ah, Never Enough," I pointed out.

"Yeah, right. Anyhow, he can say he's been hiking the Appalachian Trail. Or that he had a spiritual insight and realized that he didn't want to be remembered as a greedy sleaze. He could say he's had trouble sleeping because of all this. Now, I did say he would have to lie and those would all be lies if what you guys say about him is right."

We all nodded. O'Riley, I'm convinced, is a case of what you see is what you get. There was no substance behind that façade of avarice and selfishness. He didn't care about anybody else. All he wanted was more. More money. More girls. A bigger yacht, one even larger than the Never Enough, which is more boat than anybody this side of Donald Trump may own.

But I still didn't understand why he would agree to this.

"You guys have to make it clear to him," Troxie said. "Either he agrees to this or there's another option if you let him go and he weasels out of the deal. There's something about each of you that I can't quite pinpoint. What about you, big fella?"

She pointed her glass at Sal. It was time for everybody to reveal something about their pasts to Troxie.

"I was nearly a made man in the north Jersey mob," Sal said. "Got out just before that when the Feds closed in. The Feds offered a deal. Sing like Tweety Bird or it's prison. I sang like Tony Bennett. Sang a lot better than Tweety Bird.

"I'm in witness protection and some of my old friends – Snubnose Fazio, Fatso Laguardia and Shinbone Rizzuto – well, they're in prison. And they ain't leaving. And it's because of what I told the Feds. They'd love to see me again, let me tell you."

"I figured it was something like that," Troxie said. "What about you, Nigel? You wear that Frenchy beret but you got an Irish accent. What's up with you?"

"Well," he said, "that accent has a touch of Belfast, where my uncles trained me as a boy to become an IRA operative. That's all I'll say about that. But I was a good welterweight fighter, good enough to fight a few pro bouts. Won a couple. Lost a couple. Figured out pretty quick I didn't have what it took to be anything approaching a title contender. Especially when people started calling me Canvasback Claymore. Claymore is my last name. So I got out of boxing and the IRA and left Northern Ireland."

We all nodded, respecting Nigel's silence about some of his past. Then it was Ahmad's turn.

"I don't want to talk about my days with Al Qeada of Yemen," Ahmad said, sipping his tea. "They taught me a lot. A lot of skills that most employers don't need. Most companies don't need suicide bombers and IED makers. I'm sure you get the picture. Do Google or Apple need workers proficient with an AK-47? I don't think so. But I also learned the printing trade. And ended up working for Yemeni security services as a sort of double agent.

"They're the ones who got me out of the country because there was a price on my head for helping capture and kill some of my former friends. The Yemeni security folks and their American counterparts got me out and got me a job in New Jersey, and a new name. The one I use now."

Troxie nodded.

"And you, Monique?" Troxie asked.

"I grew up in the woods of Canada, hunting and fishing," Monique said. "My dad and uncles were lumberjacks and worked in lumber mills. I just followed them into the work and competitive weightlifting. Nearly made the Canadian Olympic weightlifting team. Still enjoy the training. I'm thinking about teaching O'Riley some basics so he can get in decent shape."

"Well, Scott," Troxie said, "That leaves you."

"I majored in American lit and tried out for my college baseball team but got cut on the first round of cuts," I said. "My parents were high school English teachers. I'm something of a baseball trivia expert and have tried out for Jeopardy! a couple of times. Didn't make it. But I'm really good watching Jeopardy! on TV."

Troxie chortled and couldn't help spitting out some of that $20 a bottle Kendall Jackson pinot grigio on her lap as she guffawed.

Then, after cleaning up the spat-out wine with the napkin that had seen previous duty hiding the .38, she looked serious and was about to say something when Sal spoke.

"What about you, Troxie?" Sal asked. "Don't you have a job or family to go back to in St. Pete? How come you're just wandering around down here in Everglades City and Chokoloskee?"

"I did have a job," she said. "I was managing a surf shop on Treasure Island. Liked the job and the people. Been there for years. Lived nearby so I had time for shuffleboard and runs on the beach and played in a co-ed softball league in St. Pete.

"My husband, Ralph, left me for a younger woman. I'm sure you've heard that story before. My last name when I was married was Kluszewski. But when Ralph left me for Charlene, a waitress from the Thunderbird Lounge, I went back to my maiden name."

I interrupted with a stupid comment.

"Ralph left you for a temptress waitress?" I said. "Some beer-peddling comely wench from the Thunderbird?"

"Scott, what the hell is a temptress?" Troxie asked.

"A woman who entices or tempts, I guess," I meekly said.

"Who talks like that?" Troxie asked. "Who uses words like temptress and comely in conversation? And wench? When was the last time you had a date?"

I said it had been a few years.

"Well, stop using words like temptress and wench and comely and your chances might improve," she said.

I nodded and kept my mouth shut.

"Now where was I?' Troxie asked.

"The Thunderbird Lounge," Monique said.

"Oh, yeah, so anyway, when the economy went south the surf shop owner was very sorry but said he had to let me go. Just as a temporary thing, he said. He said once things turned around he'd take me back. I believe him. I know he will.

"Last I heard, things are picking up on the beach and he may hire me back in the spring. So for now, I'm just sort of focusing on shuffleboard and getting to know Florida. That's how I ended up down here."

Everybody nodded again and we all felt like we knew each other a bit better. Then Troxie got to the task at hand, our CEO quagmire.

"You got to make it clear to CEO Boy this deal is some sort of sacred pact," Troxie said. "Make him understand that if he backs out and says he was kidnapped that somebody will come for him. That he can run but he can't hide. That if you guys go to jail somebody else will come for him."

"Sort of like what Joe Louis said, right?" I said.

"Huh?" Troxie said.

"He can run but he can't hide. That's what Joe Louis, he was heavyweight champ at the time, said about a challenger, Billy Conn. It was 1941, I think."

My boxing trivia didn't seem to impress anybody or make anything clearer. Troxie didn't respond, just ignored my Joe Louis reference and seemed to be thinking I'd never get another date. Nigel didn't even say anything about the boxing reference.

"Anyhow, what we got to do is make sure that somehow O'Riley understands what we mean," Nigel said. "But what about the future of Grabmore?"

Nigel had a point. If O'Riley is gone – either dead or retired - won't the board appoint some jargon-spouting, bean-counting MBA to take his place? Somebody who doesn't care about anything other than the next quarterly statement and the next bonus for coming up with brilliant, insightful managerial moves such as layoffs and furloughs?

If O'Riley agrees to step down what will become of Grabmore? Top management will just follow his managerial style. Nothing will really change.

The soulless corporate system is in place. The levels of bureaucracy are entrenched. Hand grenades would be needed to dislodge some of the bureaucrats from their fortified corner offices in Buffalo and throughout the Grabmore empire.

The people who schemed and connived to reach power have the power and won't give it up. Why would they? Why change a corporate culture that rewarded their wretched behavior? It's that very same culture that will keep them sending out self-serving statements and flatulent platitudes cut and pasted from an introduction to Business 101 survey course.

"I still don't get it," I admitted. "How does getting rid of O'Riley change things for the better? The company president, Carlotta Gutman, is as vile as O'Riley but she's smarter and a lot more devious and ruthless.

"The same goes for the CFO, Milo Heller. Heck, you don't reach the top levels of Grabmore by playing nice. All the top brass are smart folks. The only way O'Riley was able to become CEO was to inherit the title and own the 54 point-whatever percent of Grabmore stock his dad left him. He chose his parents wisely."

Troxie looked stumped. We all did. Was this kidnapping fiasco for naught? All we could do was continue attacking the platter of cheese and crackers and fruit and sit in silence.

After a minute or so, Nigel spoke.

"So O'Riley owns something like 54 percent of Grabmore, right?" he asked.

We nodded.

"So if he leaves he can do anything he wants with it, right?" Nigel asked.

We nodded again.

"What if he sold it to somebody or just gave it away?" Nigel asked.

This was an interesting thought.

"He has more money than everybody in Everglades City and Chokoloskee combined," I said. "He's not giving anything away.

Unless it was at gunpoint. I believe we have a gun right here on this porch."

"But if he gives away controlling interest," Monique asked, "who gets it?"

"It can't be any of us," Sal said.

More silence followed.

We found a way to get rid of O'Riley and in theory a way to get him out of the hurricane shelter without murdering the money-grubbing bastard. As part of our plan, O'Riley would give up that 54-point-whatever percent. It couldn't be parceled among Grabmore's grasping corporate officers. Things would only get worse if they got it. If getting worse is even possible.

"What if he gives the 54-percent whatever percent to some college or university journalism program?" Nigel said. "The professors could run it the way they think newspapers and TV news program and online news websites should be run."

We liked the idea. I knew a couple of journalism professors and could ask them hypothetical questions about this scenario. If O'Riley left their schools controlling shares of Grabmore, what would they do with it?

First, before that, we needed to talk with our captive in the hurricane shelter.

"Put down your pinot grigio," I told Troxie. "It's time to meet CEO Boy."

CHAPTER TWENTY-EIGHT

I hate the sight and sound of a grown man whimpering. Yet, that's what we witnessed and heard when I pulled open the door to the hurricane shelter. CEO Boy was curled up in a fetal position on the floor, clutching two or three blue rolled up Bed, Bath & Beyond towels. Between sobs and after taking the end of a towel he was gnashing out of his mouth, the weepy CEO began begging.

"You got to let me out of here," he said, his watery eyes looking at each of us in turn. "I can't take it anymore. I need some fresh air. I need to see sunshine. Please. Please."

Troxie spoke first.

"That's why we're here," she said. "We're going to take you outside for air and a little exercise."

"Who are you?" he asked. "I've never seen you before. Have I?"

"No, I'm new," Troxie said. "And there's no need for you to know my name."

O'Riley got to his feet a bit wobbly, leaning on the back of an orange couch that one of Uncle Orville's wives gave as a gift. The CEO shuffled along barefoot, still holding the towels, looking somehow shorter than he did just a few days ago. We escorted him through the kitchen and out the back door to the small yard and the shuffleboard court. He sat in a lawn chair, taking in gulps of fresh air and sipping water.

After several minutes of rubbing his eyes and looking around, his mood gradually brightened a bit. He also noticed the backyard shuffleboard court and began jabbering away, the last traces of that whimpering having vanished.

"I love shuffleboard," O'Riley said, his mood seeming to improve by the minute. "When I was a kid my grand-parents would take me on cross-Atlantic cruises on the QE2. And we played shuffleboard all the time. Those were the best times ever. Best milkshakes I ever had were on the QE2. Butterscotch milkshakes. The best things ever. Served in these big metal containers and poured into a big glass. I still dream about those butterscotch milkshakes.

"I had my own stateroom and grandma and grandpa were across the hall. And we'd go up on deck and play shuffleboard. Did that every summer from the time I was 6 until I was 12. We'd go over to a summer home in England in June and come back in August."

He stopped speaking for a moment and then softly said what seemed magical words to him – "butterscotch milkshakes and shuffleboard. I miss those days."

While O'Riley was going on and on about butterscotch milkshakes and the QE2 and his stateroom, I couldn't help thinking about his great-grandfather, the man-child who crossed the ocean in the stinking steerage of a much different ship. I'm sure butterscotch milkshakes weren't available in steerage on the City of Cheaters.

Troxie, though, was suddenly in a shuffleboard reverie as soon as she heard O'Riley talk about playing on the QE2.

"You play shuffleboard?" she asked.

"Not in years," O'Riley said. "Not since I was a kid."

"Wanna play again?" she asked.

"Can we?" he replied.

"Sure, let me get the tangs and biscuits out of the storage shed."

Troxie walked around the corner of the house. O'Riley, wearing blue cargo shorts and a Miami Dolphins jersey we had purchased for him, was beaming.

Nigel nudged me and whispered, "Let them play shuffleboard."

I agreed. A little R & R would be good for O'Riley. Troxie would put him at ease and I suspect her usual killer competitiveness on the court would be tamped down. So the rest of us pulled up lawn chairs and watched the shuffleboard expert and the CEO play a friendly match. She played casually and let O'Riley knock a biscuit or two into her kitchen before she took control of the match.

O'Riley was getting color back in his pasty face with some sunshine and mild exercise and an encouraging word or two from Troxie.. When they finished playing, Troxie invited him to pull up another lawn chair in the cool shade under the eaves of the house and join us, his kidnappers. He looked us over. No whimpering or trembling now. He seemed composed.

"What are you going to do with me?" O'Riley asked.

"That's one of the reasons we brought you out here," Monique said. "To tell you something."

"What?" he asked.

"Frankly," Sal said, "we felt sorry for you cooped up all the time in that room. We figured we had to let you out for fresh air and sanity. And the other reason."

"What's that?" O'Riley asked.

"We got an offer for you," I said. "One that will let you out of here and allow you to go home. You won't be harmed. But you have to agree to all our conditions or you're going to stay here indefinitely."

O'Riley sat there for a moment, a light sheen of sweat on his face, which all of a sudden was a bit ruddy from the sunshine and light exercise.

"I can't stay here any longer," he said, sounding weepy. "I got to get out of here. What do you want me to do?"

Sal walked over. He was an imposing presence, a former offensive guard at Parsippany High School in New Jersey, one who might have been good enough to play small college football if his grades had been better.

"Give up Grabmore," Sal said, staring O'Riley right in the face. "Give it up. Get rid of all your shares. Give them away. And go away."

O'Riley took that in and seemed to be processing it. But it was too much for him to comprehend.

"Give up Grabmore?" he asked. "It's been in my family for generations. For decades. It won't be Grabmore without an O'Riley. O'Riley wouldn't be O'Riley without Grabmore."

All of a sudden O'Riley seemed to be speaking in the third person.

"What if I don't give it up?" he asked.

"Then, you'll stay here indefinitely," Ahmad said. "We don't enjoy this. We don't like the idea of keeping you cooped up in that room without sunshine. But we hold all the cards. You don't have any bargaining chips."

"I don't understand," O'Riley said. "I own 54-point something percent of Grabmore shares. They were left me by my father. My great-grandfather started the company about a century ago."

It was my turn to speak.

"There's no way for you to know this but since you disappeared every Grabmore paper has published every day," I told him. "Every one of your local network affiliates has broadcast local news. The websites are up and running. The trees in the Grabmore forests are still growing. The company is going to continue with or without you. Think about it."

"Can I have some more water?' O'Riley asked.

Nigel walked in the kitchen and fetched a bottle of Zephyrhills water from the refrigerator. O'Riley guzzled down some of the cool water and then used the sleeve of his T-shirt to wipe his mouth.

"I don't get it," he said. "You want me to just give it away? It could be worth billions. Is that what this is about, you guys kidnapped me for my money?"

The anxiety returned to his face.

"No," Sal said, "you won't give it to us. That's not the point."

"I'm not going to give it to Carlotta Gutman," he said. "She's the company president. The meanest person I ever met. And that Milo Heller, the CFO? He's almost as mean. I heard employees call him Yeller Heller. He yelled at a chef in the executive dining room because the angle on the cut of his tuna on toasted rye sandwich was wrong. Yeller Heller.

"He wanted the sandwich cut diagonally instead of straight across. And he wanted it on Jewish Rye, not marble rye. I happened to stop by the executive dining room that day, I normally eat in my private dining room next to my office but popped in that day.

"Yeller Heller was screaming at the chef, who had lost both legs in Iraq. He hollered that the guy was fired and threw the sandwich at him, sitting there in his wheelchair. One of the vice presidents, I don't remember who, told Heller the guy didn't have any legs and Heller shouted, 'I don't care if he doesn't have any arms, either. I wanted my sandwich cut diagonally not straight across. Is that so tough? You don't need legs for that. He's fired. And that's that.'

"Just then Carlotta walked in and heard the chef get fired. She barked. 'Who is this person?' she said, pointing at the vet. She then said, 'Does he work here? No? Then why is he here? Somebody push this unemployed half-man over to the elevator and make sure he's out of the building in 30 seconds. Now, what kind of soup do we have today?'

"Like I said, Carlotta is the meanest person I know. Even worse than Yeller Heller. Of course, he wouldn't dare yell at me. He's too scared. Even Carlotta is too scared. But who should I give all those shares to them? And how can I trust you? I can't trust those two. They're always up to something. Can't trust them. That's for sure. Can't trust anybody at Grabmore.

"Maybe it is time to move on. Oh, by the way, I found out the vet's name. It's Grant Lincoln. A Marine. Won a Silver Star. Saved four guys in Iraq. I got him a job at my country club. For more money, too."

Something was missing from the story – the vet's reaction to the thrown tuna sandwich. So we all seemed to ask at the same moment.

"Well," O'Riley said, "he just caught the sandwich that Heller threw at him. Then he looked at Gutman and Heller for a second or two and took a bite and said, 'It tastes the same whether it's cut straight across or diagonally. I can make it to the elevator myself. Thank you very much. Semper Fi.' And then he rolled out the door and to the elevators.

"I'm not sure what Semper Fi means."

Semper Fi, the U.S. Marine Corps slogan, means always faithful, or always loyal. I told O'Riley that and he nodded. His unexpected show of thoughtfulness, if he was telling the truth, scored some points with me.

"I'm glad to hear it," I said of his getting the Marine a job. "Now as far as the trust part, you don't have any choice. Nobody's coming to rescue you. Nobody other than us knows you're here. Trust us or just stay in that room all by yourself. There's a choice for you."

"Who do I give it all to? And what do I do then?"

This entire kidnapping endeavor has been marred by failure to plan and think things through. The resolution, the way out for all us, was another example.

"We don't have it all figured out," I told O'Riley. "But we won't get those shares. Neither will anybody else with Grabmore. Our plan, at least we like to think it's a plan, is to give the stock away to some college journalism program.

"Let the professors run the company. Let them decide how to run the newsrooms. But it won't be a charity. We believe in profits. We're capitalists. We'll make that clear. Making money, a healthy profit will still be a prime goal. But we don't want the idea that anything less than a 40 percent profit margin is reason for panic."

"We haven't had 40 percent in a few years," O'Riley said. "We're lucky to be much above 10 percent now."

Sal pretended to cry and wipe away make-believe tears.

"Oh, boo-hoo, poor little Chesterfield," Sal said. "Probably doesn't have enough money for a butterscotch milkshake. Maybe your granny will buy you a butterscotch milkshake."

O'Riley was too scared of Sal's size and menacing glare to respond.

"What we want you to do is write a letter of resignation," Monique said, chewing on a toothpick. "As part of that letter you're going to give all your stock to some university. Can't think of what it's called."

"Florida Gulf Coast University," I said, referring to a school near Fort Myers. "You're going to announce it's all going to the school's journalism department to run as it sees fit. As part of your resignation you're going to write that you left the Never Enough for some soul seeking. Got it? That you just wanted time alone to think. Got it?"

"Not really," O'Riley said. "I've never written anything. I got people who do that for me. Write my press releases and what not."

"Didn't you write any term papers in college?" I asked.

"No, whenever I had papers to write I asked some kid on scholarship to write them for me," O'Riley said. "And I paid them for it. Can you guys help me? I'll pay. I usually paid the kids in college $20. I'll give you guys $25. Each."

"Well, we do have two professional writers here," Monique said, pointing at Nigel and I. "Of course, they're just sports writers so I don't know if that counts."

"Very funny, Mo," Nigel said. "Don't you have some trees to cut down or bench pressing to do?"

"We'll help," I said. "Do you want to stay outside or you want to come back inside?"

O'Riley said, "I'd like to sit outside. It's really nice. I forgot how blue the sky is. You forget that when you're locked up inside for a few days. Can I play some more shuffleboard?"

Troxie walked over and handed CEO Boy a tang and said, "You go first, big boy. The winner gets a butterscotch milkshake. The loser buys."

Sal stayed outside to keep an eye on O'Riley and make sure he didn't escape. Troxie, our gun-packing, third-degree black belt shuffleboard shark could have easily handled O'Riley by herself but it's always good to have backup in these situations. At least that's what Sal, Nigel and Ahmad told me. They know a lot more about these things than I do.

Nigel and I went in the kitchen to craft some sort of resignation letter/press release saying that Chesterfield Ebenezer O'Riley IV was stepping down and handing over his 54 point-something percent of the company to a university. The letter would also address Grabmore's future and what O'Riley would do in the future.

So we sat down at the kitchen table. First, Sal popped his head inside and said, "Don't forget, the Giants-Saints game starts at 4:15. I don't wanna be out here watching shuffleboard when a trip to the NFC title game is on the line."

We nodded.

"We're both used to writing on deadline," I said. "It's only about 2. We'll bang this out in a jiff. Just keep an eye on Troxie and Chesty."

So, Nigel and I, two sportswriters, sat down to write what became one of the most famous press releases in journalism history. Some would call it perhaps the most infamous press release in journalism history.

CHAPTER TWENTY-NINE

Nigel and I each had a yellow legal pad and scratched out a few thoughts. Then we compared notes and noticed immediately we were on the same path. Sal walked in as we were reading over our notes and I asked, "How's the Butterscotch Kid?"

"He's playing shuffleboard and looked thirsty. So I came in for some water. How's the press release coming along?"

"We'll have it done in no time," Nigel said. "As soon as do we'll print out a few copies for everybody to read. We want to make sure everybody agrees on the main points. Then we need to destroy the copies. Don't want to leave any evidence behind. We'll give O'Riley one copy to take with him and he'll order it distributed by the weasels in Buffalo headquarters. It will not be emailed from here so there won't be any electronic copies zipping and bouncing around cyberspace."

Sal said, "Or else. …"

Exactly.

We would again make it clear, very clear, that O'Riley must do what we say. That we had the means and friends to do anything, anything up to and including murder, if he didn't follow directions.

Sal went back outside with his three bottles of Zephryhills water and Nigel and I cobbled together our news release, the one that would signal the farewell of Chesterfield Ebenezer O'Riley IV from Grabmore. We researched basic facts such as what percent of the company he actually owned. This release would signal the end of a famous American business dynasty and a reign of corporate pettiness and unalloyed, unparalleled galloping greed, or so we hoped.

That was the goal. After we cobbled together our outline on legal pads I sat down at an old desktop computer that belonged to Uncle Orville and typed up the release. Below is the text of the news release O'Riley ordered the Grabmore public relations staff to send out several days later.

Copies went to the Grabmore blog and The New York Times media writer David Farr and to business publications and to all employees with a grabmore.com email address. And to the Associated Press and Fox News and to MSNBC and even, I believe, The Onion.

Here is the text of that release:

Chesterfield Ebenzer O'Riley IV announced today he is resigning as CEO of Grabmore Publications, the nation's largest newspaper publisher.

Mr. O'Riley said he plans to donate his 54.802 percent of outstanding Grabmore stock to the Florida Gulf Coast University journalism department. That means, Mr. O'Riley said, the company will be controlled by the department's professors and instructors.

Mr. O'Riley said he has been in seclusion for several days. He apologizes to concerned employees and law enforcement if anybody thought he had been kidnapped.

"I've been doing a lot of thinking," Mr. O'Riley said. "I thought it best to get away and clear my head. I've been staying in an out-of-the-way corner of Florida where my corporate colleagues and responsibilities couldn't distract me. I'd like to use this forum and take this opportunity to apologize to all present and former Grabmore employees who have been laid off, furloughed or bullied while I was granted numerous multi-million dollar bonuses at their expense.

"I can not, in good conscience, continue doing business this way. That includes, for example, earning a $7,100 bonus every time an employee is laid off. I've piled up tens of millions of dollars this way. I don't need any more money."

Mr. O'Riley said he intends to return to Buffalo headquarters soon to clean out his office. He declined to say where he has spent the past several days.

"Where is not important," Mr. O'Riley said. "It's what I've been thinking about that counts."

He added that a childhood love of shuffleboard was recently rekindled. Mr. O'Riley said he plans to use his wealth and organizational skills to finance and manage a new sports venture, the Florida International Shuffleboard League. He will serve as its executive director.

The league will be a modest shuffleboard tour with prize money that initially will total $50,000 for the first season. The inaugural season will start in October and run through March. Tournaments are tentatively planned for the first season in St. Petersburg, Fort Myers, Everglades City, Boca Raton, Daytona Beach and Winter Park.

"This is an exciting opportunity for me to pursue something I love," said Mr. O'Riley, who plans to reside in Florida. "I've loved shuffleboard since I was a kid."

Tentative plans call for a season-ending masters tournament at the St. Petersburg Shuffleboard Club with first-place prize money of $5,000. That is in addition to the $50,000 that will be paid out during the course of the season.

The overall champion of the season will be awarded the Mae Hall Memorial Silver Tang and the Butterscotch Cup will be awarded to the winner of the season-ending tournament.

Mr. O'Riley said he does not plan to answer media inquiries for some time. He added, though, that news releases concerning Florida International Shuffleboard League developments would soon be distributed. Mr. O'Riley said he and shuffleboard colleagues are designing a website and organizing the league.

"My focus now is making the Florida International Shuffleboard League a vibrant part of the Florida sports and social scene," Mr. O'Riley said. "I am finished with journalism."

Nigel and I were satisfied with the first press release either of us had ever written. It had taken only about 45 minutes. We thought it hit on the main points and were sure it would re-sound with a thunderclap throughout Grabmore and with a resounding boom in the rest of American journalism.

First, though, we checked with our colleagues for their thoughts. Nigel, Ahmad and Monique all read through it and approved. Then we went outside and asked O'Riley to read it. We did something neither of us had ever done before – make up quotes. We made up those O'Riley quotes for the release and wanted to see his reaction.

The Butterscotch Kid, as I was now referring to him, and Troxie were finishing a shuffleboard match. Troxie won handily. Naturally. We asked O'Riley to sit down and read through the release.

"I'm going to start, fund and manage a shuffleboard league?" he asked. "Since when?"

"Since now," I said. "Well, you'll probably start in a few weeks. You'll need to get back to Buffalo and have some financial matters cleared up and then you can find a place to live in Florida. I recommend St. Pete. It has likely the best and most historic shuffleboard facility plus there's plenty of nice homes and condos in your pricy range near the courts."

He just nodded.

"And who are these colleagues mentioned in the press release?" he asked.

"Well," I admitted, "we exaggerated there. We figured your shuffleboard pro here could help. As the league moves forward you'll have to find organizers in each city. I imagine a new shuffleboard website, Facebook page and Twitter account will help spread the word.

"Plus, we have contacts with the sports departments of papers around the state. We'll see about getting stories in those papers."

The soon-to-be-ex CEO wasn't done with his questions.

"Where's this $50,000 in prize money coming from?" he asked next.

"What's your annual salary?" Sal asked.

"Well, it varies," O'Riley said. "Like five years ago it was only $1.4 million. But this year it was supposed to be $2.5 million."

"I'm sure," I said, "you can find $50,000. And what about all those bonuses you got over the years? Oh, $50,000 shouldn't be a problem. Plus, I got some ideas for tour sponsorships, corporate tie-ins that could make the league a profitable little venture for all involved. For example, maybe we can get the Tang beverage people to put their logo on the tangs."

I was on a roll.

"A biscuit tie-in through the Pillsbury people is another possibility," I said. "Who makes Florida's best butterscotch milkshakes? I have no idea. Maybe we could announce a butterscotch milkshake contest to select the best. You would, of course, be the judge. Maybe DQ could be a corporate sponsor.

"We could have contests in each city to select names for teams. We'll have to come up with prizes. Maybe a set of tangs and biscuits to the winner in each city. And so on and so forth."

O'Riley seemed to brighten a bit.

"You know," he told me, "you're not quite as stupid and clueless as I thought."

"I'm just getting started," I said. "We could sell naming rights to tournaments and venues. Maybe Strumpets strip club could sponsor the Fort Myers tournament. Maybe the Tampa Bay Times could buy the naming rights to the shuffleboard facility in St. Pete. So on and so forth."

"I'm liking this more and more," O'Riley said. "Would I get a commission or percentage from any naming rights?"

"I suppose," I told him.

It did, after all, seem like a reasonable request.

"Do I have to spend the rest of the day in my room?" he asked.

I looked at Troxie, who nodded her head, indicating she thought it was OK for him to stay out of the room that was his prison.

"I'll tell you what, we're going to watch a football game soon," I said. "We got some frozen pizzas we're going to stick in the oven and some wine and beer. You're welcome to watch the game with us."

"Great," O'Riley said. "I don't know much about football but it sounds like fun. One thing I just don't get is when I hear the announcer say first down. Does that means the first player knocked down."

Sal heard this and was astounded.

"Geez, O'Riley, where have you spent your whole life?" Sal said. "Didn't you ever watch games with your dad when you were a kid or with the guys in college? Did you ever go to a high school football game? What that hell? How can you not know this stuff? I knew about downs in second grade. I don't remember now if it was my first year in second grade or second year in second grade but I learned about downs in football. What sort of guy are you?"

To me this first-down ignorance was more evidence of O'Riley's sequestered and privileged life. He grew up implausibly rich with his own stateroom on the QE2 and the money to pay other people to write his college term papers and the remoteness from the real world that he doesn't know how important tips are to baristas.

Nevertheless, I was patient with him with football 101.

"O'Riley, it's like this," I said, patiently. "Don't think of the word down as in knock down. Think of the word down as in try. A football team gets four downs or four tries to move the ball 10 yards. Got that?"

He nodded and asked, "What if they don't go 10 yards?"

"Then the other team gets the ball," I explained.

I didn't want to get into the whole punting thing or trying for a field goal or four-down territory or any of that stuff. That would be the next football lesson.

"This has been quite a day," O'Riley said. "I'm exhausted. If I go lay down for a few minutes do you promise not to lock me in the room?"

"I promise," I said. "But don't expect a butterscotch milkshake when you wake up. We're gonna stick frozen pizzas in the oven and then we got some Budweisers and some bottles of Barefoot merlot and pinot grigio. Nothing fancy. This is what ordinary people do. We watch football and eat pizza and drink cheap beer and wine. Go take your nap."

CHAPTER THIRTY

It was another one of those splendid Florida winter afternoons, one Floridians dream about in July and August when we're swaddled in a seemingly perpetual blanket of heat and humidity, one that envelopes Floridians in a sweaty embrace and won't let go.

Not in January. No air conditioning was required this day. The windows were flung open. The front door was propped open and the old-fashioned screen door that kept the bugs out was secured with a small latch.

A hint of a breeze flowed through the living room of Uncle Orville's house, or what used to be Uncle Orville's house. It was now mine, a reality I still had trouble grasping. We were ready to relax, watch football, eat pizza and drink cheap wine and beer.

It was a great day to be an American. The Patriots-Raiders AFC playoff game was on the TV with the volume turned low and our talk turned to sports. Troxie said she had heard I played in a rec baseball league in Fort Myers. I told her I was shortstop for a team and we had a big game the next day against our archrivals.

Then I told her something that really intrigued her. I said I had read up on her late great-grandfather, Hal Trosky, one-time Cleveland Indians slugging first baseman. I told her I was to play the next day in the very same park where great-grandpa Hal had played spring training games late in his career, in the early 1940s. A place called Terry Park.

"Really?" she said.

She said she'd like to come to the game. I told her that wasn't a good idea because the catcher on the other team was Lt. J. P. Hooper of the Fort Myers Police Department, the lead investigator on the O'Riley case.

"Oh," Troxie said. "I see."

Indeed. Hooper or somebody or everybody might wonder about Troxie if she showed up at Terry Park. Who was she? How did we meet? Why would she want to watch a knucklehead like me play?

I thought it best that we not risk her bumping into Hooper or Hooper wondering why and how this fetching woman came to see me, of all people, play baseball. Then I told her, seriously, that her great-grandfather was a crybaby, or should I say a Cleveland Crybaby?

"What are you talking about?" Troxie asked "My great-grandfather was a great guy."

"I didn't say he wasn't," I said. "Just bear with me on this. In 1940, the Indians were managed by a crusty old coot named Ossie Vitt. He clashed with the players, including Hal Trosky. They revolted. They got up a petition. They wanted to get rid of Vitt. They said he was a wild man. Management supported Vitt. Word leaked out and the team became known as the Cleveland Crybabies. Fans around the league threw baby bottles at them. The Indians also became known as the Half Vitts. True story.

"And those Crybabies had spring training where I'm going to play tomorrow against Hooper the copper."

"That's so cool," Troxie said. "I mean, it's cool you're gonna play where great-Grandpa Hal played long before I was born."

186

I then explained to Troxie and the others there's a great history to Terry Park. I've spoken to local historical societies and in public libraries about that spring training history.

And I asked if they knew who Bernard Malamud was. Nigel was sitting in the corner and half-listening and half watching the football game. Nigel said Malamud was a great American author now probably best known for The Natural.

"I saw the movie," Troxie said. "With Robert Redford. He played an over-the-hill baseball player. When he's young he gets shot by some crazy lady, right?"

"Right," I said. "Malamud, the guy who wrote the book, based it on a real incident. He once said all baseball history has the quality of mythology about it. The inspiration for the novel came from real life. There was a baseball player named Eddie Waitkus. Real guy. There was a teenage girl named Ruth Ann Steinhagen. She was obsessed with poor Eddie. Built a shrine to him."

"Wait a minute, Ruth Ann?" Troxie asked. "Like two of your Uncle Orville's wives I've been hearing about?"

"Yep. She was sort of a trailblazer, one of the first celebrity stalkers. That would be Ruth Ann Steinhagen, not any of Uncle Orville's Ruth Ann collection. It happened in 1949, when Waitkus was a Phillies first baseman.

"The Phillies were in Chicago to play the Cubs. Ruth Ann, she spelled it with two words and without an 'e' at the end. To make a long story short, Eddie wound up in her room in a Chicago hotel. They had never met. Ruth Ann, so goes the story, told Eddie, 'I got a surprise for you.' Did she ever. And it wasn't a cold beer. It was a .22 rifle. She shot poor Eddie in the chest but he survived and eventually played again. Ruth Ann was committed to a mental institution. She never went to prison.

"Maybe if we're caught we won't go to prison, either. And we haven't even shot anybody in the chest. At least yet."

We let that sink in as we watched a replay of New England quarterback Tom Brady throwing his fourth touchdown pass of the game, which was turning into a rout. The Patriots were now up 28-0. What a snoozer of a game. The subject turned back to baseball.

"The name of the league I play in at Terry Park is called Roy Hobbs," I said. "That's the name of the main character in the Malamud novel and the one Robert Redford played in the movie. This is a rec league I play in but we get to play at a place where some of the all-time greats played, some of the naturals in baseball history."

I then rattled off some of the names. Lefty Grove. Jimmie Foxx. Roberto Clemente. George Brett. They all played at the same place I play. Sometimes I think there ought to be national legislation or a baseball rule against the likes of me sullying the diamonds where the greatest ever played. Malamud talked about the mythology of baseball history and a tiny sliver of a fraction of it played out where I would play shortstop tomorrow for an over-40 team called Babykins.

I told my friends a little of that mythology, about Jimmie Foxx, the legendary slugger for the A's. Foxx was a Maryland schoolboy athletic marvel, a state sprint champ. The story goes that he wasn't scouted but trapped. A scout claims that he was driving through Maryland farm country one day in the early '20s and was lost.

This was long before GPS, of course. So he noticed a kid plowing a field behind a mule. Asked the kid for directions and he picked up the plow and pointed with it the way ordinary people might use an umbrella. The scout asked young Jimmie if he played baseball. He said yes.

Then I told the group about one of Hal Trosky's teammates, fireballing Bob Feller, one of the great pitchers ever. One who pitched on the field where I would play the following day. Feller got to the big leagues at 17. This was before radar guns but he had to be throwing 100 mph. Easy. One day he had two strikes on Leo Durocher who turned and walked to the dugout. The umpire said he had another strike. Durocher, so the story goes, conceded the final strike.

I told them I would be playing at the same field where the great Roberto Clemente had spring training with the Pirates in the '50s and

'60s. Clemente is another pillar in the baseball mythological story. Perhaps the greatest throwing arm ever on an outfielder.

Late in his career, when he was home in Puerto Rico for the winter, an earthquake struck Nicaragua. Clemente organized a relief effort but died when his plane crashed into the sea upon take off from San Juan. The last hit of his big-league career had been his 3,000th.The next day I would play at a place where Clemente played spring training games for 14 years.

The elements of mythology, indeed.

"Do you guys remember Bo Jackson?" I asked.

Everybody nodded yes. Even Ahmad, who grew up in Yemen. I told them Jackson, the Heisman Trophy winning running back, played for the Royals when they trained at Terry Park in the 1980s. I told them he's the only man to ever be an all-star in both Major League Baseball and the NFL.

"He was the fastest player with the best arm and the most powerful hitter in baseball," I said. "All wrapped up in one person. He played in the NFL as a hobby. A hobby! When baseball season ended, he went to join the Oakland Raiders. No training camp. Just traded his batting helmet for a football helmet.

"The Raiders had a Hall of Fame running back named Marcus Allen. As soon as Bo showed up, Bo became the starter. He was the fastest running back in the NFL, a man who could either out-run defensive backs or bowl over linebackers.

"Then he suffered a freak hip injury and all that glorious, incomparable speed and power vanished. This meteor of an athlete, a man who could have been a Hall of Famer in two sports, was essentially done.

"Bo Jackson embodies that mythological element of baseball that Malamud talked about. And tomorrow, I'll play baseball where those guys played. And I'll be playing there against Lt. J.P. Hooper of the Fort Myers Police Department. Hooper, of course, thinks I've had something to do with O'Riley. It will be tough to concentrate on baseball."

I was leading up to a connection here, a connection to why we were all here in Chokoloskee as the Butterscotch Kid napped, or as Troxie called him, CEO Boy.

O'Riley, though, was awake and Sal escorted him into the living room, where he nervously sat down on the couch, far from Troxie at the other end of the couch.

"We're gonna stick some pizza in the oven in a little while," Ahmad told O'Riley. "You want some when it's ready?"

O'Riley nodded and asked what we were doing.

"Sort of watching the game," I said. "But mainly talking."

"What are you talking about?" O'Riley asked.

"I know we're watching football but right now we're talking baseball," I said. "Specifically, local spring training history."

O'Riley just nodded blankly, the classic Grabmore response to anything I might find interesting and didn't have anything to do with profits or memos or power or bullying or backstabbing or Grabspeak. So, I continued with my story. ...

"In the early and mid-1920s, before the Tamiami Trail connected Fort Myers to Tampa and Miami, this part of the state was really remote, reached only by train or boat or by car somehow along some dirt roads, I imagine.

"You could take a train from New York City to San Francisco decades before Fort Myers and Naples could be reached by the railroad from the outside world. The '20s were the time of the land boom in Florida. Folks in Fort Myers were caught up in it as well and wanted to have a big-league baseball team train here. Now, remember the Interstate was some Jules Verne fantasy at the time. City leaders wanted the publicity a big-league team would bring to Fort Myers, which was far less known up north than Miami or West Palm or St. Pete and Tampa.

"So, in 1925, the Philadelphia A's came to town, starting a spring training tradition. They stayed for about 10 years and then the Indians came for a couple years. This, Troxie, was at the tail end of Hal Trosky's career."

She nodded and seemed to be paying attention. So I continued.

"In the 1950s, the Pittsburgh Pirates came to Fort Myers for spring training, starting in 1955. It was a different time. The era of Jim Crow. Black players couldn't stay in the same hotel, the downtown Bradford, as the white players. The great Roberto Clemente stayed at Etta Powell's boarding house in an area then known as Safety Hill or Dunbar.

"Anyhow, one of the Pirates' owners was Bing Crosby. One of his many casual and occasional golfing buddies was somebody named Chesterfield Ebenezer O'Riley Jr."

I paused for what I hoped would be dramatic effect.

"I see where you're going with this, I think," Sal said. "Remember, it took me two tries to get through second grade. So go slow."

"Well, I'm not sure where I'm going and I didn't exactly go to Harvard," I said. "So one day, Bing and O'Riley Junior are playing in a club tournament in Hollywood. That's the famous one, the one in California. Not the not-famous Hollywood here in Florida.

"So anyhow, Bing tells O'Riley he's going to Florida, to some place called Fort Myers to watch the Pirates in spring training and invites him to stop by. So, sure enough, O'Riley No. 2 comes to town, checks it out and likes the place. He sees the local paper and sees that it's thriving and senses there will be another boom, sort of like in the '20s but lasting longer and having a more profound impact.

"So, after spring training he goes to Buffalo and talks to his dad and tells him the company should buy this little paper in Fort Myers, the Tropical-Times, and that it would be a nice addition to Grabmore.

"So, in 1961, the local owners, the powerful Golyer family, land barons, oil men, advertising tycoons, owners of laundries and juke joints and much more, gets an amazing offer. And the Tropical-Times is sold for about $4 million. In the decades since it's meant tens of millions, maybe hundreds of millions of dollars to Grabmore.

"And it all started with the Philadelphia A's and spring training in 1925."

Meanwhile, I glanced at the screen and Brady had just thrown another touchdown pass and the Patriots led 35-0.

I felt pretty proud of myself for that story and poured a little more of the cheap merlot.

Troxie, though, asked, "Scott, how many years did you say it's been since you had a date?"

CHAPTER THIRTY-ONE

The aroma of that frozen pepperoni pizza warming in the oven began drifting out from the kitchen, filtering through the house and filling us with whiffs of anticipation.

Sure, it was just frozen pizza and probably not the healthiest thing but it was Saturday and all was right with the world. For the moment. An NFL playoff doubleheader was scheduled for the afternoon. We had plenty of beer and wine. Our kidnapped CEO was docile and even showing signs of humanity, reminiscing about his childhood love of butterscotch milkshakes. He also scored points for himself by finding a job for the fired disabled vet who cut a tuna fish sandwich improperly.

I hoped O'Riley wasn't lying about the vet.

I had a glass of merlot in me and was ready to move on to the strong stuff – malbec. I'd worry about Sunday's baseball game against the league powerhouse and the potential of a long kidnapping sentence in a federal pen some other time. Like after the Giants-Saints game.

Sal was beginning to look worried about his Giants and had staked out the best seat in the house – the middle of the couch in front of the flat screen TV.

I was in a storytelling mood. I knew plenty of local lore from years of writing history stories in addition to sports for the Tropical-Times. I told Troxie her situation reminded me of a Fort Myers case from 1939.

"Really?" she said.

"Yep. Young woman ....

"Gee, thanks, Scott, I don't feel so young. I'm 40."

"Well, you're young at heart," I said. "And you look young. Anyhow, it was 1939 when Thelma Rice and her sister Gertrude showed up in Fort Myers. Sort of like you showed up in Chokoloskee and Everglades City. Thelma got herself wrapped up in something pretty big and definitely illegal. Sort of like you.

"Thelma was 25 that year and a waitress. I don't know if she was a temptress waitress or not. Anyhow, she met a guy named Earl Randolph Haskew. Sounds like a great old southern name, doesn't it? He owned a black, four-door 1938 Plymouth. Practically a new car at the time. They went drinking in town at a place called, as I recall, the Parkview Lounge. They had set-ups, which are whiskey and Coca-Cola."

"I'll stick to pinot grigio," Troxie said.

I returned to the story.

"Around 11 o'clock on that summer Friday night, they drove out to Fort Myers Beach and went skinny-dipping."

"This is getting interesting," Troxie said.

"Wait," I said, "it gets better. Actually worse. A lot worse. Haskew, according to news accounts at the time, asked for what was termed an 'unusual intimacy.' You can use your own imagination for what the euphemism meant.

"Thelma felt threatened by Haskew, who she had just met. She noticed a .32 in the Plymouth. It was Haskew's gun. She grabbed it and shot him. He didn't go down.

"Should have had a .38," Troxie said.

"She should have had a V8?" Sal asked. "How would some sort of tomato juice drink help?"

"No, a .38 like my .38," Troxie said.

"Oh, got it," Sal said. "Sorry."

"So, anyhow, Thelma shot the guy a second time," I said. "He still didn't go down."

"A .38 would have done the trick the first time," Troxie said.

"Well, the third time was the charm with the .32," I said. "Haskew went down. He didn't get up. Around dawn the next day somebody walking the beach found Haskew's body rolling in the small gulf waves lapping on the beach. Thelma was long gone by then. Initially, she jumped in the car naked and started driving. She threw the gun out the window at one point.

"A statewide dragnet went into effect. Rice drove north. This was long before I-75 so I guess she went up U.S. 41 and then maybe cut over to U.S. 19 somewhere north of Tampa. She stopped in Cross City and contacted cops in Tallahassee and said she had shot a man in Fort Myers but it was in self-defense.

"Despite her self-defense plea, an all-male jury took only 90 minutes to convict her of manslaughter. She was sentenced to 10 years and was paroled four years later. I don't know what happened to Thelma after that. I doubt she became a shuffleboard champion."

"Quite a story," Troxie said.

"Oh, the best parts may be what Thelma said. I can recall, just about word-for-word what she said when she came back to Fort Myers. 'Now I'm back here to face the music. If I ever get out I am going to write a true story of how I got myself in a spot where I had to kill a man. It may make a little money for me and it should be a lesson to other girls not to drink with strange men.'"

"Here I am drinking with about as strange a group of men as anybody can imagine," Troxie said with a smile. "But I got a .38, not a .32"

Then we heard O'Riley clear his throat and he said, "I promise not to ask for any unusual intimacies."

That broke up the place. We chortled and Nigel said, "Our gourmet meal is ready."

Three of those frozen pizzas had been cooked and Nigel and Monique carried them into the living room and placed the steaming hot pies on the coffee table in front of Sal. That may not have been the best place to put the pizza if anybody other than Sal wanted more than one slice.

Ahmad gestured to O'Riley and said, "Help yourself." O'Riley grabbed a paper plate and towel and a slice of pizza and retreated to his end of the couch.

"Can I have something to drink, too?" he asked.

"I'm sorry, we don't have any butterscotch milkshakes," I told him. "But help yourself to a Bud or glass of wine or bottle of water."

He poured some malbec into a plastic cup.

"Is this how regular people live?" O'Riley asked.

I shrugged and said, "I guess. Never really thought about it."

It was almost time for kickoff. Troxie put down her glass and started speaking.

"You know, I told you guys all about myself. About how I lost my job and how Ralph left me for Charlene from the Thunderbird Lounge. I don't really know anything about any of you. Anybody here married? What's everybody's story?"

I got myself in trouble again.

"Well, the main thing to know is to never trust a woman named Charlene," I said.

Nigel, Sal, Ahmad and even O'Riley thought that was hilarious. Monique and Troxie? Not so much.

"I don't think that's funny," Troxie said.

Monique just shot me an angry look. I apologized, as did the rest of the guys.

"I'm serious," Troxie said. "How come none of you talk about wives or girlfriends back home? How come you got time to come down here to kidnap this guy?"

She pointed at O'Riley. Troxie had a point. We owed her that much. It would probably be cathartic as well to unburden ourselves.

Monique started the storytelling just as the Giants kicked off to start the game. They had won the coin toss but deferred to the second half.

"I had a steady girlfriend for years," Monique said. "Her name was Astrid. We lived together. I thought we always would. Then she started spending a lot of weekends with her mom. At least that's what she said. She was lying.

"Astrid left me, left me for a man, some guy named Pierre Bocabella, an accountant from Montreal. Now they're married. Mr. and Mrs. Bocabella. Even got a little girl, from what I hear. Haven't met anybody since and it's been three years."

Saints quarterback Drew Brees had just thrown a 43-yard touchdown pass to Marques Colston and Sal sank back in the couch and moaned. We watched in silence for several minutes, concentrating on pizza, our beverages, the game and our fears. Jail was an ever-present fear at that point.

While Sal worried about the Giants, Ahmad started talking about his wife, or, I guess ex-wife.

"Her name is Amal," Ahmad said. "We met in Sana'a. That's the capital of Yemen. We got married nine years ago when I returned home on vacation. She moved to Montvale with me and got a job in a Starbucks and worked herself up to assistant manager. Then, a couple of years ago she returned home to visit family.

"She hasn't come back to Montvale since. She became radicalized and now wears a burqa and says I'm a tool of the Great Satan. On a trip to Sana'a a couple of years ago I told her to, use some American lingo, to get a grip and lighten up. That was the wrong thing to say. She slapped me in the face and her brother, a real fanatic, said if he ever saw me again he'd strap a suicide vest to my chest and send me straight to a place without 72 vestal virgins.

"I got the hint and flew home the next day. Haven't heard from Amal since. And so, here I am in Chokoloskee, eating frozen pizza, drinking Earl Grey tea, watching American football and babysitting a CEO."

Eli Manning was intercepted by the Saints and Sal held his head in his hands and rocked back and forth on the couch. He looked on the verge of tears. The Giants were down 7-0 but it was early in the second quarter. We left him to his misery and torment. The rest of us weren't nearly as emotionally invested in the game as Sal.

Where Nigel grew up in Northern Ireland this game of American football must have seemed like some sort of barbaric ritual dreamed up by the colonists. So Nigel, who likes our football well enough, started talking about his ex-wife, Fiona.

"She was a dental hygienist, for some dentist in Hackensack," Nigel said. "I traveled quite a bit and worked lots of nights. That's what you got to do covering boxing and football, or as you Americans call it, soccer.

"More than once, even when I was home, she said there were emergencies that required her to stay late at the office. There must have been an epidemic of impacted molars in north Jersey that summer. Well, it didn't have anything to do with molars.

"I think you know where this story is going. They went to a Holiday Inn down in Raritan. And I got a lawyer. So I now can devote my vacation time to kidnapping CEOs."

The Giants scored 13 points in the final five minutes of the first half and took a 13-7 lead into halftime. Sal sat back, somewhat relieved and guzzled some Bud.

"All right, you guys wanna hear my story?" Sal asked.

We responded by not saying anything, which he correctly interpreted as a collective yes.

"We met at Parsipanny High," Sal said. "I started at right guard my junior and senior years and she was a cheerleader. Her name is Roma. Her parents, Mr. and Mrs. DiNardo, knew my parents. They were mobbed up. Pretty sure.

"We all went to the same church. Anyhow, we went to the senior prom together. She went off to Montclair State to study something and I went to work for my uncle Tony in waste management. Roma and I connected again a couple of years later and got married. This was after she dropped outta college.

"When I told her about going into Witness Protection, she didn't want any part of it. Or me. I told her I didn't have any choice. It was either 20-to-30 in a federal pen or a one-way fishing trip out of Atlantic Highlands.

"So here I am. And Roma is still in Parsipanny. I think she's dating Biff Beiderbecke, who was the quarterback at Parsipanny High when I played. We were the Red Hawks. That's about it, I guess."

"What does Biff do?" I asked.

"He owns a bunch of sun tan parlors in north Jersey and down the shore," Sal said.

The second half was about to start and the Giants would receive the kick. Sal's attention was back on his favorite team and he seemed somewhat confident. His boys were up 6 and would get the ball to start the second half.

The pizza was done. And I hoped the confessional. After the Giants returned the kick to the Saints' 47 and quickly picked up a first down on an 11-yard run, Troxie pointed out something.

"Scott, or Dashiell, we haven't heard your story," she said.

"I don't have a story," I said.

"Everybody has a story," Troxie said.

The Giants' drive had stalled and they were lining up for a 40-yard field goal attempt. It was good and Sal's team led 16-7.

"Come on, Scott, your turn," Sal said.

I took one final swig of malbec and told them my story, which isn't much of a story.

"I knew from an early age I would never have kids," I started.

"Now how can you know that?" Troxie asked.

"Well, I was so painfully shy I never went on dates in high school and college and remember thinking to myself, I'm never going to have kids.' Even going out to lunch with a girl seemed beyond the realm of possibility. I had to be a world-record holder for insecurity.

"So, I just kind of figured that dating and marriage thing was for other people. And that's it. End of story."

"It's not much a story," Troxie said.

"My life would have been the most boring reality show ever contemplated," I said.

"Or the most pathetic," Troxie said.

Just then the Giants intercepted a Brees' pass and returned it 77 yards for a touchdown and a 23-7 lead early in the fourth quarter. Sal jumped off the couch and pumped his right fist. It looked like the Giants were moving on to the NFC title game.

We didn't know yet where we were going with our plot. We'd hash out details in the morning. Everybody was tired. Nigel escorted O'Riley back to his cell/hurricane shelter and locked the door.

Monique walked over and double-checked the lock. Me? I was worn out. It was time for a little more of Poet, Pugilist and Pressman and sleep.

CHAPTER THIRTY-TWO

Troxie hadn't had a sip of pinot grigio since the first quarter of the game and was able to drive back to her temporary home in the Fisherman's Cove Mobile Home Park on Copeland Avenue, up in Everglades City.

Sal, Ahmad, Monique and Nigel went upstairs to the four bedrooms. I think Sal had the master bedroom, the one that used to be Uncle Orville's. I don't know how the others decided which bedroom each would use.

I stayed in the living room, opened up the couch, grabbed a pillow and sheets out of a closet, turned on a lamp and curled up with Poet, Pugilist and Pressman. There was a lot, though, to think about before I could focus on the book.

Babykins, my geezer rec baseball team, had a big game the next day in Fort Myers against the league powerhouse. Did we have any chance? Not really.

My kidnapping confederates would all be flying home Monday, the following day, and I would be on my own. Not entirely. Thankfully. Troxie was now part of our conspiracy. She didn't participate in the actual abduction so if we were caught certainly wouldn't face as harsh a charge as the rest of us. But prison was certainly a real possibility for the shuffleboard queen. Accessory after the fact is the legal term, I think.

Sometime soon, maybe in two or three days, I would likely drive O'Riley back to Fort Myers and drop him off close to the Never Enough and let him walk from wherever I dropped him off to his 99-foot yacht. And then he would send out that news release, the one announcing his resignation and the end of Grabmore as it's been known.

That, at least, was our plan. Would he follow through? He better. We would have to emphasize to O'Riley once again, one final time, this was a sacred pledge on his part to stick to the plan. That if he reneged we had friends, friends meaner than any of us, friends with special skills, friends unafraid to use those skills, would find him. Friends perhaps nearly as mean as Grabmore president Carlotta Gutman.

And that would be it for O'Riley. He couldn't expect any pizza or malbec from these characters. A butterscotch milkshake? Out of the question.

Did our scheme with the resignation and handing over of Grabmore stock have a better chance of success than my baseball team had the next day against Bartley's, the team with the ex-major-league pitcher? Absolutely.

I took a swig of water, forced myself to chase all those other thoughts out of my mind and picked up the book written by the first O'Riley in America and disappeared for a while into his world. I couldn't stay awake for long but wanted to read a bit of the book's final chapter, the one titled Legacy.

Now, my race is nearly done. It's been 53 years since I walked off the City of Cheaters, through Ellis Island and on to the Brooklyn Daily Eagle's front door.

More than a half-century of hard work and striving and surviving and prospering beyond my wildest hopes when I boarded that ship and slept on a urine-stained bunk and ate weevil-infested biscuits. So much has happened since I came ashore in America and couldn't afford a bar of Ivory soap.

I became an American citizen, seen two world wars, survived that horrible Spanish Influenza epidemic, weathered the Great Depression, endured the caterwauling calumny of pandering cretins on the House Un-American Activities Committees. When I came to America there was no thing such as commercial radio let alone television. The movies were silent. I sure wasn't.

Mr. Kent, the Daily Eagle editor, gave me a chance. He died a long time ago but I still refer to him as Mr. Kent, as you may have noticed. Mr. Kent didn't like surrounding himself with sycophants and scheming careerists and jargon-spewing opportunists and backstabbers.

I like to think I learned from him and tried from the early days of my company to make it a meritocracy, not a confederacy of bootlicking supplicants. Now my son runs the company and his son is a teenager in boarding school and Grabmore may his someday.

Junior – that's what I call my son – recently invited me down to Fort Myers to look around the place because he thinks we should buy the local paper, the Tropical-Times. Everybody in town seems to make a big deal out of Thomas Edison, who used to spend winters there at a home on the river and supposedly said someday everybody will learn about Fort Myers and 90-million people will live there.

I hate to drop names but I met Edison, back in Menlo Park in the late '20s. We were introduced and that was it. Nothing dramatic was said or happened. He was polite and said something like "Nice to meet you, Mr. O'Riley."

In Fort Myers they have streets, restaurants, schools and a big festival named after Edison. Junior advised me to take a trip to this place. He emphasized I should go in the winter because it's too hot and humid in the summer and summer lasts at least six months, despite what the calendar decrees. So that's what we did.

The Tropical-Times is a fine little paper but I think we can make it better.

More importantly, after spending a few days in the area, I know this part of Florida is ready to take off. More and more people are moving there every day.

Soon, I was told, there will be a bridge to Sanibel Island and another one linking Fort Myers to Cape Coral, a new town that someday could have 50,000 people. My corporate officers think I'm insane to say that but it's going to happen. Mark my words on Cape Coral. The bridges will be built. More people will come to the area. That means more readers and more advertisers and more money. As if I need anymore.

But I'm thinking about the future. Grabmore needs to go where the people are going and they're going to Florida. I hope the company follows the same plan that Mr. Kent and I used with that weekly in Poughkeepsie so long ago. Give people a compelling paper, one run by decent and honorable professionals and provide accurate yet interesting stories and people will part with their pennies to purchase it. Well, back then it was pennies. Now, they need nickels and dimes. Someday it may cost a quarter.

I certainly hope Grabmore's core principles don't change after I'm gone and I know I won't be around much longer.

Over dinner one night as we planned our trip to Fort Myers I told Junior I hope he keeps Grabmore true to what made it great. I don't think he was listening. Oh, he heard the words but rolled his eyes, sipped some more of that '46 Chateau Petreus and nodded. He seemed more interested in another California trip, golfing again with Bing Crosby and then going to parties with Hollywood starlets.

I worry about my grandson, too. Young Chesterfield is at Phillips Exeter Academy and seems to surround himself with other rich kids who have never worked or worried or knew anybody who worked with their hands.

How can that prepare him for the rough and tumble of the world? How will he deal with working people and help run a newspaper empire that depends on the nickels and dimes of waiters and barbers and stevedores to keep us living in mansions and attending exclusive prep schools?

I wonder.

That's where I stopped reading for the evening and reached up and turned off the light. Another big day awaited, a ride back to Fort Myers and our baseball game against the league powerhouse.

CHAPTER THIRTY-THREE

I heard the scuffing of feet, the whistle of a teapot, the whishing and whooshing of the refrigerator door opening and closing, the clank of spoons and caught a whiff of brewing coffee drifting out of the kitchen. I pulled the comforter up around my neck in the chill of the morning and curled up with a shiver.

Even way down in Chokoloskee, many miles south of Florida's frost line, which is just north of Tampa, January mornings are cool and we had left the windows open the previous night. Lows in the 50s are typical in January, even here, within perhaps 80 miles of the Florida Keys. I noticed through half-closed eyes Sal walking through the living room closing the windows with a soft schussing sound as they clicked shut.

Thanks, big guy.

I couldn't dawdle long on that foldout bed and under that big fluffy comforter, which I'm sure was yet another gift to Uncle Orville from yet another one of his wives. Uncle Orville may have been a kingpin in the import/export world but he hated shopping for himself or his homes, either here or on Central Park West. Or was that Central Park East? I can never remember which is the real fancy one.

I crawled off the couch, jammed the linens and pillow in the closet and settled down for breakfast with my confederates. Nigel walked over to the door to the hurricane shelter and unlocked it.

"Come on, Chesty, breakfast time," he said. "Eggs wait for no man. Or CEO."

O'Riley was just waking and snapped, "I hate that name. Don't call me Chesty."

"OK, your lordship, I'm sorry," Nigel said.

O'Riley just glared. I think he's overcoming his fear of us.

I had a bowl of Wheaties, the alleged breakfast of champions. I like Wheaties but they never made me a champion. I would need something stronger today in our big game, something along the lines of anabolic steroids. If they made a difference with real athletes could they help me? Nah. I'm not going to dabble with that stuff. I'll just muddle along like always, being a bit too slow, a bit too weak and with reflexes a tick or two or maybe three behind where they should be with whatever sport I was playing.

The game was still about four hours and a 90-mile drive away.

For now, it was breakfast. We wouldn't spend much more time together as a group, kidnappers and kidnapped. Unless some of it was in a federal courtroom. Sal, Ahmed, Monique and Nigel would all fly home tomorrow, back to their jobs scattered about the Grabmore empire.

I'm sure focusing on their jobs would be tough with O'Riley still here and the ever-present possibility that men and women wearing windbreakers with the letters FBI etched on the back may come banging on their doors. I didn't know it then as I gobbled up spoonful after spoonful of Wheaties that I was just four hours or so away from meeting and talking with a real-life, genuine, badge-toting FBI agent.

We all sat at that big round table in the big kitchen in that big yellow house in this sub-tropical outpost. Ahmad sipped his tea. O'Riley and the rest drank coffee. I had orange juice. Sal had thoughtfully placed small bowls of blueberries at every table setting and I recalled reading in Poet, Pugilist and Pressman that O'Riley's great-grandfather had never even seen a blueberry until his first day at the Brooklyn Daily Eagle more than a century earlier. That's when Mr. Kent provided him the finest breakfast he had seen in his 17 years.

Nigel put down his coffee and said, "We should review this one more time. Everybody agree on that?"

We nodded and all looked at O'Riley. We sat in silence for a few seconds.

"You want me to say something?" the CEO asked.

Again more silence from the table.

"What do you want me to say?" O'Riley said.

"It's not that difficult," Monique said. "We want you to understand what you're going to do when and if we return you to that ridiculous yacht of yours."

"If?" O'Riley asked, starting to look nervous.

"No messing around," Monique said. "We want to be clear that you'll do what you're supposed to do and that if you don't thing will get real messy. The Royal Canadian Mounted Police won't help you."

"Or the FBI," I said.

I poured a few blueberries over my Wheaties.

"OK, I got it," O'Riley said. "Somebody's going to drive me back to Fort Myers and drop me off near my boat."

"Boat?" I said. "That's no boat. Folks here in Chokoloskee and Everglades City have boats. That's a yacht."

"OK, near my yacht," O'Riley said. "I'm going to stroll back to the yacht like nothing happened. I got the press release you guys wrote for me. I'll type that up in my laptop and burn the original to ashes. Then I'll email the press release to the Grabmore Public Relations/Propaganda Division of Corporate Communications, Employee Purification and Information Dispersal. Right so far?"

He looked around.

"That's one thing that's going to change," Nigel said. "No more of this corporate BS. Just call it public relations. Journalism is supposed to be about clarity. Can't you just have common sense names for your departments? Names with clarity?"

O'Riley nodded, apparently not understanding Nigel's point.

"OK, so I send it out. I'll send it to all employees, too. Then I'll call Longstreet at the Tropical-Times and apologize for not making my appointment last week. Right so far?"

We all nodded.

"There's one thing you forgot," Sal said.

"Oh, yeah, if I don't I'll be sleeping with the fishes," O'Riley said.

"You got it," Sal said.

"I got it," O'Riley said

Did he really?

"I'm sure you're going to be tempted to call the cops and turn us in when you get back," I said. "I don't blame you. But like we've been saying all along, you turn us in, you'll unleash the hounds of hell. Got it?"

Something about those words "hounds of hell" seemed to register. And unleash struck me as a good, strong active verb that may have helped get the message across.

O'Riley gulped and said, "Got it."

Then came a familiar tapping at the front door. We knew who it was.

Sal yelled, "It's open. Come on in."

It was Troxie, of course.

"Everybody ready for a big day?" she asked.

"Not really," O'Riley said. "Just another day as a prisoner in my little cell. But I do have nice towels. I have to admit that."

I think that was an attempt at humor by the CEO. I did chuckle a little bit. After all, I picked out the towels. Troxie was holding a cup of coffee from a convenience store.

"Well, what about everybody else?" she asked.

We all sort of nodded. I was headed to Fort Myers to play baseball and the others were going sightseeing in Naples and Troxie was working a lunch shift at City Fishhouse.

"You know, we never heard about Chesty's significant others," Troxie said. "You ever been married, Mr. CEO?"

He said yes and didn't appear on the verge of revealing any details.

"Come on, we wanna know more," Troxie said. "How often? What were their names? How long were you married? What happened? Come on, Mr. CEO."

"You guys want to hear all this?" O'Riley said.

"You betcha," Troxie said.

So we heard the tales of woe and excess of O'Riley two weddings and marriages.

"My first wedding was to Susan," O'Riley said, looking around the table. "Susan Biddle. Of the Philadelphia Biddles. I'm sure you've all heard of the Biddles."

"I've heard of the Phillies," I said, referring to the city's baseball team.

"Well, anyhow," he continued, "the Biddles came from old money and big money. We met at a yacht club in Newport and got married on a Greek island. It's called Krypton or something. And the resort is Villa Faros. Very fancy. We flew in Jimmy Buffet to sing. This place, this island, is right where two seas meet. What are they called? The Asian and the Inner or something."

Nigel, our geography whiz, interrupted and said, "I think that would be the Aegean and the Ionian."

"Oh, yeah, right," O'Riley said. "So we rented the island for a week. Any of you folks ever spent a week on a Greek island?"

"I used to work in a surf shop on an island right off St. Pete," Troxie said. "It was close to a Burger King."

"I've heard of Greece," I said, always trying to be helpful.

"We were married about two years, Susan and I," O'Riley said. "But being CEO is demanding. Lots of travel and meetings and stuff."

"Travel to places like Iceland?" Monique asked.

"Well, yes, we were thinking about buying a TV station there," O'Riley said. "But I really like the place. The most beautiful girls I've ever seen. That's Iceland. You know I got lots of money and those girls were so pretty and heard about my yacht and my money. Well, I'm sure you can guess the rest.

"So did Susan. But she didn't have to guess. She knew. She hired a private detective. End of the first marriage."

O'Riley took a sip of coffee and then took a forkful of scrambled eggs.

"I guess you also want to hear about No. 2," O'Riley said. "That was Constance. Constance of the Boston Lodges. I'm sure you've heard of the Lodge family."

"I've heard of the Masonic Lodge," I said.

"Well," O'Riley said, wisely ignoring me. "We met at the Monte Carlo Casino in Monaco. I remember meeting some famous movie director there. Anyhow, that's where Constance and I met. We borrowed her dad's yacht and went to Ibiza for a week and then to Naples. That's not the Naples here in Florida."

"We kind of figured that," Sal said.

"Things were going great," O'Riley said. "It was a kind of whirlaway romance."

"Ah, you mean, whirlwind?" Nigel asked.

"Right," O'Riley said. "We had only been dating a few months and decided to get married in Tahiti."

"Well, it's nice to know all those furloughs and layoffs went for a good cause," Monique said. "I'm sure all the folks who lost their homes and were living on Spam and beans will rest easier on those park benches knowing about your weddings and trips on yachts and all that other stuff. I bet you ate caviar, too."

"Actually never liked caviar," O'Riley said. "It's fish eggs. Awful stuff. But Constance loved it. Ate it by the case. I didn't even like to look at it. But I like truffles. She never cared for truffles."

I flashed back to reading Poet, Pugilist and Pressman and how O'Riley's great-grandfather crossed the Atlantic subsisting on little more than weevil-infested biscuits and tins of corn beef.

"So, what happened with Constance?" Troxie asked.

"Same thing," O'Riley said. "Too many trips to Iceland and some trips to Ireland and even Lapland."

"Where the hell is Lapland?" Sal asked.

"Real far north," O'Riley said. "That's about all I know. And it gets cold. And lots of pretty girls."

"Maybe I'll visit someday," Monique said.

"I guess you and Constance got divorced," Troxie said.

O'Riley just nodded.

I couldn't stick around any longer. I had to drive to Terry Park in Fort Myers for our noon game. I always like to get to the park at least an hour early to go through an elaborate warming up and stretching routine and take some cuts in the batting cage. I'm sure I'd see Lt. Hooper of the Fort Myers Police Department and this new fireballing pitcher his team just snagged.

I said goodbye and added that I'd be back in time for dinner and to catch a bit of the late NFC playoff game between the Cowboys and 49ers. The winner would face Sal's Giants for the NFC title.

"Oh, one more thing," I said. "If I'm not here by 5:30 or so just assume I've been arrested and they're coming for the rest of you. Have a nice day. And wish me luck. My team will need it."

"Good luck," Troxie said. "Try not to get beaned."

"I'll certainly try not to stick my head in front of any fastballs," I said. "After the game, assuming my head isn't conked by a fastball, I'll head back here, to Troxie-loskee."

Troxie laughed at that, the way I mingled her name and the town's name. Maybe we'll switch out the Chokoloskee street signs for ones that say Troxie-loskee. But first, I had many miles to go and maybe three futile at-bats against Buck Belinksy, the new pitcher Bartley's signed up.

CHAPTER THIRTY-FOUR

My uniform, the one with the white baseball pants and garish orange jersey, was in a small bag in the Camry's trunk. My glove, spikes and cap were in another bag. The gas tank was full and I left Chokoloskee behind for a few hours, for the Sunday baseball game at Terry Park, where I'd change in a rest room from cargo shorts and T-shirt and into my Babykin's uniform.

The drive north on S. R. 29 and then I-75 to Fort Myers and then east on Palm Beach Boulevard didn't seem to take long on a Sunday morning. It was still nearly 90 minutes but the time raced by. I knew what awaited me on the field – 6-foot-4 former big-league pitcher Buck Belinsky. He wasn't much of a big-leaguer, a journeyman pro who pitched parts of a couple of seasons with the Tigers, compiling a 1-5 record and 4.99 ERA. Well, at least he won a game. And kept his career ERA under 5.00.

But he was entirely different level of ballplayer, a former University of Florida second-string quarterback who wasn't quite good enough to start in the SEC and a marginal big-league pitcher who wasn't quite good enough to last in the majors. Me? I was a marginal high school player.

It was, though, a pre-game meeting that would unnerve me more than facing 85 mph fastballs that whizzed by my late and feeble swings. After I pulled into the parking lot and changed into my uniform, Lt. Hooper of the Fort Myers Police Department, the catcher for the opposing team, was leaning on a batting cage while guys from both teams took turns taking warm-up swings. The crack of bat on ball served as a sound track to our chat.

Hooper grumbled one of his typical grumbly hellos.

I tried to make my hello sound cheery and upbeat. I think I failed.

"Hey, Bond," Hooper said, "There's somebody I want you to meet."

It wasn't his team's new, hulking 6-foot-4 pitcher. No, this guy was about 6-feet, solidly built, close-cropped, greying hair and wearing a red Bartley's jersey and the team's white pants. I walked over.

"This," he said, putting a hand on the right shoulder of the stranger, "is Agent Rizzo. That's as in Agent Rizzo of the FBI. He just joined our team. He was a DH at Auburn and played a couple years in the Red Sox system."

I was impressed. I wasn't good enough to have played Division I college baseball let alone minor-league ball.

"Oh, Hooper told me about you," Rizzo said. "I've seen your byline in the Tropical-Times. F. Scott Bond. What's up with that first initial? It's like something you'd see in the New York Times. R.W. Apple. R. J. Wingate IV. Thurston B. Howell Jr. Or whatever. Hooper told me the F stood for the grades you got in school. I thought that was pretty funny. Not real funny. Just kind of funny."

"He's a card, that Hooper," I said.

I then excused myself and said it was time to start my elaborate warm-up ritual of light jogging and stretching, then some sprints and warming up the arm, by throwing lightly and building up speed and distance and then a few cuts in the cage and finally infield practice.

As I walked over to our dugout, I noticed Belinsky warming up. It was unnerving. Non-baseball fans probably don't realize the pitching mound is 10 inches higher than the batter's box. So that makes a 6-4 pitcher like Belinksy seem 7-foot-2. He'll essentially pour his fastballs downhill, firing rock-hard baseballs that could break wrists and forearms or give a concussion. That was one of the reasons I was such a poor hitter. I never came to terms with, frankly, my fear of those fastballs crashing into my head or arm.

I watched Belinksy warming up and knew I'd have no chance. As I lay on the cool outfield grass stretching, Rizzo and Hooper came by.

"So," Hooper said, "have you heard from your favorite CEO?"

"You mean our beloved Dear Leader?" I said. "He just texted me. Said he's going to come by the game. He'd love to meet you fellas."

"You know, for a guy who got all those 'F's' in school, you're kind of funny," Rizzo said.

Hooper and Rizzo were now on the grass, stretching out their hamstrings. For all the world we looked, I suppose, like three typical aging rec baseball players trying to get loose before a Sunday afternoon game.

But we weren't talking about the game or the NFL playoffs or going to Hooters. They quickly moved to the topic I didn't want to discuss – the missing Grabmore CEO.

"Before we kick your team's ass, no offense, Agent Rizzo and I were wondering, seriously, if you've heard anything," Hooper asked. "Or know anything."

"Nope," I said by way of explanation. "Want me to text him?" They ignored that.

"You want to know what I think?" Rizzo asked.

"Sure, Agent Rizzo, what do you think?" I asked.

"I think somebody kidnapped your CEO," he said.

"I heard there hasn't been a ransom note," I said. "You're the FBI agent but I thought ransom notes usually go hand-in-hand with kidnappings."

"Or maybe whoever snatched O'Riley just killed him," Rizzo said. "What do you think of that, F. Scott?"

"If that's the case just about everybody who works for Grabmore is a suspect," I said.

"Not everybody," Rizzo said. "Most of them have rock-solid alibies because they were working in Portland or Buffalo or

Poughkeepsie. Or someplace. It would be easy to narrow it down to Tropical-Times employees and whatever Grabmore employees might be here on vacation."

"That's interesting," I said. "There's another option."

"Oh, and what might that be?' Hooper said.

"Maybe O'Riley is on some spiritual quest, a journey of the soul and mind to re-think the way he lives, a Godly re-thinking of life's purpose and meaning," I said. "A re-connecting with some metaphysical desire to bond with mother Earth and do good for all mankind."

Rizzo and Hooper both thought that was hilarious and rolled over on the grass laughing.

"Good luck, Bond," Hooper said after regaining his composure. "You're going to need it."

"You mean in the game?" I said.

"Well, that too," Hooper said.

Oh, yes, the game. I think I'd just like to gloss over that, if you don't mind but, briefly, Bartley's beat my team, Babykin's 9-1. Belinksy started and pitched six innings, allowing a couple of hits and a run. Rizzo was 2-for-4 with a double and a line-drive single just beyond my diving reach. I struck out three times, as expected. But played a solid shortstop. Or else we might have lost 11-1.

When the game ended, both teams lined up for the traditional post-game hand shakes. Hooper asked if I was going to Hooters for lemonade. I said I was kind of tired and thought I'd skip the traditional post-game activities. He shrugged and said, "I'm sure we'll talk again soon."

I grabbed my glove and threw it in my equipment bag. Took off my spikes and put on my sneakers and walked back to the car for the long drive south, back to Chokoloskee. I drove back in my uniform.

It was time to speed up the CEO return timetable. We couldn't risk holding onto O'Riley any longer. We'd have to make Monday the big day, the day we returned Chesty to the Never Enough.

We would discuss it when I got back to the big house in Chokoloskee. The drive back to Chokolosee seemed to take longer than the drive to Fort Myers. I drove and drove and each mile seemed to take an hour.

Eventually, I made it to the big house in that little town at the end of the road, down where Florida's earth dissolves into a watery mangrove maze.

Nigel was on the front porch reading The Grapes of Wrath when I pulled in the driveway. He put it down when I walked up the steps.

"Well, how'd you do?" he asked.

"About as I expected," I said.

"That bad?" he said.

"Yep," I said. "How's the book?"

Nigel placed a bookmark about midway in the book and said, "Steinbeck's prose is something. Majestic, powerful, regal yet simple and straightforward. He makes you care about the whole Joad family."

I nodded and asked him if he thought O'Riley had ever read The Grapes of Wrath.

Nigel chuckled and said, "That's a good one, Scott."

"What's everybody else doing?" I asked.

"This and that," Nigel said. "O'Riley's in his room. Ahmad went for a walk. Sal and Monique are watching football. Troxie worked a later lunch shift and should be by soon. Anything new?"

"This is new. I met an FBI agent. At the field. He's a new player on the team we faced. He had some questions. So did Hooper. We can't wait any longer. They may show up here any day. We can't hang on to the Butterscotch Kid any longer. We got to get him back tomorrow."

Nigel just nodded.

"Will O'Riley turn us in?" he asked.

"I think we've made it plain what will happen if he does," I said.

"I think we need one more reminder this evening," Nigel said. "Maybe Sal can give him a not-so-subtle reminder."

We walked in the living room and Sal hit the remote's mute button.

"How'd it go," the big guy asked.

219

"About as expected," I said.

"That bad?"

"Yep."

"Get any hits?"

"Nope."

For some reason, that interchange seemed awfully familiar.

"Something's up, right?" Sal asked.

"Yep," I said again. "We got to get this wrapped up tomorrow. I met an FBI agent at the field. It doesn't take Sherlock Holmes to find out I got a big house in Chokoloskee, one big enough to hide O'Riley. If they really think I'm part of something they'll come snooping around soon. Real soon. And I think they think I'm involved. And that means you and everybody else could be here when they come calling. If you're home and not here, the neighbors will have seen you all."

"I hear you," Sal said.

"I think O'Riley needs to hear from you again, hear you talk about witness protection and your friends," I said.

The big guy nodded and asked, "Now comes the important question: What's for dinner."

Nigel said Troxie was bringing dinner by.

"She is?" Sal asked.

"That's what she said." Nigel said. "When she got off work she went back to her trailer and placed a to go order at the Rod and Gun Club. That place is pretty pricy. She said she was placing three orders of conch fritters and three of gator nuggets as appetizers and then six entrees – three pasta dishes and three steak dinners. Plus six slices of key lime pie."

"Who's gonna pay for all that?" Sal asked.

"Troxie said it was her treat," Nigel said.

"That's too much," I said. "It's got be to be $200 or $300. Easy. Probably more. We'll all chip in. We'll even ask O'Riley to chip in. He hasn't paid for anything all week. He's got to have some money on him."

Sal walked over to the door to the CEO room and opened it.

"Hey, Chesty, we need some money," he said. "Like $200. Or $300."

O'Riley couldn't help himself and blurted out, "You guys got jobs. You're not getting a handout from me. I'm a job creator."

Sal was steaming now.

"Job creator? You're a job destroyer, you little weasel. By the way, we're not asking for a handout, you overfed twerp. It's for everybody's dinner. Including yours. You haven't paid for anything all week. You got to have some cash on you, right?"

"Well, ah," O'Riley said, starting to tremble again.

"Do you, Butterscotch boy?" Sal asked again and stepped into the room and loomed over O'Riley.

"OK, you win," O'Riley said. "I make it a habit to keep ten one hundred dollar bills in my wallet at all times. For emergencies, you know."

He reached into his back pocket and pulled out the wallet.

"Here," he said, twitchy-like, clutching a couple of those bills in a shaky right hand, handing them to Sal.

"Now we're talkin'," Sal said. "Make it $300. There's the little matter of a tip. Now that we got that all settled, want to come in and watch the second half of the Cowboys-49ers game? Dinner will be delivered shortly."

About five minutes later, the mini-Cooper pulled into the driveway. The food was excellent. The game was a rout. The 49ers were up 31-7 as the third quarter wound down and Sal said, "Got one more thing to mention, Mr. O'Riley."

Interesting how he knew when to be polite and when to be dismissive. He had O'Riley's attention.

"You know how this is gonna work, right?" Sal asked.

O'Riley nodded.

"If you rat on us, I got some friends who will pay you a visit. I'll tell you their nicknames. Scarboil. Ratchet Face. Two-Ton. The Happy Assassin. Smilin' Jack Sprat. Nothing can protect you from them. There will be nowhere to hide. We clear on that?"

O'Riley nodded.

"OK, then, you're going back tomorrow," Monique said. "You got the press release. You type it up and send it where you're supposed to send it. Right?"

O'Riley nodded again.

"And everybody lived happily ever after," Troxie said with a grin. And then she took a bite of key lime pie and a sip of pinot grigio.

CHAPTER THIRTY-FIVE

Today would be a first for my career. Calling in sick when I wasn't actually sick. I left a message on sports editor Bo Lowe's office phone and told him I wasn't feeling well and wouldn't make it in today.

I hoped he remembered how to check voice mail. I'd follow up later and double check.

Calling in sick when you're not actually sick is against my code of honor and perhaps mentioned in the Grabmore employee handbook. I wonder if there's anything in that employee handbook, which no employee has ever actually read, that says it's against company police to kidnap the CEO. If not, maybe we can point that out in our defense.

"Your honor, we checked the employee handbook under kidnapping/CEO and couldn't find anything. So we figured it was OK."

Somehow, I don't think that would help our case if we're caught and eventually brought to trial.

The 2009 Chevrolet Suburban was gassed up and in the driveway of the big yellow house in Chokoloskee. Ahmad, Monique, Sal and Nigel were packed and ready for the ride to the airport.

I asked Nigel what he was bringing along to read. He said he'd likely finish The Grapes of Wrath in the terminal and then had a volume of Raymond Chandler that included two of my favorites, The Big Sleep and Farewell, My Lovely.

Sal unlocked the door to O'Riley's room and said with a nearly brotherly tone, "It's time to go home."

O'Riley didn't say anything, just walked over to the door. The toothbrush we bought him would be thrown in the trash later. DNA evidence of his presence would be found on the toothbrush if the cops came calling so I'd make sure it was destroyed. We'd do a deep cleaning soon on the room that was once home to a missing CEO.

I'm sure he has a toothbrush on his yacht so his dental hygiene wasn't a concern. He didn't have a bag to carry and walked through the kitchen and into the living room.

"Now what?" he said, looking at Sal.

"Now we get in the car," Sal said.

On the drive to Chokoloskee the previous week, we kept O'Riley on the floor so he couldn't see anything except angry and muscular Grabmore employees. On the drive back to Fort Myers, betting everything on our plan, we let him sit between Sal and Nigel in the second row.

We piled into the Suburban. Monique and Ahmad were in the third row of the SUV. The front-row passenger seat was empty for the moment. There was room left over for everybody's bags. I sat in the driver's seat, fired up the Suburban, pulled out of the driveway and turned north.

"Are we there yet?" O'Riley asked.

At first, we all thought that painfully stupid. Then we laughed. We realized it was another stab at humor by the Butterscotch Kid.

In less than 10 minutes we pulled into the Everglades City mobile home park where Troxie was staying. She saw us before we noticed her and came bounding over to the car as we rolled along slowly through the lane between trailers. I stopped and Troxie opened the passenger door, her blond hair tumbling from under the Rays baseball cap and a smile on her face.

"Boy, this is fun," Troxie said. "It's not every day I get to return a kidnapping victim. What now?"

"Now," I said, "we drive and tell stories. What about you, Chesty? Got any stories about the 2002 Miss Iceland pageant or fun and games at board meetings or yachting through the Aegean Sea?"

O'Riley was silent, the radio played a little James Taylor and the hum of the tires on S.R. 29 became hypnotic as we approached the scary intersection with U.S. 41. This spot with the flashing signal was unnerving. Traffic whistling east and west on the road barreled through at 60, 70, 80 mph and even faster.

I pulled to a stop. Looked each way two or three times and punched the gas to zip north through the intersection. We were across 41 and on our way to I-75 but still had another stretch of two-lane S.R. 29 to go.

Troxie turned around in her seat and looked at O'Riley for a second or two.

"What are you going to miss about being CEO?" she asked.

I glanced in the rear-view mirror and noticed O'Riley take a slug of Zephryhills bottled water.

"You know," he said, "this might be the best thing ever to happen to me. Really. Nigel let me borrow his copy of my great-grandfather's book. I've been reading that when I haven't been watching the Kardashians or Dancing with the Stars.

"The thought of going back to corporate headquarters permanently makes me queasy. Now that I've had time to think about things I realize what awful people I've surrounded myself with. Maybe that's part of the reason I was going to Iceland all the time. Well, plus those Icelandic girls are real pretty."

"What about Irish girls?" Nigel said.

"Oh, they're right up there, too," O'Riley said.

Ahmad asked, "Have you ever met any Yemeni girls?"

"I'm surrounded by pigs," Troxie said.

I think she was kidding but didn't have the guts to ask if she was serious. I wisely stayed quiet and didn't ask about the attractiveness of girls in Lapland.

From the back seat Ahmad asked, "Why did you promote those people?"

He didn't mean young women from Iceland, Lapland or Ireland. He meant the corporate officers who handled most of Grabmore's day-to-day activities.

"I don't know," O'Riley said. "I was advised to. They begged me to promote them. They said I was a genius and the best-looking CEO in America. So I promoted them."

I glanced in the mirror again and could see him sort of shrug his shoulders.

"I don't know," he said.

We rode in silence for a few miles and came to the interchange with I-75 and turned west toward Naples. It was fearless Troxie who asked the next question.

"How much money have you made?"

Another shrug.

"I got financial people who handle that," O'Riley said. "I'm not sure. A couple hundred million, I suppose. Maybe a little more."

Sal whistled.

"We're talkin' Tony Soprano money here," he said.

"But I didn't kill anybody," O'Riley said.

Well, we had to give him that. And we weren't going to kill him, either.

Soon we came to the big bend in I-75 where it turns north. If one stayed on 75 long enough it would take you to the Canadian border. We were going only as far as the Southwest Florida International Airport, which is between Fort Myers and Naples. It was a quiet ride for the most part until Troxie turned around in her seat and asked if everybody had fun on vacation.

"Of all the times I've been kidnapped, this was the best," O'Riley said.

Some latent comedic tendencies were percolating out of the guy and forcing us to almost sort of like him.

"That's a good one, Chesty," Troxie said. "How's your shuffleboard game coming along?"

"A lot better than it has been for a long time," he said. "You know, running a shuffleboard league sounds like fun. It will be good getting away from Carlotta Gutman and Milo Heller, that's for sure."

"Who?" Troxie asked.

"Oh, Gutman is the company president and Heller is in charge of financial matters," O'Riley said. "Meanest people I've ever met."

"I guess you won't hire them to help run the shuffleboard league," Troxie said.

"I wouldn't hire them to work for the Mafia," he said. "Oh, sorry, Sal. No offense."

"None taken," Sal said.

We crossed county lines, going from Collier to Lee. We were getting close to the airport. Troxie turned around again.

"It's been cool meeting everybody," she said, her voice cracking slightly. "I hope you all come back here sometime to see me play shuffleboard."

From the back I heard Monique say, "Can you get me a deal on a tang and some biscuits?"

"I'll see what I can do," Troxie said.

"What about an official Troxie Trosky set?" Monique said.

"I'll see," Troxie said with a slight chuckle.

We were coming up on the airport exit. Soon, my pals would be going home and resuming their lives.

Sal would go back to delivering the Panama City Globe to retirees in that Florida Panhandle community. Monique would go back to those Canadian forests and working in a lumber mill. Nigel would resume covering boxing and soccer for the Bergen County Bugle, where Ahmad worked in the pressroom.

Spring training would start soon and I'd be busy covering the Red Sox and Twins.

Troxie? I'm not sure what her plans were. Back to working in a surf shop near St. Pete or continue waiting on table in Everglades City. One of those two, I guess.

Other things had to be taken care of first. I turned into the airport entrance and began the short drive to the terminal. When I dropped off my four colleagues would O'Riley make a run for the nearest security guard? We'd find out. I pulled up to the curb and my four fellow Grabmore employees climbed out. Troxie got out as well.

She gave each of them a hug and I watched as they wheeled their bags through the doors and into the terminal. Troxie climbed back in. O'Riley stayed where he was and asked, "OK, now what?"

"Well, I said, we got one more stop before we drop you off," I said.

"And what is that?" he asked.

"It's a surprise," I said.

We drove a good 20 minutes and were well into Fort Myers when I pulled up to a fast-food restaurant.

"What's this?" O'Riley said.

"It's called Cheeburger Cheeburger," I said. "A place where your employees can afford to eat. Plus, it has something else."

Just then I pulled up to a box and a voice crackling with static came on asking how he may be of help.

"Yes," I said. "Three butterscotch milkshakes, please."

We pulled up to the next window. I paid for the shakes and handed one back to O'Riley.

"Yum," he said. "Thanks."

"Hey, not bad," Troxie said. "Wonder how many calories in one of these."

"It's probably better not to know," I said.

She nodded and we pulled out of the parking lot and began the short drive up McGregor Boulevard to where we snatched O'Riley the week before.

"Hard to believe it's only been a week," O'Riley said. "Seems much longer."

I could hear him slurping his butterscotch milkshake through a straw.

"Well, you'll be back at your yacht in a few minutes," I said. "I hope you remember what Sal said. What Sal said about his friends with all those scary nicknames."

"You mean like Smilin' Jack Sprat?" O'Riley asked.

I didn't say anything. We were just about downtown. I drove under the U.S. 41 overpass and turned left toward Centennial Park, where I found a place to park on Edwards Drive.

"Well, Mr. O'Riley," I said, turning formal and polite toward him, "this is it. This is your stop."

He stepped out of the Suburban. Troxie got out as well and gave him a tentative hug. He clutched his Cheeburger Cheeburger butterscotch milkshake in his right hand, stepped up on the sidewalk, gave me a small wave with the shake and walked away, toward his yacht.

The last I saw of him that day was his waddling backside as he strolled through the park toward the Never Enough. And then what? Would he do as we directed or immediately call the cops? We'd find out.

For now, Troxie and I were still free.

We were also exhausted. I pulled out of the parking spot there in downtown Fort Myers, within sight of the Caloosahatchee River, and began the long drive back to Chokoloskee.

First, though, I told Troxie, "I need some caffeine." We drove a couple of blocks and parked again and went back in the downtown Starbucks, the one next to the federal courthouse, the one where we might be tried for kidnapping, the one where Hooper and I discussed the case.

We each ordered an espresso for the road. A cappuccino for Troxie and one of my skinny, no-whip mochas for me. We walked around downtown for a few minutes.

The drinks and the walking revived us. We climbed back in the Suburban and made the big push back to Chokoloskee.

We rode in silence. Not even Troxie had the energy for chitchat. There would be no shuffleboard this evening. I dropped her off in Everglades City and drove on to the big empty yellow house in Chokoloskee, arriving a few minutes later.

I made a turkey sandwich on pumpernickel, gobbled that down, guzzled some cranberry juice out of the bottle and then collapsed on the living room sofa. That was about 7 p.m. I awoke about 5 a.m.

It was a new day. What would it bring? Agent Rizzo and his FBI colleagues, perhaps? We would see. I opened up my laptop to see if anything was on the Tropical-Times website, tsquared.com, about Chesterfield Ebenezer O'Riley IV.

CHAPTER THIRTY-SIX

I woke up on the couch in the pre-dawn dark. The napkin with the detritus of the previous night's turkey sandwich and the cranberry juice bottle were still on the coffee table.

It was cool in the house and I still wore the clothes from the previous day, the grey cargo shorts, the white button-down long sleeve shirt and little white socks. I had taken off my Asics running shoes before conking out there on the couch in the Chokoloskee house.

I sat up, rubbed the sleep out of my eyes, grabbed the napkin and cranberry juice bottle, went to the kitchen and pulled out a bottle of Tropicana orange juice and took a swig. Bachelors do that all the time. Just swig out of bottles. Why use a glass? At some point you might want to clean the glass and that just means more work. Drink from the bottle and you have fewer glasses to wash. Can anybody argue with that logic? So I'm going to continue drinking straight from the juice bottles and spend less time cleaning.

Of greater importance to the story I'm recounting here is that at the moment I wasn't in jail as I tipped the bottle back and guzzled. That's a good sign. No swarm of heavily-armed local, state and federal officers was descending on the house by sea, air and land. Another good sign.

I once went to the state prison in Raiford north of Gainesville on assignment many years ago. I was just visiting for the afternoon and knew I was leaving when the tour ended and I had concluded several interviews. Yet, despite the knowledge that I was a visitor, an overpowering sense of confinement enveloped me in that place. I was happy to leave.

I can't imagine being confined for so much as one night behind bars. Let alone the thousands of nights that kidnapping convictions certainly carried. I took another swig of the orange juice and turned on my MacBook to see if any news had been reported on O'Riley while I slept for 10 hours.

I sat there with the laptop on the coffee table and started with tsquared.com, the Tropical-Times website. Right there on the home page in black letters was the news: "O'Riley Safe!"

It was accompanied by a photo of O'Riley on his yacht, smiling and waving with his right hand, the little captain's cap perched on his head and a cold bottle of Starbucks Frappucino in his left hand.

I read the Ace Hamill piece, the first few paragraphs of which are re-printed here.

Chesterfield Ebenzer O'Riley IV, the missing CEO of Grabmore Publications, returned to Fort Myers on Monday, a week after he disappeared.

Authorities had feared foul play but O'Riley appeared healthy late Monday afternoon when he walked on the deck of his yacht, the Never Enough, which is moored in downtown Fort Myers.

O'Riley smiled and waved but declined to answer questions shouted at him by television reporters. The where and why of his disappearance aren't known. Where did he go and why? Was he abducted or did he go on his own?

The CEO of the Tropical-Times' parent company sent out a news release about his week away but it has not been released by Grabmore officials. Other media outlets have confirmed its authenticity and published its contents but not Grabmore.

"We need to know that the nonsense attributed to Mr. O'Riley in this alleged news release are actually his thoughts and words," said

Grabmore president Carlotta Gutman in a statement released through the company. "Meanwhile, until Mr. O'Riley's state of mind and his physical health are found to be sound I will be in charge of all Grabmore newspapers, television stations, advertising agencies, forests and lumber mills."

Fort Myers Police Chief Bubba Tippins said that no arrests have been made or are anticipated.

"As far as we know at this point no crime has been committed," Tippins said. "No crime. No arrests. Seems to make sense to me."

O'Riley was in town for his annual inspection of the Tropical-Times offices and to meet with employees when he vanished a week ago.

"We don't know yet if Mr. O'Riley will visit the office," Tropical-Times executive editor Nate Longstreet said. "The main thing is his health and safety. He appears healthy and Grabmore security officials told me the detail normally assigned to the Never Enough has been tripled, from three to nine. All nine, I'm told, are former police officers."

This was all good news, especially the part about the police chief saying no arrests are anticipated. I breathed easier and took my laptop with me from the living room to the kitchen. I poured a pile of Wheaties into a bowl, sprinkled some raisins on top and then added milk. The bottle of O.J. was next to the milk.

I was getting hungry, especially now that things were looking up for a long-term future that didn't include prison. My next online stop was the Grabmore blog, which was humming with activity. Blog master Brad Beeswax had posted the news release Nigel and I had written, the one in which O'Riley said he was retiring and leaving his 54 point-something percent of Grabmore stock to the Florida Gulf Coast University journalism department.

That's the press release that said a new day was coming for Grabmore and that O'Riley's future included a Florida shuffleboard league. The blog was bursting and aflame with about 300 comments posted. Here are three:

From whoseparanoid: "Don't beleeve this for a second. This press release is some sort of trick by O'Riley and Gutman and Heller. They're up to something and it stinks. Give all that stock to some college nobody outside of Florida ever heard of? Are you kidding me? O'Riley all of a sudden got a conscience? Never happen. He's been happy firing and furloughing people. This is some sort of test of employees. Anybody who sez anything nice about the press release will be punished somehow. Mark my words."

From noozdude: "I don't know. I read that news release twice. It doesn't reek of the usual Orwellian Grabmore language. It sounds like it could have been written by human beings and not produced chemically through robotic corporate weasels. Whoever wrote the release knows a little bit about writing. Not a lot. A little. And I emphasize a little. The usual Grabmore obfuscating mumbo-jumbo isn't there. I didn't find one word of Grabspeak in the whole thing. O'Riley had to have help. He couldn't have written this by himself.

"There's got to be a puppet master behind the scenes pulling O'Riley's strings. But who? And why? What's next?"

From ukiddingme: Let me get this straight: One of the biggest sleazebags in the history of corporate journalism is going to give up all the millions he pockets every year to run a shuffleboard league in Florida? Shuffleboard? Why would he do that? And he's going to donate more than half of Grabmore stock to some Podunk school nobody heard of north of where alligators roam golf courses? I don't see it. There's some sort of scam being run here. Not by O'Riley. He's not smart enough. We'll figure this out at some point."

That was the general tenor of blog comments the morning after O'Riley's return.

My next online stop was to see what media writer David Farr of The New York Times had written. He had a refreshing angle. Here was his take:

By DAVID FARR

His name is Honus Roberto Schwartz and his title is journalism professor at a place called Florida Gulf Coast University.

Mr. Schwartz said his parents, lifelong fans of the Pittsburgh Pirates baseball team, named him for the two greatest players in the history of the team – Honus Wagner and Roberto Clemente. His first two initials are H.R., as in Home Run.

On Monday, Mr. Schwartz learned his department would be endowed with the most generous grant ever bestowed on an American journalism school when outgoing Grabmore CEO Chesterfield O'Riley IV announced he would award nearly 55 percent of company stock to the school's program.

That's a tape measure grand slam by any measure. A Home Run with a capital H and capital R.

"I'm flabbergasted," Mr. Schwartz said. "At first I thought it was a prank pulled by my some of my students. Then Mr. O'Riley said if you don't believe me, come by my yacht. I was just grading papers at the time so I said sure, I'll come by your yacht."

Mr. O'Riley's 99-foot yacht, the Never Enough, is currently moored in Fort Myers, a short drive from the FGCU campus.

"I figured it would be a waste of time," Mr. Schwartz said. "But it was a beautiful afternoon and if there was no yacht or CEO on the river, I'd at least go for a walk along the riverfront before going home to finish grading papers."

FGCU is a young school and its journalism program is quite small. It will soon grow by orders of magnitude that were unimaginable just two days ago.

The impact on Grabmore's more than 90 newspapers isn't yet known.

"Don't bother me," Grabmore president Carlotta Gutman snapped when reached by a reporter. "Don't bother me with trifles and trivia."

Ms. Gutman announced in a Grabmore news release she plans to run the company until the legality and what she characterized as dubious psychological underpinning of the announcement is determined. In that news release she also said she doubted the authenticity of the quotes attributed to Mr. O'Riley.

That comment was relayed to O'Riley by reporters on the dock in Fort Myers.

"I say what I mean and mean what I say," O'Riley shouted to reporters from his yacht Monday evening. "Don't listen to Gutman!"

That has been the only comment from the soon to be former CEO.

Meanwhile, Mr. Schwartz, who finished grading papers late last night, plans to meet soon with the university president and other department leaders to discuss the astonishing bequest that has fallen into their laps.

They plan to invite Mr. O'Riley to the school for a tour and to meet instructors and students.

That's where I stopped reading. It's also where I finished my Wheaties. It was time for one more long drive to Fort Myers, back to The Hovel, my very modest home. There I planned to pop in, shower, don slacks and a decent shirt and report to the Tropical-Times office.

I called in sick the day before. It was time to get back to work and get a pulse of how things were going now that O'Riley was back in Fort Myers.

CHAPTER THIRTY-SEVEN

I thought about driving by the yacht club on the way to the Tropical-Times but decided why risk it. Isn't there some old saying about criminals returning to the scene of the crime?

I would return later in the day but under different circumstances, startlingly different circumstances. We'll get to that shortly. On this morning, though, the day after O'Riley was returned to his yacht, I headed straight to the office and hoped to resume my pre-kidnapping life as a sportswriter, settling into the routines of covering games, interviewing ballplayers and dodging the sports editor and everybody else in management.

The place looked the same but somehow felt different. Oh, the relentless corporate mendacity and backstabbing hadn't disappeared overnight. There was no chance of all that dissipating so swiftly.

One can't change the direction of oil tankers or aircraft carriers like racecars. It takes time. Maybe it was my experience of the past week that had changed me. Grabmore, I'm sure, was the same as it ever was.

Curiosity compelled me to detour by Mabel Borgia's desk in the online department to see if she still had a jar on her desk asking for donations to save our Dear Leader. It was still there but the hand-scrawled message taped to it was different. Instead of asking for money for a ransom fund she was now asking money for counseling for O'Riley. Counseling? I had to ask Mabel about this.

"Well, Bond, did you read that manifesto O'Riley was forced to sign?" she asked. "Do you really think our Dear Leader would leave us in times like this to run a Foosball League?"

"Shuffleboard," I said.

"Whatever," she snapped. "That's not the point. Shuffleboard. Foosball. Skeeball. Twister. Whiffle Ball. How can we go on as Grabmore without Mr. O'Riley, our beloved leader?"

"Well, you got me there," I said. "We'll just have to muddle through somehow."

I noticed the pile of money had grown significantly since the last time I checked. The Save O'Riley jar held $20.06 last week. The Get Counseling for O'Riley fund now had, I could see, two twenty-dollar bills and more change. I asked Mabel what the pot was up to now.

"Well, I put in the $40 and some other people put in, let me, see," Mabel said, shuffling through the change. "It looks like 11 cents. So we're up to $40.11. What is wrong with people around here? Don't they care about our Dear Leader? I'll never understand this place and people like you."

I shrugged and said, "It's a mystery. I'm a mystery. Good luck with the fundraising."

As usual, I walked away as swiftly as my size 11 sneakers could carry me away from Mabel. Tess, my sports department confidante, was beaming when I approached my desk.

"What the hell?" she whispered. "What the hell did you guys do to O'Riley? Brainwash him? Torture him?"

"It's a long story," I said. "I'll tell you sometime. But not in the office."

I sat down at my desk, unpacked my laptop, fired it up to check emails and begin organizing research for my spring training preview story on the history of Florida spring training. Before I could get going on all of this, Longstreet came by my desk. I don't think I've ever spent more than five seconds chatting with him in all the years we had both been at the Tropical-Times. He asked me to come in his office. This was a first. What was going on?

"Close the door," he said, when I walked in.

So much for dodging management.

"I got an email from O'Riley," Longstreet said. "He wants to meet you."

I didn't have to feign surprise.

"Me? Why me?"

"That's what I want to know," Longstreet said. "Any ideas?"

"Maybe he's intrigued by my occasional use of onomatopoeia in some of my features," I said.

"Very funny," Longstreet said. "Any other bright ideas? Any more half-baked theories?"

"Nope," I said.

"Anyhow, O'Riley's coming by the office this afternoon to meet with employees," Longstreet said. "You're a last minute addition to the list. Along with the usual folks like Mabel and a few other hand-picked favorites."

"I'm honored," I said, lying as I never lied before.

"OK, get out of here," Longstreet said. "And don't mention onomatopoeia around O'Riley. He might think you're pronouncing his name wrong. And sure as hell don't use big words like that around Lowe, that moron."

"You know he's a moron?" I asked.

"Of course," Longstreet said. "You'd have to be a moron not to know he's moron."

"But how does he keep his job?" I asked.

"You know, I really don't know," Longstreet said.

"But couldn't you fire him?" I asked.

"No, for some reason, Lowe gets to keep his job," Longstreet said. "I'm not sure I understand why and how but my hands are tied. It's easier for me, frankly, being surrounded by morons like Lowe and suck-ups like Mabel."

I didn't know what to say to that and got up and told Longstreet I'd be around the office all day.

"Oh, by the way, I'm looking forward to meeting O'Riley," I said.

"Don't try being a suck-up, Bond. You're not cut out for that. That's Mabel's gift. She's great at it. Now, get out of here."

I was tempted to say gladly but thought better of it and walked back to my desk.

"What was that all about?" Tess asked.

"O'Riley wants to meet me," I said.

"But you've already met."

"I know that. You know that. But nobody else around here knows it. Except O'Riley.'

"What do you think he wants?"

I shrugged my shoulders and didn't say another word.

The morning crept along like rush-hour traffic in the middle of the tourist season. I sort of worked on my project. Sort of checked and responded to emails. Sort of checked the Grabmore blog.

But I couldn't keep my mind off the 1 p.m. meeting with the CEO. Should I run while I had the chance? Was he bringing the FBI along with him to say Bond is one of the people who kidnapped me? Why would he ever want to see me again?

So I waited and dawdled and dawdled more and would have doodled if I had the slightest whisper of artistic talent. I checked news and sports websites. Grabbed a turkey pita in the Tropical-Times lunchroom and wolfed that down at my desk while reading sports websites.

Finally, 1 p.m. arrived.

And so did O'Riley and his beefed up entourage. The meeting was upstairs in a conference room that featured a portrait of O'Riley and numerous photos from the Tropical-Times photographers. Nature. Sunsets. Sports. Those photos were reminders that good work is done at the paper despite the presence of the folks I was about to spend time with in that room.

I didn't want to be with them. They were the sorts if I saw them on a downtown sidewalk I'd cross the street to avoid. If I spotted them in a grocery store as I entered I'd leave and do my shopping later or someplace else.

These were the worst of the worst, the Grabmorons, the jargon-spouting weasels, the backstabbing opportunists, the shallow and the craven and the ambitious. Now, I had to sit through a meeting with them.

From marketing came Frank Seicht, a master of the meaningless phrase and scourge of many in the local business community. He spouted the empty Grabspeak lingo and always wanted to attach the Tropical-Times logo to every event and arena in the area without the paper paying for it.

"What the hell are you doing here," he asked when I walked in the door. "Who the hell invited you?"

"Ah, O'Riley," I said.

"I'm sure he has his reasons," Seicht said and turned away from me.

Next I spotted Vic Balboni from IT. He sported a suit and shiny shoes. He normally wore jeans and a T-shirt but whenever the corporate brass was in town he dressed for the occasion and never let a chance slip away to ingratiate himself.

When he spotted O'Riley in the hallway before the meeting began, he walked over and said, "Oh, Mr. O'Riley we were so worried about you. We didn't know what happened. Please don't leave the company. I don't know how we can continue without you."

O'Riley thanked him for his concern and turned back to chatting with Longstreet.

Mabel was already in the room and carrying flowers for O'Riley.

"Oh, sir," she said, actual curtseying to the CEO, "I was so worried when we didn't hear anything from you for so long. Please tell me some bad men made you sign that awful document and that you're not going to leave the company."

O'Riley said he appreciated the concern and backed away from Mabel.

Then in came Brunhilda Kravenwood, a sales rep and department head from the Cape Coral office. She epitomized the Grabmore sales culture, one that was all about always increasing profit margin and always setting impossibly high sales targets for the reps.

That way when it came time for their annual evaluations it could be pointed out they failed. Failed miserably. No pay raise for you. And they could be hustled out the door and replaced by a younger and prettier sales rep.

From the lifestyles department came Daniel (Don't Call Me Danny) Scheiss, sometime writer and sometime assistant editor. Nobody knew exactly what he did except write about one story a month, attend a few meetings and from time-to-time copy edit some stories.

But he was one of those fair-haired boys, even though he was bald. Another Grabmore mystery. But at least he wasn't a moron. He did fine work when he actually worked. The low and mid-level staffers such as Mabel and I were joined by the top Tropical-Times executives such as Longstreet, publisher Oscar Unger, production chief Bruno Zellsheimer and advertising manager Victoria Messersmith.

The meeting was scheduled for an hour, an hour I'm sure that would be the longest of my career. Even longer than sitting out rain delays at Little League playoff games and having to listen to parents who don't know anything about baseball complain about their son's coach, who had played collegiate and minor-league baseball.

I sat there, squirming, sweating and wondering. What would O'Riley say? Would Hooper, Rizzo and a gaggle of FBI agents follow him into the meeting room and haul me out?

O'Riley walked in by himself while two burly, sweaty Grabmore security goons lingered in the hall. O'Riley was wearing a charcoal grey, pinstriped bespoke suit, something that would likely cost the equivalent of a month's salary for me. He didn't look at me sitting there as large beads of perspiration popped up on my forehead.

"Good afternoon, folks," he said. "I'm sure you have questions. I'll try to answer them as best as I can."

"What's going to happen to us?" Mabel asked.

"I really don't know," O'Riley said.

"It can't really be true, can it, that you're going to run a Frisbee league?" she asked.

"Shuffleboard," he said.

"For real?" Mabel asked.

"For real," O'Riley said.

"I don't get it," Mabel said. "A lawn bowling league?"

"Shuffleboard," O'Riley patiently said.

Mabel looked stupefied and, blessedly, didn't have anything more to ask.

"I'm sure everybody has questions," O'Riley said. "I just felt I needed a change and the company needed a change. Grabmore is all I've known. It's been great for me, made me a millionaire. Heck, I was born a millionaire so I've just added millions. I got more than I could ever spend. Besides, I live in Buffalo. It gets cold up there.

"So I'm going to retire, sort of. I'm giving away my stock and will move to Florida. Questions. Anybody. What about you?"

He pointed at me and said, "What's your name and what do you do?"

"My name is Bond and I'm a sportswriter."

"Oh, right, you're the one I requested attend the meeting. I came across a couple of your stories on the Tropical-Times website and thought it would be refreshing to get a different viewpoint on the situation. What do you think?"

"Oh, change is good," I said, not looking directly at O'Riley. "Everybody needs change. It can be refreshing and liberating. And Florida isn't as cold as Buffalo. Or so I heard."

"Exactly," he said. "How do you think my leaving and the stock going to that college will affect you and the people in your department?"

"I don't know," I said, telling the truth. "Just heard about this so I don't know. I guess a lot depends on how the people at the college run their newsrooms."

O'Riley looked around the room and then the comments started flying. My colleagues were more interested in kissing up to O'Riley than in anything else. He was still CEO and had the power to affect their careers. I tuned it all out and just endured it all as the seconds dragged by.

Finally, it was nearly 2 p.m.

"I'm going home tomorrow, leaving on the corporate jet in the morning," O'Riley said. "You know, I've never invited low-level employees to my yacht. Maybe I'll invite somebody over for dinner."

Mabel nearly leapt out of her chair in anticipation. I glanced around the table and her fellow brown-nosing suck-ups were all but thrusting their arms in the air and shouting "Me! Me! Pick me!"

"What about you, Bond?" O'Riley said. "That is your name, isn't?"

I nodded.

"Well, I'm sure you got work to do but can you swing by around 6?" O'Riley asked. "I'll provide dinner. And drinks."

I nodded again. O'Riley turned around and walked out into the hall where the security goons escorted him out of the building. I walked back to sports and wondered what the hell the invitation was all about. Mabel was nonplussed, to say the least.

"After all I've done for this company, after the fund-raising for Mr. O'Riley, after kissing up to Longstreet, you get invited on the Never Enough?" Mabel said. "It's just so wrong. It's not fair."

I shrugged my shoulders and said, "I don't know what to tell you."

And I didn't. The afternoon appeared as if would drag out as slow as the morning. I went back downstairs and again pretended to work all afternoon, waiting for 6 o'clock so I could drive the mile or so to the yacht club. And dinner on the Never Enough with Chesterfield Ebenezer O'Riley IV.

CHAPTER THIRTY-EIGHT

I wasn't sure about the proper attire for dinner on a 99-foot yacht. I didn't own an ascot, monocle or one of those little captain's yachting caps and even if I did there wasn't time to drive home and change.

Instead, I drove straight from the office to the Royalty Supreme Yacht Club and found a parking spot on West First Street, about a quarter of a mile away. I was now officially on my own. Nigel and Ahmad were in New Jersey. Sal was way up in the Florida Panhandle. Monique was in Canada and Troxie was down in Everglades City.

No backup. No emotional support. Nobody to bounce ideas off of or the comforting physical presence of my pals in case things got rough. It was just me. And O'Riley. And who else?

Hooper of the FMPD and Rizzo of the FBI? A few Grabmore security goons? An Icelandic paramour or two? An Irish lass? Any young ladies from Lapland? I'd find out.

I didn't see any police cruisers or gaggle of federal agents wearing the windbreakers of various law enforcement agencies as I stepped out of the car. Would this be my last meal as a free man? That's assuming O'Riley would actually feed me when I stepped on the Never Enough.

I walked slowly along the sidewalk, glancing left and right, approached the yacht club's gate and told the security guard I had an appointment with Mr. O'Riley on the Never Enough. He let me in and directed me to the yacht. It was easy to spot. The Never Enough may have been the largest boat on the Caloosahatchee all winter.

O'Riley was on deck as I approached his slip.

"Permission to come aboard?" I asked, thinking that's what one is supposed to say when approaching a boat or yacht.

He seemed to groan, placed a hand to his forehead, then simply waved me ahead and I stepped on deck. The yacht towered another 20 or so feet above me with a deck or two. O'Riley came forward but didn't offer to shake hands.

"You know, I thought about turning you in," O'Riley said. "I thought about turning all of you in. I don't think Sal's so-called friends could find me and hurt me. I think he might have made them all up."

"Why didn't you?" I asked.

He didn't respond to that and waved me up a stairwell and we went into what I guess was the stateroom.

"See this furniture," he said, gesturing at beige sofas and recliners and a fancy coffee table. "This is Armani furniture. That coffee table is made out of mahogany and marble and probably costs more than your pathetic car."

I couldn't argue with that.

"See the floor?" he said, pointing down.

I looked down and the floor was hard to miss. It was right there below my feet.

"That's maple hardwood," O'Riley said. "This thing has six suites and an elevator. There's a Jacuzzi on the sundeck. Each suite has a flat screen TV. When we get in open water this baby can cruise at 40 knots. Impressed?"

I had to admit I was and simply said "Yep."

"So why haven't I called the cops and say that ridiculous news release you and Colin...." O'Riley said.

I had to interrupt and said, "You mean Nigel?"

"Whatever. I don't care what his name is. Or your name. I'm still thinking about turning all of you in and saying that news release was a hoax and I was forced to sign it by disgruntled employees."

"Why don't you?"

"Well, I'm just not ready. This may be a good way out of Grabmore for me. It's clean. It comes at the right time. I come across looking like a good guy for a change. I get tired of being hated all the time. And I need a change. Come on, let's go back to the galley."

We walked into the next room, which was a big kitchen, or galley, I guess they call it in the nautical world. It was all stainless steel, from the sink to the refrigerator nearly the size of my Camry to the stove.

It was also where I met three stunningly attractive young women. They weren't wearing any of the costumes of O'Riley legend. Not itsy-bitsy bikinis or French maid outfits or short shorts with tank tops.

They wore jeans and T-shirts. Two had blond hair and one was a redhead. O'Riley introduced me.

First there was Annika, who came from Iceland, where she won Miss Congeniality in a recent Miss Iceland pageant. She seemed very congenial, indeed, saying hello in English with a trace of an accent that I figured had to be Icelandic.

"Nice to meet you, sir," she said and we shook hands.

Then I was introduced to Brigida, who is from Lapland, which is basically northern Scandinavia. I asked her how she liked Florida.

"Oh, it's a lot warmer than Rovaniemi, that's for sure," Brigida said.

"Rova-a-what?" I asked.

"Rovaniemi, my hometown," Brigida said. "It's in northern Finland, just south of the Arctic Circle. Your winters here are warmer than our summers. I love it here but I miss my parents a little."

"Why did you come here?"

"Well, I met Chesterfield when he came to visit and he told me about his yacht and Florida and the beaches," Brigida said. "So, here I am. And I'm not going home again until the summer."

Annika and Brigida were the blonds. That left the red head, whose name I found out is Bonnie, which is a nice old-fashioned name. She told me she's from Dublin and left an abusive boyfriend when she met O'Riley in a pub.

"He hasn't hit me once," Bonnie said of O'Riley. "He doesn't even yell at me. Or ask me to do things I don't want to. That's a lot different than Malachy. He slapped me around and called me names and drank all the time. I mean Malachy."

Well, I had to give O'Riley that. He may be greedy and self-absorbed and not very bright but apparently he's not violent or abusive or an alcoholic lout.

"So you like it here?" I asked.

"Oh, very much," Bonnie said.

Annika was cooking something and it smelled really good. She had steaks smothered in onions going in a sizzling pan. Potatoes were roasting and asparagus was in a pot.

A large salad bowl contained what appeared to be a heaping pile of arugula. Somebody was going to have a fine dinner.

O'Riley had been quiet while I chatted with his girl friends.

"Bond, we're going to go up top to chat," he said. "Annika, Brigida and Bonnie will stay down here to eat. How's that sound?"

"It sounds fine," I said.

I would have preferred dining with the girls but O'Riley and I had serious business to discuss.

We helped ourselves to slabs of steak, helpings of potatoes, some asparagus and a salad and went outside for a chat as night began falling upon the river. The sun was settling over Cape Coral as we sat on the Never Enough's top deck. It was another splendid Florida winter evening, the temperature dipping into the upper 60s and the lights of North Fort Myers twinkling across the way.

He didn't offer me wine but did have bottles of Poland water in a bucket on the table so I took one of those.

"Why does everybody hate me so much?" O'Riley asked.

"How can you not know that?" I said. "Look around you. You got this yacht and all that money and you fire people and lay people off and keep getting richer while they get poorer. People like me and Sal and Nigel. How could people not hate you? No offense."

I felt bad about that jab but it was true.

"But it's not personal," O'Riley said. "I don't know any of the people we lay off or furlough."

"Don't forget fire," I pointed out.

"OK," he said. "And people we fire. I just do what's recommended. Gutman and Heller tell me we need to lay off 250 people this quarter so we lay off 250 people this quarter. If they tell me we need to make all employees take a week of unpaid leave next quarter, that's what we do."

I changed the topic for a moment.

"You know, this steak is really good," I said.

"Oh, thanks, Annika has become my personal chef," he said of the young woman from Iceland.

"That's another reason a lot of people hate you – your girlfriends," I said. "Women hate you because they think you're a sexist pig taking advantage of your girls. Ah, no offense. And guys who have daughters or sisters hope you don't entice one of their daughters or sisters onto to the Never Enough. Or else the guys are jealous and hate you because you have prettier girlfriends and more of them than they do."

O'Riley guzzled some of the Poland spring water.

"Like I said, I need a break. It's tiring having people hate you. It's tiring worrying about Gutman and Heller stabbing me in the back. I need out. So that's, I guess, why I didn't call the FBI. What you guys did was wrong. It was scary. I thought you were going to kill me."

He paused and took a deep breath.

"I'm sorry," I said. "We were just fed up with everything. From the layoffs and furloughs and people like Gutman and Heller running the company and promoting people almost as mean as they are. Maybe it will all turn out OK. Maybe the company will be a better place and you can move on to a less stressful life. You got all the money you'll ever need. And then some."

"That's why you're here eating my steak and drinking my water and sitting on my yacht," O'Riley said. "And not locked up waiting trial."

"You know, we could have easily killed you and gotten away with it. But we didn't. We treated you well. Plenty of food and wine and even a butterscotch milkshake."

"Well, yeah, thanks for the milkshake. It was good but not as good as the ones on the QE2."

We ate in silence for a few minutes, polishing off our dinners and could hear the low hum of conversation from below where Annika, Brigida and Bonnie were eating. We couldn't make out what they were saying.

"So, what's next?" I asked.

"Next? I'm flying back to Buffalo in the morning. The girls will stay here on the yacht. Don't expect they're going to invite you back. And when I get to Buffalo, I'll start arranging things for the transition.

"We need to meet with people from the university. I need to get with my investment adviser to get everything in order so that when I leave I get all the money due me."

Here, I stayed quiet. Money due him? All that bonus money for firing people and laying them off and ordering furloughs? It could be tens of millions of dollars. I was tempted to say something but instead stayed quiet. Maybe I should have spoke up for the people who were dismissed from the company with nothing or a few hundred or a few thousand in severance packages. I let it go.

"Then I want to find a place to live in St. Pete. I've been there before, to the yacht club. Great place, that yacht club. It's been around for more than a century. Did you know that?"

I nodded and O'Riley continued talking.

"I went online and found condos right downtown near the yacht club that I could get for maybe $1.5 million. Seems like a good deal."

That $1.5 million is just bit more than the price I paid for my 1,100-square foot condo that I call The Hovel. Like $1.45 million more. O'Riley seemed excited about leaving Grabmore and moving and even shuffleboard.

"You know, the condo I was looking at is real close to the shuffleboard club there. It's almost perfect. Overlooks the yacht club and maybe a half a mile or so from the shuffleboard courts. And there's a Starbucks right next door."

"Well, congratulations," I said.

"When do you think we should start organizing the shuffleboard league and tournaments?" he asked

"We?" I said, astonished. "We?"

"How would you like to go to work for the shuffleboard league? You could be some sort of marketing or public relations or promotions person. Or all three. "

At that point you could have knocked me over with a fistful of arugula.

"How much do you make working for the Tropical-Times?"

"Well, ah, $48,000."

"A month?"

"No, a year."

"Really? How do you live on that?"

"Hell, I make more than a lot of employees. Didn't you ever look into that? Weren't you ever curious what employees make?"

"No, Milo Heller as CFO said he would take of all those details."

"Oh."

This company was a bigger mess than I ever realized and I always thought it was messier than my condo.

"So, what do you think?"

"Well, I really like writing sports."

"OK, what about if we pay you, say, $65,000?"

"What about $75,000?"

"How about $70,000?"

"OK, it's a deal if you promise not to turn me is in for kidnapping you."

O'Riley went along with that, cementing the agreement. We talked about how soon we should start organizing the Florida International Shuffleboard League. We decided to start in April, after spring training and after O'Riley left Grabmore and after the professors started running the company.

We carried our plates back into the galley and O'Riley told the girls they'd be sailing soon for St. Petersburg.

"Russia?" Brigida asked, looking astonished.

"No, the St. Petersburg here in Florida not the one in Russia," I said. "Florida is a weird place. There's a big city here on the west coast named after a city in Russia and near here there are cities named after Italian cities, Venice and Naples.

"You're now in Lee County, which is named after one of the biggest traitors in American history, the general who led the South during the Civil War. There's a town up the coast called Dunedin that is named after a city in Scotland. Well, you get the idea."

The girls nodded.

Speaking of women. …I had a lot to tell Troxie. I promised her I would call. Assuming, of course, I wasn't in jail.

If I was in jail and allowed one call it would be to a lawyer, not to a .38-toting, karate black belt, semi-employed waitress and shuffleboard wizard. As I was leaving, O'Riley shook my hand. I waved goodbye to Annika, Brigida and Bonnie, walked back to my Camry parked on West First Street and drove home to The Hovel.

CHAPTER THIRTY-NINE

I drove in a bit of a daze. Well, I'm almost always in a bit of a daze but even more so on this evening. Good thing I didn't drink anything stronger than that Poland spring water.

Our hare-brained scheme had apparently worked. I was still free. O'Riley was leaving Grabmore and handing his stock over to journalism professors and not soulless, bean-counting, jargon-spouting corporate bureaucrats. I still had a job. And my freedom. Nearly as encouraging, I recalled I had a bottle of malbec at The Hovel.

All was right with the world. I had to get the word to my co-conspirators and let them breath easier. Boy, I hate that word co-conspirators but it applies. We conspired. And we were co.

I reached The Hovel, walked inside, turned on a light, went to the kitchen, grabbed that bottle of malbec, opened it, poured a glass, stepped on the lanai, sat down in a 20-year-old wicker chair, took off my grey Asics sneakers, sipped a bit of malbec and then took a deep, very deep breath.

Whew!

My first call was to Troxie. We had all agreed that we would not discuss on the phone what we had done. You never knew who might be listening.

When we talked we didn't use O'Riley's name or the word kidnap or the abbreviation CEO. To anybody out there it might be a casual conversation not a reason for exhalation of breath and celebration.

"How's the shuffleboard game?" I asked.

"It's coming along nicely," Troxie said. "I think I'm primed for some tournaments. Never played better."

"I'm sure you could knock those biscuits into those kitchens," I said. "Kitchens on every court in the state. Or country or cruise ship."

That was our code. That meant things were going well and that we appeared to be home free and it was time for her to spread the news to Sal, Nigel, Ahmad and Monique. Tell them it appeared we got away with it.

If, on the other hand, I had said, "Don't let anybody knock your biscuits into the kitchen" the message would have been different. That meant the cops were closing in and that she should run, run fast and run far, run farther away than St. Petersburg, run as fast as her Troxie legs could carry her and as far they could carry her.

If she didn't get a call at all from me by 10 p.m. it would signify I was in jail and that it was time to sprint out her front door and to the nearest dock, steal a cigarette boat and get away at a very high rate of speed.

"So, how are things in Everglades City?" I asked, another seemingly innocuous question.

And it was just that. We had no more code words or phrases. No magic decoder rings or drop boxes in the Everglades where we had deposited microfilm. Troxie said things were well but she was ready to go home to St. Pete and prepare for a big shuffleboard tournament. I wished her well and promised I'd keep up with her shuffleboard career.

I walked in the living room and TCM was carrying Casablanca. I never miss a chance to watch it again and that's what I did. For a while. Until I fell asleep on the couch with an ounce or two of malbec left in the glass, sitting there on the coffee table.

I woke up in time to hear Claude Rains as Capt. Renault say, "Major Strasser has been shot. Round up the usual suspects."

Nice timing there. Nobody in our little band had been shot and we weren't being rounded up.

And no matter what happened after this, all of us, Troxie and Monique, Sal and Ahmad and Nigel and even, I suppose O'Riley, can say "We'll always have Chokoloskee."

The next morning I felt better than I had in years. I knew my Grabmore career had only a few weeks remaining. I believed Grabmore would begin becoming a saner and more compassionate place so if I stayed it wouldn't remain the same suffocating place it had been for decades and throughout my career.

I now knew I could put up with anything and anybody, even Mabel Borgia, the most insufferable sycophant I had even encountered. I walked in the office the morning after my dinner with O'Riley with a figurative bounce in my step. There are never literal bounces in my steps. My walking gait is more a lurching, un-even, disjointed strolling style where the legs and arms never seem to be in synch. So much for bouncing and bounding. And definitely not sashaying. Not that there's anything wrong with that but it's not my style.

Yet again, I detoured by Mabel's desk in the online department. The jar where she collected money initially for O'Riley's ransom and then for counseling was empty. Mabel was nowhere in sight.

I asked Stephanie Winchester, one of the put-upon, bullied, abused, over-worked and under-paid members of the online staff, where her boss was on this fine morning.

"She called in sick," Stephanie said.

"Really?" I said. "She never calls in sick."

"Well, she called in sick today. I talked to her. She sounded fine. Except she seemed to be weeping."

"Did she give a reason for calling in sick?"

"She said she had a touch of melancholia and distemper," Stephanie said.

"That's an odd combination, But I'm not a doctor. Just a sportswriter. Still, it seems she might be making medical history with that combination. Enjoy your day, Stephanie. If you need anybody to call you names or make fun of you or suck up to Longstreet, let me know and I'll swing by and call you some names or mock you or whatever it is you're accustomed to here. Just so the day doesn't seem too unusual for you."

Stephanie found that amusing, smiled and said, "If we need anybody to call us names you'll be the first person we call."

I asked if Mabel said anything else when she called

"All I could make out was shuffleboard, shuffleboard, shuffleboard," Stephanie said. "She just kept repeating that word. What do you think it means?"

"Maybe she's got a new hobby. But I think it had to do with O'Riley starting a shuffleboard league."

"Oh yeah, I forgot about that," Stephanie said.

I congratulated Stephanie on her Mabel-free day and lurched over to sports. Tess was already there working on her boating column.

"Well, how was dinner?" she asked.

"The steak tar-tar was a trifle tough, the caviar was second-rate and bland but the champagne was delightful," I said.

"I mean really"

"Actually, pretty damn good. Real food. Food I recognized. And you ought to write about that yacht for your boating column."

"I've tried. Gone through corporate and up the chain of command but they've always denied me access to the damn thing."

"Figures. Maybe things will change in the future."

Maybe.

I think things will change. How much? We'll find out. Maybe things will get worse. Maybe Mabel will be promoted to publisher and the new regime will continue downsizing and gutting the operation and crushing the souls and spirits of employees. But I don't think so.

In a way, I kind of wished I hadn't agreed to the shuffleboard league job offer. Is there a future in that?

Sticking around the Tropical-Times and seeing it evolve seemed intriguing. I was reminded of something that was said about another newspaper chain. It was said that this other chain could buy a bad paper and make it mediocre or buy a good one and make it mediocre. Sounds a lot like Grabmore.

But I wouldn't stay. I was leaving for a new adventure and maybe a new career.

The Tropical-Times would have to get along without me. And Grabmore would have to get along without Chesterfield Ebenezer O'Riley IV.

EPILOGUE: PART ONE

It's been a year now since the events I've described in this account changed so much for so many people.

O'Riley is gone from Grabmore and running the Florida International Shuffleboard League and I'm his Public Relations Wizard. That's my official title. Really. It says so right there on my business card, the one with the crossed shuffleboard tangs and photo of a butterscotch milkshake. I didn't want any Grabmore mumbo-jumbo title such as Executive Assistant In Charge of Public/Corporate Communications And Promotional Fluffery Double Speak.

Pubic Relations Wizard. That's it. Thank you very much. I like the sound of it even if I need lots of work and experience to become an actual public relations Wizard with a capital W.

Now that a year has passed since my steak dinner with O'Riley on the Never Enough, so much has changed with so many people that I hardly know where to begin.

I guess I'll start with former Tropical-Times executive editor Nate Longstreet, or Col. Longstreet. Yes, I said former executive editor. He would have been fired even if O'Riley remained as CEO and Grabmore had remained as it was before the big changes.

Longstreet's troubles began at a Civil War reenactment he participated in last summer. The Battle of Antietam, as it's widely known, was perhaps the bloodiest conflict of the Civil War.

Col. Longstreet, as he liked to be called, was portraying Confederate Major General A. P. Hill. When the reenactment was over and as he sipped an Iron City beer, Longstreet was approached by a Baltimore television news crew covering the reenactment and looking to do a harmless, fluffy feature stories about re-enactors and why they do what they do.

The trouble started when Longstreet was asked about Antietam.

"You mean the Battle of Sharpsburg," he said, referring to the battle's name in the South at the time of the war and for years after.

Longstreet was still wearing his grey confederate uniform and was still very much in character. But even in Fort Myers wearing slacks, a white shirt and a tie with a topless hula girl on it he was always in character as a Civil War officer.

The interviewer nodded and said, "OK. Why do you like participating in these Civil War reenactments?"

"I don't call it the Civil War," Longstreet said. "It's the War of Northern Aggression."

"But," the flummoxed TV person said, "didn't the war end slavery?"

"That was one of the bad things that happened because of that war. States right have been gutted ever since. Now, black people can vote and all sorts of things."

"You're not saying ending slavery was a bad thing are you?" the astonished interviewer asked.

"That's exactly what I'm saying," Longstreet said. "Ending slavery was a bad thing."

The segment aired that evening on the 6 o'clock news on that Baltimore station. By the next morning, it had gone viral with the added oomph that the knucklehead defending slavery was the top editor of a paper in the nation's largest newspaper chain.

He was fired that afternoon, less than 24 hours after his incomprehensible comments. Last I heard Longstreet had retired to his Georgia plantation and was bemoaning how the Tea Party had been taken over by a gang of wild-eyed liberals.

The bumper sticker on his BMW has these words: The South Will Rise Again. I don't think Longstreet will ever rise again.

The new executive editor is a fellow who was banished from Grabmore several years ago because he didn't play the corporate games. He was the best editor I ever worked for, a veteran who cared only about quaint concepts such as accuracy, storytelling skills, solid reporting and fairness.

He held the corporate weasels in contempt and they forced him out. Joe Clanton had been bouncing around journalism for the past few years and I was always mystified why he was unacceptable to upper management. Now, he is upper management.

He had no use for people such as Mabel Borgia, the former online editor. After Longstreet left, Mabel had a complete breakdown and started wearing the same clothes to the office every day.

White sneakers. Khaki slacks. A white shirt that got grayer and grayer each day. She wore a NASCAR baseball cap and her grimy, matted brown hair tumbled out of it in stringy clotted locks. She began talking to herself in a sort of mumbling way that scared others in the newsroom.

Oh, yes, the term information nexus is now gone. The newsroom is called, simply, the newsroom.

Mabel's behavior and lack of personal hygiene was off-putting to say the least. She was demoted from online editor to producer. Her lack of rudimentary spelling and grammar skills and common sense led to way too many basic errors showing up on the website.

Using eminent when the word imminent was meant.

Spelling the name of the city wrong – Fort Meyers. Instead of Fort Myers.

Spelling Red Sox as Red Socks.

It kept on like this. Way too many errors. Mistakes that made the website a local laughing stock.

Mabel was warned and warned about the errors but didn't stop. She was asked to use soap and wear clean clothes. Please.

She responded by saying over and over, "Oh, I miss Col. Longstreet. Oh, I miss Col. Longstreet. Shuffleboard. Shuffleboard. Shuffleboard."

In her previous role as online editor she didn't need to know anything or be able to do anything. She brownnosed bosses and stabbed lower-ranking people in the back and it was enough for her to thrive in the corporate world. Not any longer. She was supposed to do actual work.

She was asked to resign. She had no choice. Last we heard Mabel had moved in with her sister, Myrtle, a spinster schoolteacher with 10 cats who lived in Tampa.

Stephanie Winchester was promoted to online editor. Stephanie knows how to spell Fort Myers and Red Sox and the website is cleaner and more accurate.

I know Stephanie can also spell the name of the company's former president – Carlotta Gutman. Yes, former president.

Gutman didn't exit Grabmore with the same stunning stupidity and racism of Longstreet. She did it the old-fashioned way – she embezzled and was caught.

The $1.2 million annual salary and the perks and stock options that totaled nearly another million weren't enough for Gutman, the meanest person O'Riley ever met. No, she was siphoning off cash from the company's 401K program for her personal use.

Gutman is now serving an 18-year sentence in a federal prison camp in Alderson, West Virginia. It's the same facility that once housed Martha Stewart, the housekeeping tycoon. Both are listed under the category of financial fraudsters on the prison's website. Gutman is 50 and if she's lucky and behaves herself will be out of prison in her early 60s.

Good luck, Carlotta.

Milo Heller, the former Grabmore CFO, is not in prison. Yet. But his screaming and ferocious temper got him into serious trouble and a civil rights lawsuit. It was a Tuesday in March last year, shortly after O'Riley left the company. Yeller Heller, as he's known, was bitter, or so goes the story, that some folks in the company now had the clout to fight against his repeated moves to lay off people and avoid giving pay raises and ordering furloughs a couple quarters every year.

You may recall this is the guy who summarily fired a disabled vet who worked as a chef in the executive dining room for cutting his tuna sandwich straight across instead of diagonally. Heller was known to fire janitors or grounds keeping people or payroll clerks for the slightest perceived violation of Grabmore policy.

He reveled in his power and after O'Riley's departure and the naming of a college professor as CEO, that power was stripped away. He was in a foul temper that Tuesday evening last year as he drove home from corporate headquarters.

Heller's driving habits were as mean-spirited as his manners at the office. He was road rage personified. On that evening, he was, as usual, speeding, tailgating and weaving in and out of traffic and leaning on his horn.

He got stuck behind a black sedan of some sort and began blowing the horn and flashing his high beams. This kept up for a mile or more. Finally, when the car pulled into a Mobil, Heller's rage was more out of control that usual.

When the car stopped at a gas pump, Heller stopped right behind it. Two men wearing suits got out. The driver was a black man.

"Hey, boy!" Heller screamed, "where did you learn to drive?"

The driver was so astonished he was speechless. His companion, though, said, "What did you say?"

"Who asked you, Chico?" Heller yelled at the other man.

The black man asked, "What's your problem, pal? And don't call Carlos by that term."

Some other gas station patrons were taping the encounter with their cell phones and this also went viral.

"You drive like a little old lady," Heller screamed.

"Hey, I shouldn't admit this but I was actually about 5 miles per hour over the speed limit."

Heller wasn't mollified and walked over to the man and poked him in the chest with his right forefinger.

"Sir, don't do that again," the man said as he continued pumping gas.

Heller did it again.

That's when the black man pulled out his badge and introduced himself as Agent Covington of the U.S. Marshals Service. The other man also pulled out a badge.

"I'm Agent Rivera," he said. "Also from the U.S. Marshals Service. And you, sir, are under arrest. For assaulting a federal agent."

The other gas station customers applauded the two agents. Don't we all wish we could deal with road rage bullies that way?

Covington and Rivera have filed civil rights complaints against Heller. He's also facing six months in prison for physically and verbally assaulting a federal agent. He was fired the next morning.

Lt. J. P. Hooper of the Fort Myers Police Department is now a captain. He was promoted several months after O'Riley returned to his yacht. Sadly, his team continues to beat my team in the old guys rec baseball league but in our most recent game we were leading 6-5 with two outs and the bases loaded in the final inning when Hooper hit a routine ground ball to me at shortstop. Routine even for me. The ball, though, hit a pebble or divot or something and took a very bad hop over my head. Two runs scored. We lost again. I could hear Hooper cackling with delight as he ran to first and noticed the ball rolling into the outfield.

Honus Roberto Schwartz, the Florida Gulf Coast University journalism professor, has taken a one-year sabbatical from his duties at the school. He's renting a townhouse in Buffalo and running Grabmore the way he always thought a newspaper chain should be operated.

The emphasis is on producing good newspapers and solid local news reports on the Grabmore television stations. Making a healthy profit is also a cornerstone of the new Grabmore. That's a change from the days when making obscene profits was the prime directive, an absolute obsession of pathological dimensions.

Schwartz couldn't go in to the office the first day and – abracadabra - change everything. It's been gradual. Grant modest pay raises. Hire more reporters and photographers. Provide readers with a thicker paper in all those cities, giving them more reasons to buy the papers instead of fewer reasons.

One of his first moves was a plea to cut down on the Orwellian corporate jargon that made Grabmore a laughing stock in journalism and to anybody anywhere with any respect for the English language.

"Clarity in language should always be our goal," Schwartz wrote in a brief memo to all employees. "Few words are better than lots of words. Keep sentences and titles short and clear. Thank you."

Speaking of short, the Tropical-Times now has a new sports editor. Bo Lowe, the semi-literate, pint-sized, inarticulate philandering nitwit former sports editor, finally went too far. Under the old regime, nothing would have happened.

He often wore polo shirts to the office. When he showed up one day wearing one with the logo of an exclusive local golf course. Olde Scottlandia Links and Golf Club by the Sea, the new editor, Clanton, got to wondering and asked Lowe where he got the shirt.

"Oh, this shirt?' he supposedly said as he tugged on it.

"Yes, that one," the editor said.

"I got it at Old Scottlandia," he said.

Nothing happened that day. Calls were made. Lowe not only got a free polo shirt but free membership at the club, where annual dues are $15,000. He was fired two days later.

My friends from the kidnapping adventure are all doing well.

Monique has been promoted to general manager of all Grabmore forestry and lumber operations in Canada. She wants to come back to Florida for a vacation next winter, which is the best time not to be in Canada and the best time to be in Florida.

Ahmad has also been promoted and is now a foreman in the Bergen County Bugle pressroom. He's also met a woman, the ex-wife of a New York City politician who was swept up in a sexting scandal. They plan to honeymoon on Sanibel Island. We'll probably get together for lunch.

The folks in the Witness Protection Program have moved Sal again. They were worried for his safety. Sal can't say where he is or what he's doing but I occasionally got cryptic postcards from western states wishing me well.

I hope Sal is safe and his old friends and enemies from the north Jersey mob don't find him.

Nigel is no longer at the Bugle. The New York Times hired him to cover soccer. It's a great opportunity for Nigel, one of the best sports writers I know. He's traveling more than ever, going to Europe and Brazil and all over the country covering his favorite sport.

He's the paper's No. 1 writer on the world's No. 1 sport. His future assignments will take him to the Olympics and the World Cup.

I've asked him to take time out of his schedule to do a feature on the Florida International Shuffleboard League. He said it might be a tough sell for the sports section but a lifestyle writer from the Times may come down to Florida next winter to profile our little league.

The first season of our league is now over and we're planning season No. 2. The first year will likely forevermore be known in shuffleboard lore as the Year of Troxie. ...

EPILOGUE: PART TWO

This was the life Troxie Trosky had dreamed about ever since she first heard the name many years ago of shuffleboard legend Mae Hall.

Troxie was excelling, even dominating on the first pro shuffleboard circuit that the world may have ever seen. The prize purses weren't like golf or tennis but money could be made. All those hours of practice were paying off for Troxie. It's said that 10,000 hours of practice is the magic threshold to master anything, whether it's the violin or hitting a baseball or singing. Or shuffleboard, I suppose.

Troxie zipped past 10,000 hours of pushing biscuits with a tang long ago. She was meant for the Florida International Shuffleboard League.

That first season there were six tournaments in six cities. Troxie won in St. Pete, Fort Myers, Everglades City and Boca Raton. She was runner-up in Winter Park and Daytona Beach.

First-place prize money at each event was $5,000 and runner-up prize money was $2,000. She cashed in $24,000 in prize money.

Then she won the season-ending tournament and another $5,000.

That's not Tiger Woods or Serena Williams money but not bad for a few weekends.

Plus as the league's Public Relations Wizard I ordered Troxie T-shirts made and sold at each venue. She picked up a percentage of every T-shirt sale. I don't want to say how much but it was a nice little pile of change, a lot more than the tip money she was pocketing in that Everglades City seafood restaurant.

Troxie Trosky dolls were also on sale at venues and fans sometimes waved them in support as she prepared to slide biscuits in various shuffleboard tournaments.

"I've never been happier," Troxie said at the St. Petersburg Shuffleboard Club.

This was right after she won the season-ending tournament. She was holding the Mae Hall Silver Tang and the Butterscotch Cup. The tang signified her ranking as the No. 1 player on the regular-season circuit and the Cup was awarded for winning what we call the Masters Shuffleboard Showdown in St. Pete.

Sure, the league was a novelty but it was going well. Hundreds of people came to the matches. DQ set up kiosks at the venues to sell butterscotch milkshakes and other treats and we split the revenues three ways – DQ, the league and the host site. We secured a modest corporate tie-in with Tang.

Pillsbury was on board for a biscuit tie-in. We sold naming rights to the tournaments for several thousand dollars. They were to local businesses such as a newspaper in Southwest Florida called Florida Weekly, which sponsored the Fort Myers tournament.

The paper was allowed signage and a kiosk to give away papers and talk to potential advertisers. They paid a modest fee and people got to know their paper and advertising reps met potential advertisers. We found our demographic was fairly upscale, people who had played shuffleboard on cruise ships or in retirement communities. They had money to spend and enjoyed hanging out at the tournaments and meeting attractive shuffleboard players such as Troxie, who wore white shorts and blue T-shirts as her playing attire.

We politely tried to separate fans from a little of their money. We sold shuffleboard equipment and caps and ballpoint pens and those Troxie T-shirts and butterscotch milkshakes.

Troxie was profiled in a few newspapers and our website, shufflepros.com, was getting regular traffic and some advertising. Through ticket sales and advertising and merchandise we were making money.

Our old kidnapping accessory after the fact pal was the public face of Florida shuffleboard.

Folks were noticing. We were contacted by shuffleboard clubs in other Florida cities about staging tournaments in their communities. We're considering Sarasota, Jupiter, Dunedin and Cocoa Beach for tournaments next year. A nudist camp in Pasco County invited us to hold a tournament there but we politely declined. It would be too controversial even if our players kept their clothes on. Thanks but no thanks.

park a couple mornings a week to play a patty-cake, slow-motion version of the game. But he's moving around and the pounds continue dropping.

The day after the season ended we chatted briefly at the shuffleboard courts before he walked the three-quarters of a mile home to his condo.

"I should have left the company years ago," he said, standing there on the sidewalk across the street from the downtown St. Pete public library. "It wasn't a healthy environment."

"Didn't you help make it that way?" I asked.

"Well, I did," he admitted. "You got me there."

"No, we got you in downtown Fort Myers," I said.

As soon I said it I regretted that comment. O'Riley, though, laughed and said, "Good one, Scott. Esmerelda and I are going to dinner tonight at Moon Under Water. I want to go home and get cleaned up. Next week we can start planning the next shuffleboard season."

"Sounds like a plan," I said.

For not having a plan on the kidnapping adventure it sure worked out well, exceeding all our expectations.

There are some things I miss about sports writing but not much. I don't miss waiting hours in the hope that some utility infielder will grace me with a five-minute interview during spring training. I don't miss the arrogance and egos of some of my fellow media members. I don't miss the sham 38-hour workweeks. That was the deal at Grabmore. One worked 38 hours and not a second more. Or a second less.

You'd get in trouble either way. There was no way to win. Go over and ask for overtime and you'd get in trouble. Walk out of the office two minutes before the 38th hour was up and you'd get in trouble.

I filled out my own timecards and wrote down my first 38 hours of the week. Then just kept working. Most weeks it was around 50 hours. Some weeks 60 hours and on some occasions I inched past 70 hours without a penny of overtime.

Working the extra 10 or 20 or 30 hours a week was easier than dealing with irrational Grabmoron editors, or God forbid, asking for an hour of overtime pay when you worked an extra 15 hours.

So, no, I don't miss it. Not at all. I sold my house in Chokoloskee, the big house that once belonged to my Uncle Orville. I don't want to say how much I got for it but let's say it was more than half a million but less than a million.

I loved the house but unless one was really into fishing, kayaking or kidnapping there was no point in owning a Chokoloskee home. So I sold it, paid off my little condo and I'm in better financial shape than I ever expected to be. Ever.

In addition to working for the Florida International Shuffleboard League I'm doing a little freelance writing for local publications. My goal now, though, is to write a novel. I have the time. I have some financial security. I'm not sure, though, what to write about.

There's an old saying that one should write what one knows. Well, I don't know nothin' so that makes writing what one knows very difficult.

I've been pondering this for quite a while now and I've found a story, of sorts. I worked a long time for a large, impersonal, soulless corporation. Maybe I could write a novel based on my experiences at this big company.

If I write this novel, though, I wonder if anybody would ever believe it.

ABOUT THE AUTHOR

Glenn Miller is a long-time Florida sportswriter whose work has appeared in several state papers. This is his debut novel. He resides in Fort Myers in a humble, book-filled home he calls The Hovel.